THE SLAVES of ALMVS

STEVE DIXON

Other books by the same author:
Out of the Shadows
What the Sword Said
The Empty Dragon

Scripture Union, 207–209 Queensway, Bletchley, Milton Keynes, MK2 2EB, England
Email: info@scriptureunion.org.uk
Website: www.scriptureunion.org.uk

Scripture Union Australia
Locked Bag 2, Central Coast Business Centre, NSW 2252
Website: www.scriptureunion.org.au

Scripture Union USA
PO Box 987, Valley Forge, PA 19482
Website: www.scriptureunion.org

British Library Cataloguing-in-Publication Data
A catalogue record of this book is available from the British Library.

Printed and bound in Great Britain by Creative Print and Design (Wales) Ebbw Vale

Cover design: Phil Grundy

Scripture Union is an international Christian charity working with churches in more than 130 countries, providing resources to bring the good news about Jesus Christ to children, young people and families and to encourage them to develop spiritually through the Bible and prayer.

As well as our network of volunteers, staff and associates who run holidays, church-based events and school Christian groups, we produce a wide range of publications and support those who use our resources through training programmes.

Contents

For Susan
with thanks for days by the sea

1

Amisso

Amisso loved the cries of seagulls. They sounded like freedom and adventure. And he loved the look of the birds. Although he had lived in the seaport of Mercatorius all of his 16 years, the size of the seagulls never ceased to amaze him. They walked the harbour side, perched on pillars, masts and spars, and fed on bits of gutted fish, but they weren't tame birds, like sparrows. They were big-bodied birds of the sea, their wings broad and powerful enough to carry them off to the glittering horizon, and their yellow eyes were hard, proud and dangerous – a reminder of their savage beaks. You didn't mess with seagulls, nor could you get too close. As you moved towards them, they simply walked away. And in their own time they would spread their enormous wings, leaving you with nothing but a contemptuous cry that turned into strange, triumphant laughter. They showed their opinion of Mercatorius in chalky white splashes all over the harbour, the sailing ships, the customs house, the scores of palatial warehouses, and the gaudy uniforms of the harbour guards. It was an opinion that Amisso shared.

Amisso was watching a seagull now as it strutted up and down one of the window sills of the great meeting room in his father's office building. The bird shot a scornful look through the diamond-paned glass, cocked its head as if puzzled by the antics of the men gathered round the long table inside, then turned away. Amisso gazed out longingly as the bird stretched its wide wings and launched effortlessly into the air. He went on watching as it soared over the buildings on the other side of Merchants' Square and banked towards the harbour.

'Amisso will back me!'

Amisso turned quickly as he heard his elder brother, Bardo, say his name.

'What's your opinion, brother?' he asked.

Bardo was standing at the table, looking splendid in his best embroidered doublet. He had his hand on a roll of lace material.

'Gentlemen, we cannot pay the price you're asking,' Bardo told the three men facing him on the other side of the table. 'Think of the profit margin you're leaving us – it's far too narrow.'

Amisso came to join his brother and looked at the lace.

'It's beautiful,' he said, running his hand gently over it.

'There you are, you see!' one of the men said.

'Beautiful, it may be,' Bardo replied coolly, 'but the price you're asking for it isn't.'

Amisso looked at the neatly made out bill from the lacemakers, which lay on the table next to their goods. He racked his brains to remember the figures in the heavy leather-bound ledgers his father had shown him in the accounts room earlier.

'But don't we charge much more than that when we sell it?' he asked his brother.

Bardo stared at him, and the words his father had spoken that morning sounded in his head: 'Try to involve Amisso in the discussions. The boy has to learn.' Bardo was confident when negotiating prices with men twice his age, but he felt helpless in dealing with his fool of a brother.

'Master Amisso,' a quiet voice said, 'there are packing and shipping and many other costs to pay for, not to mention the tariffs and taxes – we have to charge more when we sell.'

It was their father's trading agent. He was in attendance on the orders of their father, Crasto, to oversee Bardo's dealings. Bardo normally resented the presence of the weasel-faced little man, but just then he was heartily thankful the agent was there.

Amisso continued to stare at the patterns in the lace, his cheeks burning.

'The plain fact is, gentlemen,' he heard his brother continue, 'the Summata is already well laden with material just as fine as yours, for which we have paid only three-quarters the price you're asking. And three-quarters of this...,' he tapped the bill on the table, '...is all I'm prepared to pay for what you're offering.'

The three lacemakers muttered together.

'Time is pressing,' Bardo insisted. 'The Summata sails this evening. We have little space left for cargo, and there are other gentlemen of business waiting downstairs. Without wishing to be rude, I must ask you to take my offer or leave it and make way for others.'

His father's agent led Amisso to the side of the room while the three men considered.

'It won't take them long to agree,' he whispered to Amisso. 'Your brother's in the right, and they know it. They only tried to overcharge because they think he's young. They haven't come up against Bardo before, or they'd have known better. He may only be 21 but your brother's a sharp man already. He'll be a great man of business in time, like your father.'

'Yes,' said Amisso as he watched the chief lacemaker draw a line through the bill and amend the figures. 'Yes, he will.'

Bardo caught his young brother's eye over the bowed heads of the lacemakers and smiled. Amisso smiled back. Bardo's world may have bewildered him, but Amisso did not resent his brother's success in it.

'Master Bardo,' the agent called, 'shall your brother fetch the glass traders?'

A look of relief spread over Bardo's face – here, at last, was something useful Amisso could achieve. Bardo nodded, and his brother left the room.

Amisso found the glass traders in the grand reception chamber that ran the length of the ground floor of his father's business headquarters. He instructed one of the uniformed servants to escort them up to Bardo, but he did not follow. He stood in a corner, beside a marble statue of a Mercatorian warrior, and watched the scene. The chamber was full of representatives from the major manufacturers of Mercatorius, and there was a constant jabber of conversation. Some were still waiting to see Bardo, but others had already concluded their business or had no business to do at all and were just there for the excitement. The departure of a trading convoy containing the flagship of one of the most important merchants in Mercatorius was a great social occasion. And today there was an extra interest in Bardo's role – this was the first time the elder son had been given complete charge of loading one of his father's ships. Amisso heard Bardo's name on everyone's lips, and, from the snippets of conversation he overheard, the business community of Mercatorius seemed impressed.

No one noticed him in the busy crowd, and Amisso knew that he would not be missed in the meeting room, so he made his way up a back staircase to the only place in the whole building that made any sense to him – the map room. He felt at home there. Sometimes he liked to creep in when it was not in use and turn the big globes in their dark wooden frames or stare at the huge maps painted on the walls. He would mouth the names of the distant cities and countries marked on them. They were as foreign to him as the words of business his brother and father spoke, but somehow these names were full of meaning. They even had tastes – like the exotic fruits that were often on sale in the endless rows of stalls in the city market. Amisso would roll the names around on his tongue and taste their rich, sweet syrup. And his eyes would follow the trade routes marked on the maps or his finger would trace the red dotted lines on the globes over land and sea to the farthest outposts his father's trading reached.

But he was not to be left alone to enjoy his imaginary journeys today. No sooner had he entered the room than he heard footsteps approaching from his father's office across the corridor. Amisso retreated to one of the tall window alcoves at the end of the room and stood still, a silhouette made almost invisible by the sun streaming through the towering sheet of crystal panes behind him. The heavy wooden door opened with a crack that echoed from the dark panels and polished floor of the room. His father strode in briskly, followed by two men Amisso recognised as the captain of the Summata and the admiral who would be in charge of the trading convoy.

'It's here,' Crasto said, pointing to a large wall map that showed the coastal area around Mercatorius. 'That's where they were waiting - in the northern cove.'

'But we've got a garrison on that island,' the admiral replied.

'Not any more,' Crasto told him. 'The Sordesians wiped them out a month ago.'

'But that's an act of war,' the captain protested.

'Piracy - that's what the Sordesians are claiming,' Crasto explained. 'They're blaming it on pirates. Nothing to do with them, so they say.'

'They're making out that pirates destroyed our garrison?' the captain asked in disbelief.

'They are. And with our garrison out of the way, they lay in wait in that cove, then captured the pride of Senator Perdo's fleet, laden almost to sinking with cotton. He couldn't wait to get it back to our markets and had ordered his captain to race ahead of the convoy.'

'You'll not be too saddened that Perdo lost his goods, Senator,' the admiral laughed. But Crasto wasn't amused.

'Business rivalry is one thing,' he said, 'but an attack on any vessel from Mercatorius is an attack on us all. The details of the convoy's course are your own business, Admiral, but whatever you do, steer well clear of that island and be on the alert constantly. Our ships may have the speed to outrun anything Sordes can send after them, but beware of ambush and surprise and keep your ships together.'

Crasto remained in the room when the officers left. He stared at the map a moment longer, then spun one of the globes violently and strode towards the windows. The sun was dazzling and he had almost reached the alcove where Amisso was standing before he noticed his dark shape.

'Who's there?' he said sharply, taking hold of the hilt of his sword.

'It's me, Father,' Amisso replied.

'Amisso? Why aren't you with Bardo?'

Amisso turned away to look out of the window. Below him he could see the busy crowds passing to and fro on one of the broad approaches to Merchants' Square. The strong sunlight made the whole scene sparkle. It seemed cut off – an unreachable world of happy, wealthy, confident people.

'I didn't seem to be much help,' Amisso said.

His father stood beside him and put his hand on his shoulder.

'You must try, son,' he said.

'I do!' Amisso replied. 'If only you knew how hard I try, but I can't...'

'*Can't* is not a word we use in this family – or in this city,' his father told him, gently but firmly. He took his son by both shoulders and looked him full in the face for a moment. Then he sighed deeply and looked out of the window again. 'Sometimes I think you don't appreciate all this,' he went on, waving at the scene outside and spreading his arms to include the room they were standing in. 'You don't seem to want to be part of it... to contribute. Aren't you proud to be part of Mercatorius?'

Amisso didn't know what he could say. They'd had this conversation before and he knew what was coming.

'A citizen of Mercatorius is like royalty compared to other people,' Crasto went on. 'You don't just live in some stinking, second-rate seaport, boy. Mercatorius is a city, a beautiful city, and more than a city – a city-state, the centre of the most powerful trading empire in the world.'

'I wouldn't know,' Amisso replied quietly.

'What?'

'I haven't seen the world,' Amisso told him, 'so how can I tell if Mercatorius is the most powerful empire?'

Crasto knew this conversation as well as his son. Many times Amisso had asked to sail on one of his father's fleet of ships, and each time Crasto had responded as he did now.

'Amisso,' he said, 'I know you'd like to go to sea, but it's not fitting... It's not fitting for the son of a Mercatorian senator to rub shoulders with common sailors.'

Amisso sat heavily on the window seat and his father looked down at him in silence. He was busy. He had to check and countersign the paperwork Bardo had made out for the voyage; and he was due to meet the Naval Committee of the Senate in an hour, to request that a detachment of marines be assigned to the Summata in view of the threat from Sordes. And yet he lingered, and at last he sat down next to his son.

'Why won't you take an interest in the business?' he asked.

'But I do!' Amisso replied.

'You never show any sign,' Crasto said. 'Bardo's always asking questions, always trying to find things out, but you—'

'I want to know things too,' Amisso interrupted.

'Then ask,' his father said.

Amisso looked at the senator and knew in his heart that it was hopeless, but still he took a deep breath and tried.

'Laraka,' he said, rolling the word in his mouth like a sweet fruit. It was one of his favourite place names from the maps on the walls. 'What's it like?'

'Laraka?' Crasto replied, considering a moment. 'It's wealthy, that's true, but its army is weak and it has no navy to speak of. Cotton's its chief product; that's its only use to us, in all honesty. Oh, it buys a little of our wine, but there's no profit in that and there's too much competition from the vineyards of Kara – they're only half a day's journey inland. Our quality's better of course, but...'

The senator caught sight of the vague expression that was creeping over Amisso's face and he stopped.

'What is it that you want to know?' he asked.

'What does its market smell like?' Amisso replied. 'What songs do the people sing? What stories do they tell? What beasts and monsters are there in the country? How do the stars look from Laraka? That's what I want to know, Father.'

The pair looked into each other's eyes for an embarrassed moment, then Crasto got up and stared out of the window at his city. The papers needed checking. He would need to concentrate to make sure there were no mistakes. He took two steady breaths and walked away.

Amisso slipped, unnoticed, out of his father's headquarters, crossed Merchants' Square and made for the harbour. The quayside and the ships that would actually travel the trade routes were always far more effective than any maps or globes in raising Amisso's spirits. Amisso spent many hours hanging round the harbour, listening to the sailors' tales and learning their songs, or at the inland station where the packhorses assembled in caravans to travel the long routes over mountains and deserts to distant continents. There the atmosphere was very different: always hot and rank with the smell of horse sweat, leather and dung. The shouting of men and cracking of whips seemed to dominate and there was a trembling mixture of fear and bravado in the air, heightened by recent anxieties about Sordes, as if an army was getting ready for war. Down at the quayside it was much cleaner, cooler and more calm; the men's cries didn't carry as far as the seagulls', and no one cracked whips at the sea.

Amisso may have had secret doubts as to whether Mercatorius was really the greatest trading city in the world, but he was certain that her ships were the most beautiful. The slim lines of the swiftest coastal galleys took your breath away, and the strength of the ocean-going galleasses was awesome. The naval galleasses, moored in ranks in the arsenal dockyard to the west of the merchant harbour, had circular foredecks with cannons pointing in every direction. They seemed to dare the powers of the world to approach, and their banks of oars with gun platforms built out over them looked like sturdy wings. The ships had their sails furled in harbour, but Amisso knew the graceful curves the white triangles of canvas would make as they bellied in the breeze to carry the ships of Mercatorius, flags flying, to the ends of the earth. What had the clumsy cogs and carracks that came into harbour from other places got to offer in comparison? They were nothing but old bathtubs and wine barrels – their sails as graceless as washing on a line.

Amisso was just casting a critical eye over a particularly ugly old cog from Sordes, their hated neighbour state to the north, when something hit him on the back of the head. An apple core bounced on the stone quayside and plopped into the harbour. Amisso swung round ready to give the urchin who had thrown it a good hiding, but there was no ragged bundle of mischief in sight. The docks weren't the safest place for a wealthy young man like Amisso to be; down here, he frequently came in for abuse from the city's poor. But like every boy of his class, he'd been taught to box and fence and he carried a sword, so he was always able to see them off. He often thought tossing them a coin might have been an easier way of getting rid of them, but his father forbade it. 'They must work for their money, as we do,' was the senator's response to the beggars of Mercatorius.

'Pssst!' someone hissed.

Amisso peered into the shadows of a nearby warehouse front. A row of barrels was lined up across the doorway, and a hand suddenly popped up from behind them, waved, then dropped out of sight.

'Psssssst!' the sound came again, more insistent this time.

Amisso drew his sword – shorter than a duelling blade, but very handy for street fighting – and advanced towards the barrels. They were chest high and he peeked over them with caution. Then he let out a disgruntled 'Humph!' and clattered his weapon back into its sheath.

'For heaven's sake, Beata!' he said, taking a step away.

'Come back!' the girl whispered desperately.

Amisso halted and began to smile. Beata was his best friend, and he was actually glad to see her. He walked back to the row of barrels and peered down at her, still smiling.

'You look like a monkey,' she said. 'What are you grinning at?'

'You,' he said. 'If I'm a monkey, you're—'

'What?' she said fiercely.

He thought for a moment.

'A casket of jewels, hidden in a nest of straw,' he said at last.

'Oh,' she murmured and blushed.

She certainly looked out of place – the pearls and rich brocade of her dress shimmered and glowed in a crumpled heap as she crouched in a most inelegant way among the shadows behind the barrels. Beata's family were Amisso's neighbours, and like Amisso's family, they were very wealthy.

'Come on,' Amisso said, holding out a hand to help her up.

She took it and started to rise, but then she spotted something behind him.

'No!' she gasped, and shaking herself free she dropped back behind her barricade.

Amisso turned to find out what had alarmed her and saw a grand-looking young woman with a long, graceful neck sweeping towards him. She had a maid and two pageboys in tow. Although she was only four years older than Amisso, she seemed to belong to another generation and he bowed deeply, as he would to one of the matrons of the city.

'Good day to you, Verna,' he said.

'Good day, Amisso,' she replied, looking vexed and distracted. 'I'm shopping with my sister and I seem to have lost her. You haven't seen Beata, have you?'

'No!' Beata hissed desperately from the shadows.

'Yes,' Amisso replied, smiling pleasantly, 'I saw her about five minutes ago actually, in Senate Square. She said she couldn't find you and was going to walk home.'

'Walk? How can she walk?'

'One foot in front of the other?' Amisso suggested.

Verna ignored the sarcasm.

'That girl has no sense of what's right and proper,' she muttered, then turned to one of the pageboys. 'Run and tell the coachman to get ready,' she ordered. 'We'll catch her on the road.'

As Verna and her attendants disappeared in the crowd Amisso held out his hand to Beata again.

'Catch you?' he laughed. 'Not a chance!'

'Thanks,' she said, dusting herself down as he hauled her to her feet.

'And thanks for the apple,' he said, rubbing the back of his head.

'Let's have a look.'

She turned him round and picked about in his hair.

'No slimy bits stuck in it. You'll be all right.'

Amisso had curly golden hair that fell to his shoulders. He was rather proud of it and shook the locks out, running his fingers through them. Then he caught her smiling at him and stopped.

'What are you playing at, anyway?' he asked.

'I've escaped,' she whispered.

'I can see that – what's going on?'

She took his arm and led him in the opposite direction to Senate Square.

'They want me to go to my cousin's wedding.'

'So?'

'So I'll have to have new clothes – that's what we were shopping for.'

'I thought girls were supposed to like new clothes.'

'Oh yes, but not like this.' She slapped the solid front of her dress. 'You've no idea what there is under all this. Or at least you shouldn't have.'

Amisso blushed. She gave him a shove and pirouetted away, holding her arms out wide.

'I want something I can move in,' she shouted. 'Like those dancers from the south we saw at the carnival.'

'But they weren't much better than—'

'They were good dancers. They were beautiful. That's what I'd like to look like. This—' she took hold of the stiff, lifeless folds of her skirt and pulled them about impatiently, '—it's just rubbish.'

'Expensive rubbish.'

'Rubbish, all the same.'

They walked to the farthest point of the quayside, and then out along the curved wall of the harbour defences towards the lighthouse at the end – one of their favourite spots. Beata had Amisso by the arm again and was tugging him onwards. They were the same age, but she seemed almost half his size and, as she pulled herself against him, her head with its black, shiny hair just bumped against his shoulder. She often clung to his arm when they walked with each other and it showed how she felt about him – they'd grown up together and sometimes she hung on to him as the only person in her world she could possibly talk to and stand a chance of being understood. For him, having her that close always felt like carrying a bomb, and he never quite knew if the fuse was lit. But he had no inclination to throw the bomb away.

'What are you doing anyway, skulking around the docks?' Beata asked. 'I thought the Summata was due to sail. Shouldn't you be learning how to do whatever it is that men of business have to do at such times?'

'Yes,' he said miserably. They walked on in silence for a few moments, then he burst out angrily, 'It's not fair! Why don't you girls have to do all this boring stuff too?'

'Lady's privilege!' she said. 'All we have to do is get trussed up like fancy parcels, supervise the kitchens, supervise the household, supervise our husbands and look beautiful and contented. Piece of cake, really.'

She looked up at him, but he didn't meet her eyes and he wasn't smiling.

They walked on in silence until they got to the end of the long curved wall that protected the harbour from wild seas and enemy attack. A tall, elegant lighthouse marked the extremity of the wall, and they liked to sit on the broad stone blocks that made its base. Two hundred metres to their right was another lighthouse at the end of the defensive wall that curved out from the other side of the quay; and in front of them was the sea - nothing but the sea. It was a place of unlimited possibilities; anything, just anything, could be out there.

Sometimes they would sit beneath the lighthouse without speaking for half an hour or more, but today Amisso couldn't settle. Beata knew his moods in the same way any child of Mercatorius knew the moods of the sea, and after a few moments she took hold of both his hands, pulling him round to face her.

'What?' she said, fixing his eyes with her own.

Their eyes couldn't have been more contrasting – hers as dark as her hair, his bright blue as a summer sky. He squeezed her hands briefly, then freed himself, turning back to the sea again.

'Just the usual,' he said. 'But it always gets worse when there's a ship due to leave.'

'If you learned the business, maybe you could be your father's agent,' she suggested, 'then he'd have to let you sail with his ships.'

Amisso shook his head.

'No, that'd just spoil it. I want to be an explorer, not a grubby merchant, too busy counting his money to look at the world. I wish Father would let me learn to be a captain. I'd be good at it. I know I would.'

'Why don't you ask him?'

'It wouldn't be good enough for him. You know it wouldn't. Even if I got to be an admiral – which I don't want to do – it wouldn't be good enough. He's a senator of Mercatorius; he couldn't have a sailor for a son, even if he turned out to be the best explorer there ever was.'

He was silent for a while, and Beata waited patiently.

'Bardo's the kind of son my father wants,' Amisso said at last, 'someone to carry on the business. Bardo wasn't much older than me when he started doing real jobs for Father in the business. I just know he's going to try and give me some job in the office soon, and I won't be able to do it. I'll ruin everything. I'm useless.'

2
Have You Got a Plan?

Mercatorius was not all marble pillars, gilded domes and broad thoroughfares. The sea was the gateway to Mercatorius, and the city seemed to look towards the sea as if this was the way it showed its face to the world. The further back from the waterfront you went, the narrower the streets became and the smaller and poorer the buildings. It was not an area that the gentlemen and women of Mercatorius travelled far into. To Amisso, it was as foreign as a distant land, but not one he felt inclined to explore. There were, however, certain citizens who crossed the frontier into these gloomy, inland regions of the city. Fallax the taxman was one.

Fallax kept his hand on the hilt of his short sword as he shouldered his way through the dark alleys of the Poor Quarter – a mere five minutes' walk from the light and air of

Senate Square, where he had his office. His office was not actually on the Square itself, but tucked away in a yard behind it. The cream of Mercatorian society would not want a taxman's premises on open display. A man who spent time in the Poor Quarter seemed to have its smell lingering about him, and gentlepeople wanted to keep their distance. Not that Fallax felt any more accepted among the poor of Mercatorius – to them he was a foreigner who was up to no good in their territory. He was jostled as he moved among them and he heard muttered curses behind his back. But he was hardened to it. He was in his mid-forties and had been doing this work half his life, first as a clerk, then as a state official. There had been a time, as a young man, when he'd minded people's opinion of his business – but if he'd grumbled, his father had soon put him straight. His father, 12 years dead now, had been a bent-backed cobbler with a face as brown and wrinkled as the leather he worked and he had only one response to his son's complaints: 'You've crawled out of the gutter, son – don't slip back. You're a somebody now. For the love of your father, kick anyone's teeth that tries to drag you back down.'

'Open in the name of the Senate!' Fallax bellowed as he thumped his fist on a heavy wooden door.

'He's left the country!' a woman's voice called from an upstairs window behind him. A cackle of laughter followed. She may have been on the other side of the street, but the passageway was so narrow that she seemed to be directly overhead. Fallax took shelter beneath the overhanging upper storey of the house he was visiting, in case anything was thrown down or tipped on him. He pummelled the door again.

'Open to me, or I'll be back with the Guard!'

He waited a moment longer, then heard steps on the wooden stairs inside. Heavy bolts were drawn, and the door swung open.

'We can do this out here, or inside – it's up to you,' Fallax told the man who'd opened the door.

'I wouldn't let scum like you near my wife and children,' the man replied.

'Please yourself,' Fallax told him, looking up and down the street. People were standing in doorways and leaning out of windows to see what was going on, and passers-by had stopped in their tracks. The man crossed his threshold and looked around at his neighbours.

'Say what you have to,' he told Fallax. 'I've nothing to hide from them.'

'You own a pack of mules,' Fallax said. 'You have a transport business working out of the stable yard at the Northern Gate.'

'That's true,' the man replied.

Fallax took a small roll of paper from the inside of his padded leather jacket and handed it to the man.

'Your tax bill for the last quarter,' he told him.

The man looked at the paper, then laughed and thrust it back towards Fallax.

'You've got the wrong man,' he said. 'I haven't even earned that much money in the last three months, never mind owing it in tax.'

Fallax kept his hands behind his back and left the man waving the paper at him.

'It's based on the standard income for a man with a dozen mules,' he stated.

'Plus your mark up!' the woman in the window shouted down.

'But these aren't standard times,' the man argued, 'or haven't you noticed? Land trade on the northern routes is practically finished since the Sordesians made their allies stop dealing with us. My business has been halved. I've hardly got enough to feed my family, let alone pay taxes.'

'That's no concern of mine,' Fallax told him.

'No concern of yours? Who do these taxes go to? The Senate—'

'Such as he doesn't steal for himself,' the woman shouted.

'—and if Sordes isn't the Senate's concern, whose is it? If we're paying taxes to the Senate, the Senate should do something about getting the markets open again, then we could trade as we always have.'

'It's only 'cos the Senate's ordered attacks on Sordesian caravans that they've had the markets closed in the first place!' someone called out behind the taxman.

Fallax turned sharply. 'Bandits are attacking their caravans,' he told them. 'It's nothing to do with Mercatorius. It's thugs and criminals that are causing the problems, not the Senate, and we all know where thugs and criminals come from.'

He looked slowly up and down the narrow street, staring at the men leaning against walls and doorposts. They glared back but he knew, and they knew, that assaulting an officer of the State was not worth the punishment they'd receive.

The mule owner wavered. The hand that had kept thrusting the bill towards Fallax dropped to his side.

'Look,' he said, in a quieter tone, 'I don't have the money.'

'Sell something,' Fallax told him. 'You've got a nice house.'

It was true. As a small tradesman, he had a house that was slightly larger than those around it, and he owned the property, rather than renting it.

'There must be a way,' the man pleaded. 'In times like these, surely the State can reduce the taxes. I can pay a little, but not this.'

The bill was getting crumpled in his tightening hand.

'Take away your rake-off, taxman – that should halve the bill,' the woman shouted from the window.

Fallax stepped out of the shelter of the overhang and stared up at her.

'My commission is my business,' he shouted. 'It has nothing to do with this... and nothing to do with you!'

The Senate Finance Committee set the basic tax levels, but Mercatorian tax collectors were allowed to add whatever they wanted to the bills as an extra commission for themselves. This was supposed to make them diligent in collecting, which it did, but it also made them hated. The bystanders in the tiny street were infuriated by what Fallax had said and they began to crowd round him.

'You're no better than a Sordesian yourself!' a man shouted. 'Filth like you doesn't belong in this city!'

There were cries of 'Well said!'

'Don't belong?' Fallax shouted at them. 'Don't belong? Use your brains! All I'm doing is making the most I can out of the opportunity that's been given to me. Tell me how that doesn't belong in Mercatorius! It's the spirit this city's built on. I'm the spirit of this city. Learn to live with it.'

He turned back to the mule owner, but before he could repeat the tax demand he suddenly spun round again and made a grab into the press of bodies behind him. He dragged a woman forward, gripping her by the wrist. She was dressed in men's clothes, and one of her front teeth was missing. In her hand was a leather purse.

'Mine, I think,' Fallax said, pulling the purse from her fingers, 'and so are you, now. You're for the dungeons. If you can't pick pockets any better than that, it's time you looked for another career.'

The woman struggled violently for a moment, then seemed to think better of it. She drew herself to her full height and pushed herself almost nose to nose with the taxman.

'If you're the spirit of this city, I'm your spirit,' she hissed. Then she spat in his eye.

He instinctively put his hands to his face, releasing her, and she bolted.

'We're both thieves!' she yelled as she ran.

In an instant, Fallax was after her, but a bystander stuck a foot out and the tax collector went sprawling in the filth of the gutter.

'Run, Nefa!' someone shouted.

Fallax scrambled to his feet, but Nefa had already disappeared down a side alley and he knew she would find a hiding place in moments in the warren of gloomy streets. He drew his sword, and turned to the little crowd. They moved back a few paces.

'She's dead!' Fallax said menacingly. Then he pointed his blade at the mule owner. 'And you,' he said, 'payment in full at my office within the week, or I'll be back for your house.'

～～

That evening there was a party at the home of Senator Crasto. The senator and his two sons lived in a fine villa on a country estate about a kilometre north of the city, and in the autumn twilight the cobbled highway from Mercatorius rang with the sound of horses' hooves and carriage wheels: all the top names in city society had been invited to help Crasto celebrate the successful embarkation of the Summata. When the long process of arrivals and greetings was completed and everyone was finally seated and served, the host rose to propose a toast. Candlelight glowed from the golden cup he held aloft and from the huge golden dishes laid out along the length of the table. It sparkled from the jewels that decorated every one of the ladies present and many of the men.

'To our convoy! To the Summata: a safe journey and a safe return!' Crasto proposed.

'And a safe return on investment!' someone else shouted.

Everyone laughed as they repeated the toast, but Crasto wasn't paying attention. He held his cup for a moment longer before drinking and raised it slightly towards a life-size painting hanging on the opposite wall. It was of an imposing woman in the full state dress of a senator's wife – the senator's flagship bore her name. Amisso's mother, Summata, had died five years earlier in one of the epidemics that periodically struck rich and poor alike in this hot and humid land. As Amisso watched his father, he realised that this, at least, was something that they shared, and Bardo too – the love and sense of loss.

But the moment didn't last. Crasto drank deeply and turning to left and right, where his sons were sitting, he grasped them both by the shoulders of their brilliantly embroidered doublets and pulled them to their feet. Spontaneously, everyone began to applaud. Crasto was one of their most influential senators and at 55 he was at the height of his powers. He was broad shouldered, with iron-grey hair swept back from his stern, confident face and a pointed beard jutting defiantly. Flanked by two fine sons, he made a splendid sight. Bardo was already known in the city – his tall, wiry figure, straight, flaxen hair and impassive blue eyes were a familiar sight in the Exchange Building and he had even spoken in the Guild of Merchants. His young brother was still little more than a boy, but everyone agreed he looked to have the makings of another fine son – almost as tall as his father, and shaping up to be broader in the chest than Bardo. There was just something a little vague about his eyes, something slightly uncertain about his bearing, but everyone put that down to his youth. He'd be another strong pillar for his father's house in time.

Crasto raised his hands to end the applause.

'I give you my sons,' he proclaimed. 'Long life to this house. Long life to the State!'

He squeezed his sons' shoulders hard as their guests roared back this second toast, with glittering goblets raised.

When the toasts were over and the guests had ripped their way through the piles of meat set before them, there was dancing in the long gallery room in the west wing of the villa. Beata claimed Amisso as her partner, but after three dances she was bored and dragged him outside onto the veranda. They were still regarded as children and were not expected to linger and make polite conversation.

'Useless!' Beata cried, banging the heavy material of her dress. 'How can anyone dance in this stuff? I don't know why it has to have so many pearls on it, and so much gold wire. Father might just as well plate me in gold and hang me on the wall with a sign round my neck saying, "This is what she's worth, come and get her".'

'Does your father really want to marry you off so soon?' Amisso asked surprised.

'Of course. Fathers never want to let their sons go – they're needed for business – but they can't wait to get rid of their daughters before they go rotten on the shelf.'

'But surely it's Verna's turn before you.'

Beata turned back to the open windows, through which they could see the revels. Verna was not dancing. Instead, she was busy summoning drinks waiters, ensuring that everyone had all they required and making sure people mingled. The widowed senator was always glad to have Verna as his guest. In fact, over the last couple of years he had come to rely on her skill in directing banquets and always made sure she and her family sat next to his, in the centre of the great table, with Verna next to Bardo.

'I think our fathers already have plans for Verna,' Beata said quietly.

Amisso looked at the festive scene, puzzled.

'What?' he said.

But Beata walked away to the far end of the veranda and gazed out at the stars.

'Which way's north?' she asked.

Amisso pointed.

'That's where Father is then,' she said. Then a moment later, she added, 'I wish he was here tonight. I wish he didn't have to go away so much.'

'He's a diplomat, Beata,' Amisso reminded her. 'He has to go away.'

She took his arm and pulled herself close to him.

'I know,' she said. 'I don't usually mind, but this time they've sent him to Sordes.'

Amisso looked down quickly at her and saw the worry in her face.

'The situation's really getting bad,' she said, 'with all these raids on our shipping. And apparently we've been attacking their caravans – although nobody's supposed to know that. I only know because I heard Father talking to Verna. He discusses everything with her. You won't tell anyone, will you?'

'Who'd want to talk to me about trade or politics?' Amisso asked.

Beata gave him a sad little smile and gripped him tighter.

'They've sent Father to try and sort things out,' she said. 'I think it's some kind of emergency. I've never seen him so worried about a trip before.'

'He'll be all right,' Amisso told her, trying to sound confident. 'Diplomats are supposed to be protected.'

'I know,' Beata said, 'but you can never trust the Sordesians.'

***

It was the early hours of the morning by the time all the guests had finally gone. Crasto stood on the steps of his villa with his sons watching the flickering lights of torches as they guided the coaches back into the city, or branched off on the driveways leading to the neighbouring estates. After a while, the senator said a very pointed 'Goodnight' to Bardo and nodded briskly. It seemed to be some kind of signal, as Bardo nodded back and left immediately. Amisso said goodnight to his father too and turned to go, but Crasto put a hand on his shoulder and held him back.

'I want to show you something before you go to bed,' he told him.

He led the way through the entrance hall, across the inner courtyard with its gently gurgling fountain, and into the range of rooms at the back of the villa. This was where

Crasto had his private office – where he met his most important clients and fellow senators.

'Come,' Crasto said, opening the heavy wooden door.

He was carrying a torch, and he used it to light the candelabrum on a huge, leather-topped desk, before setting it in a bracket on the wall. The soft lights made the dark wooden panelling glow. The shadowy room seemed like a cave to Amisso, but he felt trapped in it rather than secure.

'Sit down, son,' his father said, and he indicated the big wooden chair behind the desk.

It was highly carved, and the seat and back were covered with padded leather that squeaked as Amisso lowered himself into it. He felt extremely uncomfortable: the chair was too big for him; the desk was too big. He half expected that his feet wouldn't touch the floor.

'Open the drawer,' Crasto instructed.

There was a large drawer underneath the desk, and Amisso pulled it towards him.

'Now, pass me the key.'

The drawer was full of rolled up papers, writing implements, magnifying lenses and measuring instruments, but to the left-hand side was a special velvet-lined compartment in which lay a large key. Amisso handed it to his father, who took it to a tall cabinet at the other side of the room. He opened it and took out a casket, which he carried back to the desk and placed before his son. It was made of gold, covered in elaborate decoration, and was clearly very heavy. A single letter was picked out in rubies in an oval mother-of-pearl panel on the lid. The letter was 'A'.

'Open it,' his father said. His voice was soft, reverent.

Amisso opened the lid and stared. The casket was full of gold coins of the highest value, neatly arranged and packed in tightly. It was a fortune.

'One day, this will be yours,' Crasto said. 'I don't want you just to carry on my business. There are agents who can do that. This is yours for yourself, to start something new, to build another business empire, to feel proud that you too have contributed something of your own to the wealth and splendour and power of Mercatorius.'

Crasto went back to the cabinet and patted another casket, glimmering faintly in the shadows.

'There's one for Bardo too,' he said. 'He's almost ready to take his.'

Amisso tasted bile rising in his throat. He was very tired, he'd drunk more wine than he was used to, and something in his father's soft, awestruck tone turned his stomach. For a moment, frustration turned to anger inside him.

'Maybe I'm ready too,' he said sharply.

His father stared at him in surprise, then his eyes brightened.

'Have you got a plan?' he asked eagerly.

There was a long, embarrassing pause and Amisso closed his eyes. Then he heard Crasto shut the casket and carry it back to the cabinet. He heard the key turn in the lock and a moment later felt his father's hand on his shoulder as the senator leaned over him, replacing the key and gently closing the drawer.

'You can have the money whenever you want,' he said gently. 'You know where it is now. You know where to find the key. This room is never locked, and the servants will never stop a son of mine from entering it.'

When the week was up, the mule owner had not presented himself at the taxman's office. Fallax went to his desk and began writing a message to the Commander of the City Guard, requesting a small escort to come with him to the man's house. But he was stopped almost as soon as he'd started by one of his clerks who came bursting through the door.

'He's here!' he shouted.

'Who?' Fallax demanded.

But before the clerk could reply, the mule owner had pushed through the door. He marched up to the taxman and dropped a small canvas bag on his desk. It clinked gently.

'There it is,' he said, 'every last coin of it. And I'll have a receipt, if you don't mind.'

He slapped the tax bill down next to the bag. Fallax looked at the man for a moment. He was not pleased. In addition to his tax collecting, Fallax had a good second income from renting out property in the Poor Quarter, and he'd been looking forward to taking possession of the mule owner's house. He opened the bag and emptied out a pile of gold coins. He prodded it with his finger.

'Where did you get these?' he asked.

'Mind your own business,' the mule man told him.

Fallax carefully examined the coins to make sure they were genuine, then slowly counted them. It was full payment. He scribbled his confirmation of receipt at the bottom of the tax bill and threw it back across the table.

The mule man took the receipted bill and went without another word. He left the taxman's office in a dream, dazed by all that had happened to him in the last twenty-four hours, and so he was nearly knocked flying as he entered Senate Square by a squad of City Guards racing past at the double. He staggered into a man wearing the uniform of a clerk to the courts.

'What's all that about?' the mule owner asked. 'Has the war started?'

'Haven't you heard?' the clerk replied. 'It's Senator Crasto. His son's gone. Not Bardo. The boy, young what's-his-name. He's taken a pile of money too. Cabinet open, casket gone, bed bare... Disappeared. The Guard's been searching since dawn but he's just vanished.'

3
Chasing the Dream

The clothes were rough against Amisso's skin, but they did their job. They made him look like any other labourer's lad from the Poor Quarter of Mercatorius. With his hair hacked short, and what was left of his golden locks stuffed under a grubby canvas cap, he was sure that no one would recognise him. Nevertheless, he felt that people were staring at him as he passed, peering round door frames at him, muttering behind his back. But he made himself keep going, not looking to right or left. A youth of his social class would normally show his confidence among these people by striding through them with his shoulders back and head held high. In this way, even a teenager such as Amisso could make poor people who were old enough to be his parents dodge out of the way. But such behaviour would not do now if he were to blend in with the crowd.

Amisso had to make sure to keep his head down. He bowed his back, and avoided barging into any of the other people thronging the narrow streets of the Poor Quarter.

He didn't want to get into an argument, but most of all he didn't want anyone to bang into the bag he carried over his shoulder. It was just a worn old leather bag, but the weight of it was straining the straps so that Amisso had to keep a hand under it for added support. If it fell to the ground or anyone knocked into it, the bag would clink in a way that Amisso was sure would betray its contents. It wasn't quite as heavy as it might have been, however. Amisso had already dipped into the inheritance he'd sneaked out of his father's study in the early hours of that morning. He'd used some of the gold to pay for the disguise he was wearing, and he'd paid for it dearly.

Amisso had entered the city long before dawn, passing through the Northern Gate – a sighting by the sentries there was the only clue that those searching for him later in the day were able to find. But then, instead of taking the broad road that led from the trading station to the prosperous south of the city, he'd slipped away among the stable yards of the mule owners, hoping to lie low until he could find a way to change his clothes. He hadn't expected to meet anyone at that early hour, but to his surprise he'd found a man in the first yard he'd come to. The man had a mule beside him, but he didn't seem to be working. He was leaning over the animal, with his head resting on its shoulder, while the mule bore his weight with an expression of great patience on its long face.

Amisso's first thought was that the man was sick, and going over to him he put a hand rather nervously on his shoulder. But when the man straightened up there were no signs of illness, just a face wet with tears. And when he saw this striking figure in his aristocratic clothes, he held his hands up as if he was surrendering.

'I didn't think you'd come so early,' he said. 'I thought at least you'd give me until the sun was up. But it doesn't matter, we're ready to leave. I'll tell my wife.'

He turned to go, but Amisso stopped him in alarm.

'Who do you think I am?' he asked.

'Hasn't Fallax sent you?' the man replied.

When Amisso told him he'd no idea what he was talking about, the mule man explained how Fallax was due to take possession of his house for failing to pay his taxes.

Amisso was horrified. 'But where are you going to live?' he asked.

The man turned and pointed to the stable behind him.

'At least it's a roof, young sir,' he said, patting the mule, 'and the company's good.'

Amisso, who had never slept beneath any roof that wasn't gilded, stared at him in disbelief. Then a thought occurred to him – a way of helping the man – and it made him feel suddenly grown up to be able to suggest it.

'I've got an idea,' he said, putting on a businesslike tone, 'a deal, a proposition for you.'

Ten minutes later, Amisso had begun his journey through the Poor Quarter, dressed in the mule man's clothes, his hair hacked by a pair of shears that were usually used on the animals, and having paid a sum exactly equal to the mule man's tax bill. But he hadn't just bought the clothes and the haircut – his most important purchase was the man's promise of silence about where the money had come from, and his agreement not to sell the expensive clothes Amisso had left bundled beneath the straw in the stable but to burn them. And as a bonus, the man had given Amisso directions to a tavern where he might be able to join the crew of one of the less well-known trading ships, with no questions asked.

~~~

The cheap wine that was served to swill down breakfast in the tavern felt sour in Amisso's stomach, but the fish - fresh from the sea - was good, and the young runaway was ravenous. It was mostly excitement that was making him so hungry. The whole adventure felt like an elaborate joke that had unexpectedly turned into reality. The sun was only just up and already he'd achieved so much - he'd escaped his home undetected, got himself a disguise, and found a place that was going to provide him with his route out of Mercatorius for good - or at least until he could return with something to show for the money he'd taken. What that something might be, or how it might be got, he had no more idea now than he'd had on the night his father had shown him his inheritance. That night had left him with a sour sense of humiliation that had outlasted his hangover, and at some time in the week that had followed, he'd lost patience. If he waited for inspiration to come to him he might wait for ever, he'd told himself; better just to take the money and go, and see if he ran into inspiration on his way.

Amisso finished his fish breakfast and scanned the room. About 20 sailors were scattered round the dark wooden tables, most staring at their plates as they ate. Those few whose heads were raised had hard, unsmiling expressions. No one seemed in the mood for conversation at that time in the morning, and the only sounds were the scraping of knives on pewter plates and distant shouts and clattering from the kitchen. Somewhere in the distance a group of seagulls started a harsh chorus of calls.

Amisso wondered how he was going to make the contact that would lead to a ship and escape. Once or twice he caught the eye of a sailor, but there was no flicker of welcome. In fact, Amisso looked quickly away each time, cowed by the hard frown he'd received. Some men left, throwing small coins on the table and grunting at the girl who collected them. Others came, muttered their orders and settled into heavy silence. Occasionally they would shout a word of greeting to another customer, but nothing more. Time was passing, and Amisso knew that he would have to make a move. The alarm would be raised by now and his father would be arranging a search. Amisso needed to be on board ship as soon as possible, and at sea before the morning was out.

A hand slapped down heavily on Amisso's shoulder and gripped it. The teenager jumped in surprise. He turned in his seat, expecting to see a soldier of the Guard behind him. But instead he found the hand belonged to a broad man in a seaman's jerkin with black, greasy hair falling round his weather-beaten face.

'Mind if I join you?' he asked.

His voice was sharp and had a slight accent that Amisso couldn't place.

'Help yourself,' Amisso replied, trying to sound gruff and manly.

The sailor relaxed his hold on Amisso's shoulder and sat down beside the lad.

'You're a stranger here,' the man said.

He'd brought a bottle of wine with him and refilled Amisso's glass from it, then poured a generous measure straight into his own mouth.

'No one comes here without a purpose,' he went on.

Amisso was silent, unsure how to respond, and tried to take a drink of the cheap wine without coughing.

'So, what's yours?' the man continued.

Amisso looked him in the face, trying to read his character in it, but the sea wind seemed to have scoured it free of expression. It was as blank as a leather mask.

'I'm looking for employment,' Amisso told him.

'You're a sailor then?'

'I am,' Amisso replied, hoping that he wouldn't be asked to name the ships he'd served in.

'Then why aren't you queuing at the booths in Chandlers' Square?' the man asked. 'That's where the masters do their hiring.'

Amisso drained his glass in a way that, he hoped, made him look like a seasoned drinker.

'I have my reasons,' he told him.

'Ah – a young man with a past,' his companion said, filling Amisso's glass again. 'There's something you need to get away from, perhaps.'

The wine was muddling Amisso's head, and he struggled to think of a reply.

'In that case, my lad,' the man went on, 'I may be able to help you. That is, if you have some money to invest.'

'I have money,' Amisso said, and he kicked the bag lying at his feet. It clinked but its weight stopped it moving. The man stared at the bag for a moment, then held out his hand.

'My name's Volpo,' he said.

By evening on the day of Amisso's disappearance, most of the boy's family and friends seemed to be lost as well. No one knew where anyone else was. Everyone had experienced the need to be outdoors and doing something. As the light began to fail, Bardo was still accompanying a detachment of guards in their hunt through every alley and yard of the city, insisting they keep searching, although every other unit had long since returned to barracks. Crasto, after exhausting himself by riding almost to the neighbouring city of Munius and back in the hunt for his son, had returned to his villa, sat in his study staring at the wall for five minutes, then left the house again without saying where he was going. Beata had joined in none of the searching, but she too had felt impelled to leave her home. As soon as the news of her friend's disappearance had reached her she'd gone out and had been away all day. Verna had gone to Crasto's villa and stayed at her post there, ready to receive any reports or news of the runaway.

Beata wasn't searching because she knew at once where Amisso would be. To her, he wasn't lost. Instead it was she who felt lost - lost inside herself, abandoned. For hours, she'd wandered on the headland to the west of the city watching the ships come and go along the seaways from Mercatorius, wondering which one was carrying her friend away from her. She supposed she should have felt glad for Amisso, that he'd achieved their dream. But instead she felt annoyed. It was a seething irritation that kept her pacing up and down the cliff paths. Running away to sea was a shared dream, but he'd gone off on his own and left her behind. And really, when it came down to it, she had to admit to herself that it was only meant to be a dream. It wasn't meant to be something that actually happened. It was a story that two teenage friends told to each other - that was all. The real world was where people's mothers died of fever and people's fathers were sent to dangerous places. That was the world where she needed her friend to be, but now he'd gone off into their dream world and left her to deal with reality on her own. Somehow he'd managed to mix up the worlds. And if that could happen, it seemed as if anything could. Beata found herself on the edge of the cliff and she noticed a seagull gliding past far below her. She watched it for a moment, then suddenly she snatched up a stone and threw it at the bird, missing by metres.

It was beginning to get dark. Beata was cold and hungry and the anger inside her eventually subsided into a gloomy depression, so she set off for home. She'd got as far as the cliffs above the naval dockyard, when she saw the shapes of two men sitting on a big rock about fifty metres ahead of her. They were engrossed in conversation and didn't notice the girl approaching. Soon she was able to recognise them and when she did she stopped in her tracks. One was Amisso's father, Crasto, but it was the sight of his companion that had brought Beata to a halt. On the rare occasions she'd ever seen him before he'd been on the balcony of his palace in Senate Square, or on the platform at the far end of the State Banqueting Chamber. But there could be no mistaking his jutting chin and narrow beak of a nose. Beside her friend's father sat His Serene Lordship, the Dux of Mercatorius – leader of the Senate and their city's Head of State.

'These are difficult times for Mercatorius,' Beata heard the Dux saying.

'And this is a difficult day for me,' Crasto replied sharply.

'Of course it is, my friend,' said the Dux.

'Then why are you troubling me with this?'

Crasto was bent over, with his arms resting on his knees and his head hanging. But the Dux sat bolt upright, staring out across the naval dockyard – The Arsenal, as it was called. Beata followed his eyes and scanned the dark shapes of the galleys and galleasses moored below, row upon row of them – the whole might of the Mercatorian navy.

'Crasto, I've authorised the Guard to search the city,' the Dux told him. 'I've had the Commander send cavalry into the hills. I've ordered my own bodyguard to join the search. I wouldn't have done a fraction of that for anyone else's son. What more can I do?'

'You know I'm grateful,' Crasto responded.

'Then show it,' the Dux insisted. 'I need you; Mercatorius needs you tomorrow. The threat of Sordes grows every day. This cannot wait, not even until your son is found, which he will be soon – have no fear.'

Beata was not in the habit of eavesdropping on other people's conversations. She had intended to leave the path and creep away behind the two men. But mention of Sordes caused her to linger. Perhaps she might hear something about her father's fate. Slowly, she sank to her knees and hid among the long grass and bushes beside the track.

'Is that the only reason you came out here to find me?' Crasto asked.

'Not entirely,' the Dux replied. 'I came for friendship's sake as well. I've not forgotten the hours we spent on these cliffs together when we were boys, Crasto. If I hadn't remembered those times, I wouldn't have known where to look for you. But that was long ago. We're grown men now – getting to be old men. There's more than friendship for us to consider. We both serve the State, and the State needs us. The State needs you tomorrow. You must speak in the Senate. We have to rearm. We must have at least five more warships before the spring. If you speak in favour, the Senate will agree – you know they will.'

Neither man had looked at the other throughout this exchange, but now Crasto glanced up at the Dux.

'Have I driven him away, Torgo?' he asked.

'You've done nothing wrong in this,' the Dux said briskly. 'The boy has simply run away. What's happened is no one's doing but his own. He'll be found soon, you'll whip some sense into him, and life will go on. We can't afford weakness, Senator – least of all now.'

Crasto was silent.

'I can count on you tomorrow?' the Dux persisted.

Crasto seemed to nod, but did not speak.

'Come along then,' the Dux said, in a surprisingly gentle tone. 'Let me take you home. And I must go home myself, or there'll be search parties out looking for *me*.'

Crasto allowed the Dux to help him to his feet. They made a striking contrast as they stood side by side: Crasto broad, barrel-chested and muscular, and the Dux half a head taller but angular and bony by comparison. They both took a last look out to sea, as they must have done many times together as children, then set off towards the city wall. Beata let them get a good start before she too headed for home.

4
A Floating Prison

Amisso was brought back to consciousness by a pain in his head. It started as a dull, pulsating ache, but the moment he tried to sit up it felt as if a burning spike had been jammed through his brain. Instinctively, his hands jerked to get at the source of the pain but he found they wouldn't move. Despite the agony in his head, he twisted and turned, but his hands were firmly tied behind his back. He discovered that his ankles were bound together too. After a few moments he stopped struggling and lay still, panting and letting the pain in his head die down again. It was dark, but the stink, the rolling movement and the gentle sloshing of water gave him a good clue as to where he was. He guessed he was below decks in the bilges of Volpo's ship. He had no idea how long he'd been unconscious or how far they must now have sailed from Mercatorius.

As he lay in the dark space, still barely conscious, Amisso's last sights of home formed in his mind like a dream. He'd been standing on the poop deck of Volpo's ship as he'd watched the gilded domes blaze in the bright rays of the morning sun, then slowly lose their lustre and shrink into the distance behind. The wind had freshened as the ship left the shelter of the promontory to the west of Mercatorius. The sails strained, orders were shouted, whistles blew and men scrambled up the rigging to set more canvas. Amisso had felt the wind get hold of the vessel and drive it forward like horses galloping away with a carriage and he'd breathed deep with pleasure. He'd turned his back on the fading smudge that was his home and faced the bows, rising and falling as they hissed through the water. He'd stood with legs apart, riding the motion of the deck, and imagined himself the captain of the vessel.

It wasn't a sleek galley or a mighty galleass, but he'd told himself it had a kind of elegance of its own and it was certainly fast. The ship was a three-masted caravel, with a mixture of square-rigged and lateen-rigged sails, and it wasn't Mercatorian. Amisso hadn't been able to make out where it was from and he couldn't remember ever having seen it in port before, nor could he recognise the words the sailors were shouting at each other as they worked. He'd realised he ought to ask Volpo more about the ship and turned to look for the captain, but as he'd done so he'd seen the figure of Volpo just behind him with his arm raised high. There'd been a bang and Amisso had felt his head jerk. He'd been aware of his body hitting something hard, then blackness.

The memory of Volpo's treachery brought Amisso out of his half-conscious reverie. He was seething with anger and wrenched violently at his bonds. The pain this caused in his limbs and his head made him draw a sharp breath.

'Best lie still,' said a male voice close by.

Amisso gasped again, in surprise.

'Who's there?' he said, unable to keep a tremble out of his voice.

'Don't worry,' the man replied, 'I won't do you no harm. I'm trussed up the same as you. So's the rest of them.'

'Rest?' Amisso said. 'How many are there down here?'

'Can't say,' the man told him. 'Maybe a dozen.'

Amisso listened carefully and gradually he became aware of the sounds of other people – he heard the occasional heaving breath, then someone muttering and, after a while, something else that sounded like sobbing. Then a low moaning started up.

'That one's seasick,' the man next to Amisso whispered.

'Can't someone shut him up?' a voice shouted as the groaning grew louder, but the man kept on and a few minutes later he started to retch. Soon the smell of vomit had joined the other stenches in their wooden prison.

Time passed, then the man spoke again.

'You sound like you're just a kid,' he said to Amisso.

'I'm 16!' Amisso said aggressively.

'Like I said,' the man replied.

Amisso didn't respond. He was glad of the blackness now, because the hint of kindness in the man's voice had brought tears to his eyes and they had started to run down his cheeks. He fought hard to prevent himself making any noise that would give him away, but in the end he couldn't help sniffing hard. He felt such a fool. He was frightened and homesick, but most of all he was so angry with himself. His tears were a bitter mixture of misery and frustration.

'Let it go, son,' the man said. 'There's grown men been crying down here since we set sail and I'm one of 'em.'

He told Amisso his name was Urso and that he had a wife and two children in Mercatorius who thought he was on his way to make their fortune.

'The captain said I could do some trading of my own on the trip,' Urso explained, 'so I signed on for the crew and brought all our savings. Soon as I got aboard they jumped me and took the lot. I should have known better, kid. That's what hurts. I should have known he wasn't to be trusted or why wouldn't he have had a booth in Chandlers' Square like all the other masters instead of doing his business round the taverns? It was greed that done for me – he said you could make three times as much trading in the places he was going.'

'Shut up going on about it, will you?' someone shouted. 'He caught us all the same. We don't want reminding.'

'What about you, son?' Urso asked, lowering his voice. 'Is that what happened to you?'

'Sort of,' Amisso replied.

Amisso pictured the scene in the tavern. Volpo had taken him to a dingy back room, poured more cheap wine for him and then fixed him with a stern, unblinking eye.

'You're no sailor,' he'd said bluntly, and before Amisso could think of a reply, Volpo had grasped both the boy's hands and squeezed hard. Amisso had returned the grip, but Volpo had simply laughed.

'Strong,' he'd said, 'but soft – soft as a lady's pillow. You've never done a day's work in your life.'

Amisso had felt his cheeks burn, but Volpo had just smiled.

'That's nothing to me,' he'd said, releasing Amisso. 'Only, it makes me wonder if cutting those hands to ribbons heaving on rough old ropes and breaking your back hauling in sail is the best kind of thing for a lad like yourself to be doing at sea. I was thinking you might be better employed in a captain's cabin – my cabin. Not as a cabin boy, mind – though that might better fit your age – but as a partner in my venture.'

Amisso had asked what the venture was.

'Something the people of this port would kill to know about and be part of,' Volpo had told him. 'Something that will add to the fame and glory of Mercatorius like nothing before in all its history – not to mention the glory of the heroes who undertake it. There'll be statues of them in Senate Square when it's over – you can count on it.'

Amisso had pictured a statue of himself in the great square of Mercatorius – the heart of the world – with his father and all the other senators gathered round it to marvel and, hungrily, he'd asked for more details. Volpo had leaned far forward over the table and put his arm round Amisso's shoulder to draw him closer.

'I have in my possession,' Volpo had murmured into Amisso's ear, 'an ancient map – passed down from a seafaring people who sailed this globe half a thousand years ago, when Mercatorius was no more than a row of cottages and a handful of fishing boats. It shows a secret route – a sea passage lost since ancient times – a passage that ships beyond counting have set out to find and have failed.' His voice had dropped until it was no more than a stirring of the air. 'It shows the sea route to the East,' he'd said.

The legendary sea route to the East – it would cut the travelling time to those distant lands by months. Silks, spices and all the other treasures of the East could be in the markets of Mercatorius in a fraction of the time and at a fraction of the cost and the risk that was currently involved. It would be a revolution. Volpo was right – statues in Senate Square would be a certainty for those involved, not to mention a fortune to match his father's and more.

'So,' Volpo had asked, 'do I have a partner? An undertaking like this is a costly business. And when we reach the East we'll need to buy in a cargo to bring back. It's going to take a lot of money. I have a ship and a map, but not a ducat to pay for the trip. If I had, I'd have gone months ago; I'd have been back already, the hero of Mercatorius! No money, no venture. So the question is: do you have the money, young man? And do you have the guts to join me?'

Amisso had shaken hands without another thought, and within half an hour he and his bag of gold had been aboard Volpo's ship.

'Yes,' Amisso said to Urso. 'He got me just like the rest of you – he jumped me for my money.'

A few minutes later, a faint light reached the dark hold and the glimmering of a lantern told them someone was coming. It was Volpo, followed by half a dozen fierce-looking sailors. Volpo searched among the bodies of his captives, then he came up to Amisso and held his lantern in the boy's face.

'I didn't kill you then,' he said with a harsh laugh.

'What's going on?' Amisso demanded.

'You're learning a lesson, Master Pillow-hands,' Volpo told him.

At that moment Amisso realised that his supposed partner had never even asked him his name.

'I'm called Amisso,' he snapped but raising his voice sent the pain shooting through his head again and he winced.

'Hurts, doesn't it?' Volpo sneered. 'I've brought you some food, Master Pillow-hands,' he told him, putting a wooden board and a leather flask down beside the prisoner.

'I'm Amisso,' he repeated, but in a sullen whisper this time.

'Your new owner will tell you what your name is, boy,' Volpo told him. 'Now I'm going to untie you so you can eat. But don't try anything. I could kill you with one hand, and I wouldn't lose any sleep over doing it – you won't fetch much in the market. To be honest, you're hardly worth feeding, but I can't stand waste and I might as well get every last ducat out of you.'

Panic seized Amisso as Volpo's words sunk in: the captain wasn't going to be content just to rob him, he meant to sell him as a slave. Now he understood why grown men had been weeping in the hold.

'I'm worth lots,' Amisso cried urgently. 'I'm Senator Crasto's son. He'll ransom me. Ask what you want. He'll give you a fortune.'

'He already has,' Volpo said, with a grin. 'It's surprising how much one old bag can hold.'

'He'll give you another then. You said you don't like waste. Why waste the chance to double your money? Think about it.'

'No, you think about it,' Volpo told him coldly as he worked at the knots that bound Amisso's wrists. 'How hard would it be to swap you for the money and get away without a galley on my tail? And how easy is it to drop you off at the next slave market? Risk assessment. Profit and loss. You've got to do the calculations. It's called business sense, and it's obvious you don't have any.'

Amisso's hands were free, and Volpo left him to his meal: rank water in the flask and stale bread on the board. The sailors had untied the hands of the other prisoners and left them with similar provisions, but their feet remained bound and as the sailors were all armed with heavy clubs, none of the captives seemed inclined to cause them any trouble.

The arrival of their meagre food and exercise times were the only things that allowed Amisso and the other prisoners to calculate the passage of time. They were fed and watered twice daily, and exercised every day. Exercise amounted to half an hour trudging round the main mast guarded by the heavily armed crew. No talking was allowed, but once his eyes had got used to the glare of the light, Amisso was able to scan the horizon, check the position of the sun and make an estimate of their location. By this method, he knew that to start with they were sailing due west. So much for Volpo's tales of a search for the passage to the East. They called at two ports en route, and each time the prisoners feared they would be led out to be sold. But instead more captives were brought to join them in the stinking bilges. Their journey west entailed five days sailing and two days in port, then there was a change of course – their floating prison turned northwards.

There were no more stops now, and during exercise on their fourth day travelling north, Amisso spied land ahead. It was close enough to make out some detail and he could see that it was mountainous with a broad coastal plain. He made some rough calculations, based on the directions he knew they'd taken, the time they'd been at sea, and the knowledge gained from his father's map room, and looking at those mountains he felt sure he knew where they were. If he was right, those craggy walls, their ravines deeply shadowed by the morning sun, were the mountains of Partak. No trade route crossed them, and beyond them were lands unknown to Mercatorius and Sordes.

The next day the prisoners were herded on deck once more, but not for exercise this time. They were stripped and given buckets of water to wash in, then they were issued with lengths of cloth to twist round their waists and made to sit on stools, three at a time, while they had their heads and faces shaved. Finally, olive oil was rubbed into their skin to make it shine and they were arranged in two lines amidships, like a parade, as the ship glided gently on towards the port that could now be seen ahead, lying in the shadow of the mountains. Amisso put on the expressionless face that he had learned to adopt as a way of avoiding the attention of the sailors who guarded them. Any show of emotion or other indication that the captives were in fact fellow human beings was likely to be met with a sharp rap from a club. But inside, Amisso's feelings were in turmoil now that the end of their journey was near.

During their days below decks, those prisoners who shared a common language had told each other their stories. Amisso had already blurted out that he was a senator's son, and there had seemed no point in hiding the fact that he'd run off with his father's money. When he'd confessed what he'd done, the full force of it had finally hit him. All the others were innocent victims, but Amisso had begun to feel that he deserved to be a prisoner. A strange silence had greeted his tale; no one had wanted to cause more distress by criticising a fellow captive, but Amisso could tell that his companions were shocked.

Amisso was frightened for his future, but it was the thought of his father that preoccupied his mind as he stood on deck watching the port growing closer. Among the reasons Amisso had told his story to the others was the hope that one of the captives might some day return to Mercatorius and send word to Crasto about his son's fate. But another part of Amisso hated the idea that his father should ever learn what had become of him. Far better that his father should think he had simply disappeared without trace. What disgrace it would bring to the house of Crasto to know that the senator's son had been sold in a slave market. As Amisso realised how appallingly he'd treated his father, he began to appreciate just how much he loved him.

When the ship was safely moored at the quayside, a gangplank was lowered and the prisoners were marched across, heavily guarded by the ship's crew. Captain Volpo was waiting on the quay, eyeing up his stock as it was disembarked. Amisso stared into the captain's face as he was paraded past him. Volpo met his eyes for a second without even a flicker of recognition, then surveyed his body for a moment before turning his attention to the next in line. And that was the last Amisso saw of the man who'd promised him the world, taken his money and his freedom and given him nothing in return but a look that seemed to say he was no more than an animal, and a poor quality one at that. If this was business sense, Amisso thought, he was glad he didn't have any.

As his bare feet touched the warm stones of the causeway that led from the harbour to the town, Amisso was surprised by a new emotion. In spite of everything, he found that the fascination of the strange sights, sounds and smells that surrounded him was mixing excitement with his distress. This place was so much more colourful than Mercatorius. Instead of white marble and shining gold and pale yellows, pinks and greens, the town where they'd landed was full of rich, definite colours. They were marching through the market area, and every stall had an awning of orange or purple, crimson, emerald or yellow as rich as an egg yolk. And the place was so noisy. In Mercatorius business was a serious matter, to be conducted in hushed voices with nods and winks and words murmured behind hands, but here voices cried out their wares joyfully – some even seemed to be singing about what they had to offer. There was laughter and backslapping, arguing and haggling that was so dramatic it looked like scenes from the theatre. It didn't seem to be a rich place. Amisso couldn't see anyone dressed in the elaborate clothes of Mercatorius. Everyone, men and women, seemed to wear simple ground-length robes, mostly in white or cream, but they had a flowing elegance that the Mercatorians lacked. Perhaps it was something to do with the way they walked – slowly, with chins high, and arms relaxed at their sides. No one was carrying any weapons, Amisso suddenly realised. But the thing that struck Amisso most was the scent of the place, a wonderful mixture of woodsmoke, cooking fish and lemons. This, if his calculations were correct, was the town of Dekan.

The captives were marched to a broad open space on the outskirts of the town. It was much larger than the squares of Mercatorius, but was simply baked earth rather than neatly cut flagstones. And business was being conducted in the centre of the space, whereas in Mercatorius the trading booths were arranged around the edges of the squares. Amisso, Urso and the others from Volpo's ship were placed in a wooden pen – just one in a row of half a dozen, all with their stock of potential slaves. To the left of the slave pens were about twenty individual stalls, each containing a small horse – black or very dark brown. They kicked and pawed the ground, looking fiery and hard to ride despite their size.

In contrast, the human livestock stood still and silent with heads bowed. They seemed to have much more in common with the bulky oxen which occupied a large corral to the right and whose only movement was an involuntary twitch of the flanks or swish of the tail when an insect jabbed into their hide. The smell of the town was overpowered here by the stench of dung and urine, and the sounds of the people were drowned in the incessant bleating from the sheep and goat pens that ran the whole length of the site behind horses, men and oxen.

Senator Crasto didn't own slaves. His galleys were rowed by free men who were all allowed to bring their own small stock of goods to trade in the ports they visited. Amisso's father claimed this made them more loyal and hard working. Other shipowners thought a whip was a better incentive, however, and manned their oars with slaves. As he stood in the midday heat, dehydrating and growing dizzy from exhaustion, Amisso found himself hoping that one of these merchants from Mercatorius might be visiting the market to re-stock his crew and would buy him. Even though he knew it would bring shame to his father, Amisso was suddenly overwhelmed by the desire to return even as a slave to the city he had turned his back on with such high hopes just under a fortnight ago. Once he was in Mercatorius, he could surely get a message to his father and beg his forgiveness. Surely his father would buy him back.

But there were no Mercatorians to be seen. He heard nothing but the jabber of foreign languages as he endured being poked and felt by potential customers and experienced the strange mixture of relief and disappointment as he was passed over and others were bought. Urso had been bought almost at once. Amisso found himself envying those who were led away by their new owners – slaves maybe, but released from the torture and degradation of this long wait.

Eventually, Amisso became aware that someone had been standing in front of him for several minutes but had not touched him at all. He raised his weary head and saw a man in his thirties, dressed in a white robe, simply looking at him. Several slaps across the face earlier on had taught Amisso that he was not supposed to look the customers in the eye, but something made him break the rule with this man. His eyes were a pale hazel colour, making a striking contrast to his dark skin and short black hair, and instead of slapping Amisso for his insolence, he smiled. Amisso smiled back.

'Would you like me to buy you?' the man said quietly.

Amisso was astonished to hear his own language.

'You're a Mercatorian?' he whispered through dry, cracked lips.

'No,' the man told him. 'But your language is well known. It's the language of trade throughout the world – every merchant's second tongue.'

'But how did you know I was from Mercatorius?'

'You haven't answered,' the man said. 'Do you want me to buy you?'

Amisso had no idea how he was supposed to reply to such a question.

'Please get me out of here,' was all he could think to say.

5
Return to Mercatorius

The cavalry squadrons of Mercatorius were legendary for their swiftness. Just as Mercatorian galleys could outpace any ship afloat, so the city's cavalry could outrun any mounted force sent against them. But a column is only as fast as its slowest member and Captain Cito was cursing the fact that his squadron had been assigned to escort one of the slowest parties he could imagine – a delegation of Mercatorian senators.

'They'd be faster walking!' he snarled to his lieutenant, as the two of them pulled their horses out of the line and rode up onto a slight rise to survey the situation. They were travelling through a broad plain and the two officers had a good view of the surrounding countryside from their mound, but more hilly terrain lay between them and Mercatorius, and Captain Cito was worried.

'Send outriders up to that ridge on the left,' he ordered, pointing to a grey, rocky shape in the distance. 'The last thing we want is an ambush so far from the city. Send your steadiest men. Tell them not to engage. If they find anything, they're to return to the column as fast as they can. We don't want any heroics.'

'Do you really think the Sordesians would land a force this far south, sir?' the lieutenant asked.

'Who knows what they might do?' Cito replied. 'I'm taking no chances. The quicker we get back to Mercatorius the better as far as I'm concerned.'

'But we're not even at war,' the lieutenant went on. 'There's nothing but rumours.'

'I don't think the shipping we've lost this winter or the outposts that have been attacked were just rumours, Lieutenant,' Cito replied, sharply. 'And what do you think this is all about, if it's not preparations for war?' He gestured towards the lumbering carriages with their cargo of senators.

They were returning from a week-long visit to the neighbouring state of Munius, and it was common knowledge that the senators' business had been to agree an alliance with their nearest neighbour. Munius was strong, but small and inward-looking. In normal circumstances it would have nothing to offer a great power such as Mercatorius, but in time of war an ally to block the land approaches to Mercatorius would be invaluable.

'Despatch your outriders, Lieutenant,' Captain Cito ordered. 'The Senate expects war, and so must we.'

The lieutenant galloped back to the line, and Cito watched as a dozen men were singled out and sent on their way to check the ridge. Cito knew every one of his men even at a distance and he approved his lieutenant's choice.

'If there's anything up there, they'll find it,' he thought to himself.

He let the whole column pass him and scanned the horizon behind to make sure there was no pursuit. All was clear, but Cito took little comfort from this – there was no doubt that the most dangerous part of their journey lay ahead. It was well into the afternoon and travelling at this snail's pace it would take them four more hours to clear the hilly terrain ahead and be within sight of home. If anyone was going to attack a travelling column Cito knew that among those hills was just where they'd do it. People had plenty of insulting things to say about the Sordesians, but Cito knew better than to underestimate their cunning or their courage. If there were Sordesian marauders in the area, he knew he'd be in trouble.

Captain Cito was just contemplating which configuration of his forces would be best if he was called on to defend the senators when he noticed that the column had stopped. At once, he spurred his horse and galloped to rejoin his men.

'What's happening, Captain?' one of the senators called, in a trembling voice, as Cito sped past his carriage. But the captain didn't stop until he had reached the head of the column.

'Well, Lieutenant?' he demanded, as he brought his charger to a skidding halt beside the junior officer.

'Someone injured by the roadside, sir,' the lieutenant replied, pointing to a figure stretched out in the dust.

A couple of troopers had dismounted and were examining the body.

'Is he alive?' Cito asked.

'Yes, sir,' came the reply. 'He's been badly beaten, but he's still breathing. Doesn't look very old. In his teens, I'd say.'

Cito swung his horse round and cantered back to the first of the three carriages he was escorting.

'There's an injured boy by the roadside,' he called in to the senator who was the head of the delegation. 'He seems to have been attacked.'

'Attacked?' the senator repeated, in an alarmed voice.

'Is it your wish that we should attend to him?' Cito asked. 'Perhaps your Honour would allow him to travel in your coach.'

'Certainly not!' the senator barked. 'Ride on, Captain! Leave him! This may be the result of a Sordesian attack – they may be waiting to attack us! He may even be a Sordesian. It may be a trap to hold us up – he may be a spy! Ride on, Captain! Ride on at once!'

'For pity's sake!' Cito muttered, turning his horse away.

He paused for a moment, then raised his voice and called his orders as he galloped back to the head of his troops.

'Ride on, Lieutenant!' he shouted. 'Leave him and ride on!'

The young victim was only dimly aware of what was going on. He had a sense of a large number of people close to him, the sound and smell of horses, someone bending over him. Then it seemed as if he was alone again. He struggled to raise his head and saw the blurred shapes of horsemen and coaches disappearing into the distance. Spring had barely begun and a chill breeze began to blow. Shivers shook his body and he knew that a night out in the open would kill him, even if his injuries didn't. But there was nothing he could do about that. The robbers who had attacked him had stripped him almost naked and had beaten him until he hadn't the strength even to crawl from the roadside in search of shelter. He tried to call out, but no sound came from his lips and he sank back into unconsciousness.

Water trickled between the injured youth's lips. He tried to swallow but failed, and his body was convulsed by a fit of coughing. He felt himself being raised and cradled in strong arms, and when the coughing had subsided the flask of water was put to his lips again. This time he managed to swallow properly. There was just enough light for him to make out a small train of packhorses standing patiently on the road and two men attending to them – probably servants. He guessed that the man who had him in his arms must be a merchant of some kind.

'You're freezing,' the man said. 'Here.' And taking off his thick woollen cloak, he wrapped it round his patient. 'Where are you from?' he asked. 'Munius?'

'No,' the victim whispered. 'Mercatorius.'

For a moment the two stared at each other. The merchant knew that it would be quite clear from his accent that he himself was from Sordes. Although they used some different words and phrases, and had very different accents, the two rival states actually spoke the same language and their citizens could understand each other perfectly if only they could get over their mutual hatred for long enough to make the effort.

'I'm bound for Sordes,' the merchant said, at last. 'My road's to the north, but I'll take you to an inn that I know. They'll look after you there.'

The merchant called one of his servants, and together they raised the youth to his feet. He clung to their shoulders and they half carried him towards the packhorses, but suddenly he started struggling.

'Wait,' he croaked.

They stopped and supported him as he freed a hand and ran it over his chest. His fingers closed tightly round a small leather pouch that was hanging from his neck.

'All right,' he whispered and relaxed again, letting them hoist him onto the back of one of the horses.

'What's your name?' the merchant asked as they moved off.

'Amisso,' he replied.

Beata hid just out of sight where the broad staircase up from the entrance hall of her home met the corridor that led to her chamber. Verna had sent her to bed, and she was furious. With their father, Ambassador Capax, still held in Sordes, their mother had withdrawn to her rooms in grief and was living like a hermit, and all authority in the house had now passed to Verna. Their mother hadn't even stirred to welcome the unexpected guest who had caused Beata's banishment. In the entrance hall, talking in a low voice to Verna, was none other than the Dux. As soon as the servants had announced his arrival Verna had ordered her younger sister to her chamber, but Beata was determined to find out what was going on. The Dux had never visited their home before. Something important was clearly happening – perhaps it was to do with their father.

Another male voice could be heard in the entrance hall, and Beata realised that Amisso's brother, Bardo, had arrived as well. She got down on her hands and knees and peeping through the railings at the top of the stairs she was just in time to see the three of them walking away in the direction of the parlour. Two members of the Dux's bodyguard were standing by the outside door and started to follow, but the Dux waved them away. Beata ducked out of sight as the Dux turned to his guards but as soon as the way was clear she came hurrying down the stairs. The bodyguards scowled at her, and one of them moved forward as if he was going to say something, but she imitated the Dux's gesture of dismissal and rushed off down the corridor.

The parlour door was shut, but Beata had expected that. She went past it and entered a small adjoining room. She knew that she would not be disturbed here if she sat with her ear against the communicating door and she would have a good chance of hearing most of what was being said.

Thankfully, the Dux had a firm, clear voice. 'I've spent an hour with him,' Beata heard him telling Verna. 'Bardo's spoken to him repeatedly. He takes no notice. You are our last hope, Mistress Verna. If Senator Crasto will not listen to sense from you then all is lost.'

'Surely he can be allowed to grieve in peace,' Verna suggested.

'Grief is all well and good,' the Dux replied, 'but Amisso has been gone for months. Crasto's return to his duties is long overdue. He hasn't been to the Senate House since the disaster of his speech on rearmament the day after Amisso absconded. There were calls for his resignation then. "A man who rambles incoherently for five minutes, then almost runs from the Chamber is clearly not fit to have a hand in governing Mercatorius," is what Senator Perdo said and there were many who agreed with him. It took all my authority to recover the situation.'

'Perhaps they were right,' Verna replied. 'Perhaps he should be allowed to retire.'

'Never!' Bardo broke in.

'Certainly not, Mistress,' the Dux added sharply. 'There is more at stake than Crasto's personal life. At a time like this, the Senate needs a man of his strength and wisdom. It's a question of duty. The Senate is not what it was. Crasto is vital to the good government of our State, and yet his enemies will have him out of his seat unless we can get him to return to the Chamber.'

'How can they do that?' Verna asked. 'They can't make him resign.'

'They don't need to,' Bardo explained. 'If a senator fails to take his seat for six months then he is automatically disqualified. Amisso has been gone more than five months now – we have very little time to persuade my father to return to the Chamber.'

'Will you help us, Mistress Verna?' the Dux asked earnestly.

'Our business has already suffered enough by his withdrawal from the Senate,' Bardo told her. 'I'm doing my best, but people don't want to associate themselves with the House of Crasto anymore. They don't trust us to look after their trade. They think there must be something suspicious about us – including me. Any reputation I might have been building up has been destroyed over these past months. If Father's forced out of the Senate, the disgrace will finish us off.'

'Mercatorius is a place of pride and honour, Verna,' the Dux reminded her. 'It values fortitude and success. The weakness that Senator Crasto has shown is crippling his business – no one backs a weakling in this city. Bardo is facing an impossible struggle. You owe it to Bardo to do what you can.'

There was a silence, and Beata pressed her eye to the keyhole of the door. She saw her sister take a step towards Bardo and rest her hand on his arm. Beata was fascinated and watched Verna's face intently. There was the look which Beata knew so well – the look that said Verna was doing her duty – but there was something else there too. Verna turned her face towards Bardo with an unusual uncertainty, as if she was searching for something – some response. But Bardo didn't look at her. His expression was anxious and distracted. He was very pale, and Beata suddenly realised how much weight he'd lost. After a moment, Verna removed her hand and went to ring for a servant.

'Fetch my cloak,' she ordered when he appeared.

Fever and delirium robbed Amisso of any memory of the days after his rescue. But when he had recovered sufficiently to take in his surroundings and talk to those who were caring for him, he found that he had one clear picture in his mind – a dusky road and a Sordesian merchant lifting him onto a packhorse.

'Where is he,' Amisso asked the innkeeper, 'the Sordesian who saved my life?'

'Long gone,' the innkeeper told him. 'He had business that couldn't wait.'

Amisso lay back in his bed and stared at the wooden rafters above him.

'He'll be back, though,' the innkeeper went on. 'He often calls here. He paid me something on account for your lodging and said he'd settle the rest next time he was passing. I don't think you'll be moving anywhere in a hurry young man, so I expect you'll still be here to see him.'

The innkeeper had sent for a surgeon from Munius – on the Sordesian's orders and at his expense – and the man had diagnosed three broken ribs and a broken arm, but no other major damage. The main prescription was to feed the patient well and let him rest. So Amisso spent his days sitting on a bench outside the inn, firmly strapped round the chest and arm, eating as much as he was able and watching the spring begin to bloom. He was in this position a fortnight later when dust on the road from the north told him visitors were approaching. A packhorse train appeared led by a wealthy looking merchant dressed in the characteristic baggy trousers and loose shirt of a Sordesian. He called a halt outside the inn and seeing Amisso he dismounted and came towards him. Amisso stood and after a moment's hesitation he gave the merchant a formal bow.

'I wouldn't have recognised you if it hadn't been for your bandages,' the man told him. 'You look so well – and who'd have thought you had such golden hair! It was like old rope the last time I saw you.'

They looked at each other for a moment, not knowing what to say or do next. Then the merchant held out his hand.

'My name's Peregrino,' he said.

Amisso looked at the outstretched hand. It sparkled with Sordesian rings. Amisso had seen Sordesians often enough. When tension was high between the two states, as it was at the present, it was not safe for Sordesians to travel to Mercatorius or vice versa, but at other times their merchants visited each other's markets. However, even during times of more relaxed relations the citizens of the two states still held each other in contempt. No Mercatorian businessman would dream of inviting a Sordesian to his home, and no Mercatorian would ever shake a Sordesian's hand, even to complete a business transaction.

Among the many reasons given in Mercatorius for hating all Sordesians was the commonly held view that they were dirty, greedy, untrustworthy, uncivilised and utterly selfish. The Mercatorians usually referred to them as 'dogs'. Amisso looked from Peregrino's outstretched hand to his face. He had pale, delicate features and eyes as blue as Amisso's own – hardly the face of a monster – and without doubt he had saved Amisso's life, at considerable personal expense.

'Thank you,' Amisso said, taking Peregrino's hand and giving his best ceremonial bow once more.

A smile flickered across Peregrino's face; then he turned away quickly to occupy himself in seeing that the horses and servants were attended to and settling accounts with the innkeeper. It occurred to Amisso that this man must be at least twice his age and yet he seemed as shy as Amisso felt himself. After a while, Peregrino ordered a meal and tentatively invited Amisso to join him. To dine with a Sordesian was something else unheard of for a Mercatorian, and there was an embarrassed silence as they sat together at table and began to eat. It went on until Amisso could stand it no longer.

'Why?' he said at last. 'Why have you done this for me? I can understand why you might have stopped, but why didn't you leave me when you found out I was a Mercatorian?'

Peregrino didn't reply at once, and looked rather puzzled himself.

'I don't suppose our two states will ever be able to be friendly to one another,' he said at last. 'How can they? They exist for business and business means competition –

winners and losers and make sure the loser isn't you. I should know; I'm a merchant myself. It's how I make money.' He chewed thoughtfully on a mouthful of chicken for a while, then washed it down with a large gulp of wine. 'It may be how we have to live,' he went on, 'but it doesn't feel good, you know. It doesn't make me feel good. Helping you made me feel good for a moment. Sitting here eating together feels good, doesn't it?'

Amisso didn't reply. To him, it just felt very strange.

'I can't believe you've spent so much money looking after me,' he said at last.

'What's money for?' Peregrino asked. 'I'm very rich, Amisso. But sometimes I feel very poor inside.' He tapped his chest with his fist. 'I feel a little richer in here for helping you.'

They ate in silence for a while. Their table had been set in the open on the veranda, and Peregrino looked out down the southern road towards the hills that rose between them and the coastal plain.

'Do you have family in Mercatorius?' he asked.

Amisso followed the line of Peregrino's gaze and felt a powerful wave of homesickness. The longing to be back in Mercatorius had driven him on during these last months and as he'd recuperated at the inn he'd been impatient to finish his journey, but there was one thing that spoiled the anticipation of his return. It was the thought of his father and how Amisso had treated him. His feelings of guilt and shame had grown over the months, so that now he could hardly bear to think of Crasto. However, if he was to go home he would have to do more than think of his father – he would have to meet him again. Amisso knew that he could make up some story about his past to tell to

Peregrino, but telling the truth felt like a way of facing up to what he had done – a preparation for meeting Crasto.

'My father's a member of the Senate,' he said quietly.

Peregrino paused with a forkful of food halfway to his mouth and stared at Amisso in astonishment.

'But your clothes!' he said. 'What little the robbers left you were just rags. What happened to you?

And so Amisso told his story: the fortune he'd stolen, Volpo's trickery, the days tied up in the hold with Urso, the slave market and the man who'd asked, 'Do you want me to buy you?'

'And he did buy me,' Amisso explained. 'Then he bought clothes for me, fed me and gave me a clean bed in a hostel on the outskirts of the town. I'd been right – we *were* in Dekan, and the next day he led me up into the Partak mountains. He seemed to know every path and goat track, and when I asked him how, he said the mountains belonged to his father. We travelled for two days, climbing all the time; then he told me how to find my way through the rest of the range and back to Mercatorius. He set me free. When I got out of the mountains weeks later, I found work in the towns and villages I passed through as I headed south for home. Volpo said I'd never done a day's work before and he was right. But when I did some labouring for a builder in the first town I came to, he told me I had a gift for working with wood and soon I was getting well-paid work as a carpenter and wood carver. I stayed for a while in a few of the towns so that I could take on bigger jobs and save some money. In the end I had quite a bit – nowhere near the fortune I'd lost, but enough to show my father that I wasn't completely worthless. But all that's gone now. The robbers took everything.'

'Everything apart from that little bag around your neck,' Peregrino reminded him. 'What is it? Some kind of good-luck charm? It must mean a lot to you. You wouldn't get on my horse until you were sure you still had it.'

Amisso didn't reply. He could sense the cord around his neck and he had to stop himself patting the bag that hung from it to reassure himself that it was still there.

'Something I don't understand,' Peregrino said, 'is why the man who bought you set you free.'

'Maybe it made him feel good,' Amisso suggested. 'Like you helping me. I really don't know.'

But Amisso did know or at least he had part of an answer. There was an important piece of the story he deliberately hadn't told Peregrino and it had to do with the bag round his neck. In it were six seeds – a parting gift from the man who'd bought him, the man he'd come to think of as his master. They were each about the size of a hazel nut but deep brown and glossy.

'They don't look like much,' his master had told him, 'but the fruit they give is astonishing. Just one is enough to give food and drink to a grown man for a whole day. And more than that, anyone who lives on it will be stronger and more active than they've ever been in their life before – and they'll find they're more contented too. It grows anywhere. It doesn't need any looking after and it germinates, grows and fruits in days.'

He'd spread his arms wide to indicate the whole mountainous vista.

'This is where it comes from,' he'd said. 'You might not think so, but there are several fertile valleys among the Partak mountains. The villagers who live there eat nothing but the fruit from these seeds. It's called Almus.'

'I've never heard of it,' Amisso had said.

'No one has, outside these mountains,' the man had told him.

His master gave Amisso directions to the first of the mountain villages and told him that the villagers there would then direct him to the next and so on until he was out of the mountain range.

'No one's been through this land for over a thousand years,' he'd said. 'I doubt that even you would be able to find your way back to these villages once you've left them. If Almus is going to reach the world, someone's going to have to take it. You are a slave, don't forget. Why not be a slave to Almus? Take it where it needs to go!'

Amisso had been puzzled.

'Why don't *you* take it?' he'd asked.

'I have other work to do,' the man had replied. 'This is your task, if you choose to take it.'

'But how will I know where to go with it?' he'd asked.

'Perhaps you'll get a feel for that,' the man had told him. 'Why not try Mercatorius to start with? After all, it is the centre of the world, isn't it?'

'So my father thinks,' Amisso had replied.

As he'd remembered his father, Amisso had wondered if these seeds could be the gift he brought back from his adventure. They seemed to be very little to show for the investment of a fortune but if their fruit really was as miraculous as the man said then surely bringing them to Mercatorius would be recognised as a triumph. And it was this thought that now kept Amisso from telling Peregrino about the strange seeds. The mountain villagers had fed him on Almus, and so he knew from his own experience how wonderful the fruit was. While he'd been recovering, he'd toyed with the idea of giving a seed to Peregrino as payment for the care he'd shown, but something hard and stubborn inside him had said, 'No'. Despite all he'd done, Peregrino was still a Sordesian and these seeds were to be for his father and for the glory of Mercatorius – they were all he had left to give and no one else should have them. He hadn't even dared grow a seed while he had been at the inn – although he knew the Almus fruit would have helped him recover – in case the innkeeper learned the precious secret.

~~~

Amisso had felt well enough to travel on for a couple of days now, and he'd only been waiting to meet his rescuer before he set off for home. Peregrino insisted on escorting his young friend as far as he could on the last leg of his journey. After all, the merchant pointed out, there might be Sordesians lying in ambush on the road. It would be dangerous for Peregrino to be seen anywhere near Mercatorius, so they set off under cover of darkness before dawn had broken the next day. When the two stopped to part company not far from the borders of Crasto's estate, the sky was beginning to turn grey and the black bulk of Amisso's city could be seen ahead of them beside the dark expanse of the sea. They shook hands warmly, then Amisso marched away without a backward look – all his thoughts on home.

The birds were singing joyfully and the rising sun had given colours back to the world by the time Amisso stood once more beneath the shade of his father's boundary trees. The olive groves and fruit orchards led in neat lines down a gentle slope to the white villa where Amisso had been born. To the left were the lands and villa belonging to Beata's family, and between the two properties was the broad, cobbled highway that led to Mercatorius. The city walls shone the palest of greys in the morning light, and the golden domes of the city's great buildings already dazzled the eyes. Amisso could make out the Senate House, the palace of the Dux, the Palace of Justice and the palaces of the Grand Admiral and the General-in-Chief. The huge watchtower still stood like a rose-coloured mast at the corner of Senate Square. The barracks, the mighty Arsenal, the cannon batteries guarding the harbour, the twin lighthouses at the harbour mouth – everything was as he had left it. And beyond it all the sea shimmered like a sheet of liquid jade, stretching to the end of the world. Amisso set off running down the slope towards his home. He'd been away for a day short of half a year.

6
Business as Usual

As he ran down the slope towards his father's villa, Amisso saw a movement among the olive trees on Beata's family estate. It was too early yet for any of the workers to be about, and Amisso stopped in surprise and alarm. Peregrino had told him all about the worsening situation between their two states and the Mercatorian fear of an attack from Sordes. Could this be a raiding party, sneaking through the trees? Amisso narrowed his eyes and scanned the grove. No, after a moment he was sure there was only one figure – a girl in a rust-coloured gown, and she seemed to be wandering about quite aimlessly. Then she sat down with her back to one of the olive trees and something in the way she settled her dark hair behind her shoulders told him at once it was Beata.

Amisso was going to call out, but then he had a better idea. He left the road and began to move stealthily from tree to tree, making a wide arc so that he could creep up behind his friend. It was a beautiful morning: the birds seemed to be bursting with the joy of being alive; the earth as it warmed in the sun smelled good enough to eat – like a cinnamon cake; and Amisso was dazed with happiness. He crouched behind a trunk 5 metres away from Beata and savoured the moment of their meeting. He realised that jumping out suddenly would frighten her and he didn't want to spoil their meeting. He wanted it to be as perfect as the morning. So he cupped his hands round his mouth and produced a soft trilling whistle. He'd learned how to do it when he was a child and when he'd wanted Beata to come out and play he'd used it to call her. It was his secret sign.

From where he was hidden, Amisso saw Beata become suddenly alert when she heard the sound. He made it again and her head turned to left and right. He let a few moments pass, then stood up silently and stepped away from the cover of his tree. He whistled again, and this time Beata too got to her feet. She turned in the direction of the sound and saw him. She gasped and stared into his eyes for a moment, then she gave a little scream, put her hands over her mouth, spun round and ran.

'Beata!' he cried, and set off after her.

'Go away!' she shouted, still running. 'Get away from me!'

She'd snatched up the bottom of her gown to free her legs and her bare feet sent the dust flying. She was fast, but Amisso caught her up before she reached the door in her garden wall.

'Beata, wait!' he panted, grabbing her shoulder.

She swung round and thumped him in the chest.

'Get off me!' she said.

He took a step backwards, and they stared at each other. Then she sank to the ground, put her hands over her face and wept.

After a moment he sat down next to her and put his hand on her shoulder, gently this time, but she shook him off.

'Beata, what is it?' Amisso asked.

She didn't answer, and he waited until her sobbing had subsided.

'What have I done?' he said, when she was quiet. He was completely bewildered.

Her head snapped up and her eyes were blazing.

'What do you think?' she shouted. 'You left me! You ran away - you left me on my own!'

'I thought you'd understand. I needed—'

'You needed? What about what anyone else needed? Have you any idea what it's been like here? Do you know what's been going on while you've been wandering round the world having your stupid adventures?'

'I've heard that things are bad with Sordes,' Amisso offered meekly.

She glared at him, speechless. Then he remembered.

'Your father,' he said. 'What's happened?'

'I don't know,' she said coldly. 'Nobody knows. He never came home. He was trying to negotiate, but now it looks as if he's being held prisoner. The Dux has sent envoys demanding his return, but they say it's "not convenient" for him to leave Sordes at the moment.'

Her eyes filled with tears again, and this time she let him rest his hand on her shoulder.

'I thought I'd never see you again,' she said. 'I needed you. Everything's gone to pieces. I can't sleep any more, and Mother does nothing *but* sleep – she spends all day in her room with the shutters closed. I have to do everything.'

'What about Verna?' he asked.

'Most of her time's been taken up trying to keep Bardo going and looking after your father.'

'Father?' Amisso asked, alarmed. 'What's the matter with him?'

Beata looked at him with disbelief.

'He thought he'd never see you again either,' she explained. 'Didn't you realise what running off like that would do? It's nearly destroyed him.'

'But I thought he'd be glad to be rid of me,' Amisso said.

'Amisso, he had half the City Guard out hunting for you.'

'I should think he wanted his money back.'

'Money?' she said. 'You're his son, Amisso – what does money matter?'

They were quiet for a while, then Beata took his hand and gripped it hard.

'Don't ever do anything like that again,' she said fiercely.

He bowed his head, unable to meet her eyes.

'Come on,' she told him. 'You must go to your father. A carriage arrived at your villa just as dawn was breaking – it had the Senate crest on it. I think there's going to be trouble. We'll get you some decent clothes first – you can borrow some of Father's.'

'No,' Amisso said, with a decisiveness she'd never heard in his voice before. 'I'll go to him as I am.' Despite Peregrino's offer to have him dressed as befitted a young gentleman, Amisso had refused anything other than the simplest clothes. 'I'll go dressed as a beggar,' he said to Beata, 'and I'll beg his forgiveness. I don't see how he can forgive me, but perhaps at least he'll accept my gift.'

'The only gift he needs is you, Amisso,' she told him.

'No,' he said. 'There's something else.'

Nothing in this meeting with Beata had happened as Amisso had anticipated. As he'd crept towards her he'd imagined sitting with her peacefully as the sun rose in the sky, telling her all his adventures. But the one thing he hadn't intended to tell her about was the bag of seeds round his neck. The adventures had gone untold, but instead he felt an unexpected urge to explain to her about Almus. Suddenly he remembered the words of his master, when Amisso had asked how he would know where to take the seed: 'Perhaps you'll get a feel for it,' he'd said. Amisso took the bag from his neck and emptied the contents into his palm. The shiny seeds seemed to radiate warmth, and he realised that their rich brown was the same colour as Beata's eyes.

'Here,' he said, and he placed two seeds in her hand, folding her fingers tightly round them. 'The rest are for Father,' he explained.

Then he told her what the seeds were and how the Almus fruit fed the people of the mountains.

'I've seen them,' he said. 'They eat nothing else but Almus. It's all they seem to need – and they're the happiest, healthiest people I've ever met.'

'We need an answer, man. Either resign today with some dignity, or tomorrow your seat in the Senate will be taken from you.'

The broad frame of Senator Perdo seemed to fill Crasto's office as he leaned over his old business rival to give this ultimatum.

'Think of the good of Mercatorius,' Senator Tundax put in. 'The State can't be governed if senators don't attend the

Chamber. That's why the rule is there: "Any senator who fails to attend for six months shall forfeit his seat".'

'And tomorrow will be six months to the day since you last attended,' Perdo reminded him. 'It can't be avoided – your only option is to resign and maintain the good name of your house.'

'Not to mention the good name of the Senate,' Senator Tundax pointed out. 'It hardly inspires confidence to be expelling members in the middle of a crisis. There's no way out, Crasto.'

'Unless you intend to join us tomorrow, of course,' Senator Lenex added.

This suggestion was met with silence from Amisso's father. He felt, and looked, like a worn-out, wounded animal surrounded by predators. He had led his three fellow senators into his office – the very room in which he had shown Amisso his inheritance – and had then sunk wearily into the seat behind his desk, but the others had remained standing for the interview and now looked down on the bowed head of their colleague. The iron-grey hair was turning to white. It was thinner, and unkempt. Crasto's once imposing figure seemed shrunken, and his clothes hung loosely. Since Amisso's disappearance, not only had he failed to attend the Senate Chamber or any of the committees on which he served, but he had also neglected his business. Bardo was doing his best to keep things going, but the senator's enterprise had been among those to lose shipping to the 'pirates' during the winter, and the lack of confidence caused by Crasto's withdrawal from public life had made customers turn away from his House as if it were afflicted by plague. The behaviour of his younger son – widely regarded as insane and criminal – had added to the effect. Profits had begun to fall dramatically and nothing

Bardo could do had been able to turn the tide. In a desperate bid to reverse their fortunes Bardo had committed a large part of their reserves on a scheme to import wine from distant Kara. But the goods had proved to be unsaleable and the whole enterprise had folded at a loss.

'You have troubles enough of your own, Crasto, without worrying yourself with affairs of state,' Senator Lenex said gently. 'None of the senators will think badly of you if you resign.'

'If anything, they'll be thankful,' Tundax added. 'After all, the Senate is supposed to represent the best of Mercatorius, and with all the goodwill in the world, you can no longer be said to fulfil that role.' For the first time, Crasto looked up. His face was thin and drawn, but his eyes were still capable of a formidable glare. 'A man whose business is failing,' Tundax continued, 'whose son is a runaway, who is the father of a thief—'

Crasto pressed his palms down firmly on the leather top of his desk and thrust himself to his feet.

'Enough!' he said. 'That is enough!'

He looked each of them in the eye, then settled his attention on Perdo. 'Might I ask what gets you out of your bed this early in the morning, Senator?' he asked. 'Couldn't you wait until a more civilised hour to bring me your message? Or were you so thirsty for my blood that you had to have it for breakfast? I'm sure these gentlemen would have been quite prepared to leave me until dinner.'

The two men glowered at each other for a moment, then Perdo turned away and Crasto sank back into his seat.

'Senator Perdo was only thinking of your good, Crasto,' Senator Lenex told him. 'The earlier your resignation's received the better—'

'A few months ago would have been better still,' Senator Tundax muttered.

'Last minute never looks good,' Lenex explained. 'Your reputation has suffered badly, Crasto. You must try to save what little remains.'

'I see,' said Crasto. 'I'm comforted to know you have my interests so close to your hearts.'

Perdo turned back to his rival and was about to renew his demands when there was an urgent hammering on the door.

'Come!' Crasto ordered.

The tall double doors opened and one of Crasto's servants came in.

'I'm sorry to disturb you, sir,' he said, 'but it's your son—' He broke off and beamed at everyone in the room, unable to keep within the bounds of respectful behaviour. 'Oh, sir!' he went on, 'it's Master Amisso – he's back!'

Crasto stared stupidly for a moment, then he struggled to his feet.

'Where is he, man?' he shouted. 'Bring him in at once!'

'Beg pardon, sir, but he won't come in,' the servant explained. 'He's out on the road and he says he's not fit to come in. He begs your forgiveness and says he doesn't expect you to see him, but if you'll send word, he'll go to the servants' quarters and work for you there until he's repaid his debt.'

'Debt? Nonsense!' Crasto cried. 'Out of my way!' he barked, pushing Perdo aside as he made for the door, and he sprinted across the inner courtyard like a schoolboy.

The three senators waited in Crasto's office, but he did not return so they went in search of him. They found him in the reception lobby of the villa, clinging to a young man dressed in the clothes of a peasant, whom the senators recognised as the runaway, Amisso. A few steps behind the father and son were the two daughters of Crasto's neighbour, Ambassador Capax. And scattered round the edges of the room were all the servants of the household.

Tundax and Lenex instinctively held back in the doorway, but Senator Perdo strode up to Crasto and stood at his elbow. After a moment, Crasto looked round and the joyful expression turned to one of anger. He took a step back from his son and faced Perdo.

'Well?' he demanded, sharply. 'What do you want now?'

'An answer,' Perdo replied.

'Senator Perdo,' Lenex said, coming forward from the door, 'I think in the circumstances we could—'

'We need an answer,' Perdo insisted. 'Do we have your resignation?'

Crasto squared his shoulders and took a deep breath.

'You have my word,' he replied, 'that I shall be in my seat in the Senate Chamber tomorrow. But not today – today is a day for feasting.'

Senators Tundax and Lenex tried to lead Perdo away, but he shook them off.

'Tell me,' he said to Crasto. 'Do you intend to press charges against this thief? Surely a senator of Mercatorius will not condone robbery.'

Crasto's muscles tensed ready to strike, but then they relaxed.

'A thing cannot be stolen if it is freely given,' he said. 'This is a day of rejoicing, Perdo, and even you can do nothing to destroy it. I believe you will find your carriage is waiting for you.'

Crasto nodded to the head stable boy, who scurried out of the room.

'Forgive us if we leave you now,' Crasto said to the senators. Then he turned to the servants. 'A feast!' he cried. 'Prepare the best of everything we have. We have fasted for long enough – tonight we shall feast!'

The servants hurried away in all directions, chattering with excitement; Crasto led his son and the two sisters away to the family rooms; and the three senators were left alone in the lobby. After a moment, they heard the wheels of their carriage on the cobblestones as it was brought up to the main door.

Preparations for the feast were soon well under way. Ovens that had been cold for months were glowing, and wonderful smells were beginning to creep from the kitchen throughout the whole villa. Verna was supervising the catering while Beata and Crasto, who had spent a considerable amount of time persuading Amisso to present himself once again in the finery of a senator's son, were now drawing up a guest list. It was going to be a select list – only family and close friends. It was short notice to send invitations more widely, and in any case the last six months had seen a sharp decline in those who were anxious to be seen at Senator Crasto's table. One member of the family that Amisso particularly hoped would turn up to the feast was his brother.

'Where's Bardo?' had been one of his first questions, once his father had persuaded him to cross the threshold of his home as a son.

'Send for him, at once!' Crasto had ordered, and a servant had set off for the city on horseback straight away.

However, the servant had returned an hour later with a message from the senator's elder son saying he was far too busy to come home but hoped to join them when the day's business was completed.

Darkness was falling, the banqueting hall had just been set out to Verna's satisfaction, and the preparation of the food was nearing completion when the footman on duty in the reception lobby heard a horse gallop up to the main entrance. The footman was bubbling with excited words about the miracle of Master Amisso's return as he held open the door to welcome Master Bardo. There was so much joy in the house that for the time being the formality between the family and their servants had slipped, but what the footman saw in Bardo's face killed any thought of conversation with the young master. Amisso's brother strode past the footman without a word, throwing his short cloak on the marble floor, and headed for the family rooms.

Crasto, Beata and Amisso were grouped round a small table in the sitting room, discussing seating arrangements for the evening when the door burst open as if the City Guard were conducting a raid. Bardo stood framed in the doorway, hands on hips and chin thrust forward. Amisso had been longing to see his brother all day. He was still finding it hard to believe that his father had welcomed him back so readily, but he felt confident of a warm greeting from Bardo.

Amisso looked up at his brother's face happily, but what he saw there shocked him. Bardo's hair hung round his face in limp, dishevelled strings. And his face was sharp, fleshless – almost skull-like – with wild, staring eyes that had anything but welcome in them.

'What's all this?' Bardo demanded.

'We're preparing a feast,' Crasto told him, 'for your brother's return.'

'I know that,' Bardo snapped. 'You do realise we can't afford a feast. We can barely afford to eat.'

Crasto moved towards his elder son.

'You exaggerate, Bardo,' he said.

'Father, you don't know how bad things are,' Bardo replied. 'You've refused to look at the books for months.'

'Things will be better now,' Crasto assured him. 'You'll see.'

'See?' Bardo exploded. 'I'll tell you what I see! I see a fool who ran off with his father's money – and has he brought any of it back?' There was silence. 'No, I thought not. I see a fool who's thrown away a fortune, ruined his father's health and destroyed his business... and now he's going to be rewarded with a feast. What is there to celebrate? Personally, I'd celebrate if I knew I was never going to see the wretch again.'

There was a stunned silence. Tears filled Amisso's eyes as he stared, speechless, at his brother, and Beata instinctively found his hand. Crasto stopped halfway between his two sons and bowed his head as if he hadn't the strength to look at Bardo in his rage.

'When did you ever give a feast for me?' Bardo asked. 'Do I deserve nothing? For six months I've worked night and day to try and keep our business going—'

'I'm sorry, son,' Crasto began, 'I should have—'

'No!' Bardo interrupted. 'It's not your fault. I've never blamed you, Father. I've worn myself out for you, but in all these months I've never blamed you.' He stopped for a moment, and Crasto looked up to meet his son's eyes. 'But I blame you now,' Bardo went on in a quiet, icy voice. 'When this fool comes home and you give him a feast, I blame you for that, Father – indeed I do.'

And he stormed out of the room.

'He's right, of course,' Crasto said, after a moment.

He looked at his younger son and Amisso saw there was only sadness in his father's eyes. Amisso realised with a shock that his father was confused and didn't know what to do. Throughout his life, he'd only known Crasto as a man in control. Looking now at his sad, uncertain face felt like looking at another man.

'Many times during these last months I've thought that I should hate you, son,' Crasto continued. 'But I couldn't do it, or even come close to doing it.' He returned to the table and put his hand on Amisso's shoulder. 'I'm just so glad to have you home,' he said, 'even if you have come back empty-handed.'

'But I'm not empty-handed,' Amisso said.

'What?' Crasto asked, a sudden light coming into his eyes.

'I've brought something back,' Amisso told him. 'It's a gift – for you. A very special gift—'

But before Amisso could say another word Crasto had hurried into the corridor.

'Ho there!' he shouted, 'Come quick!'

They heard a servant running.

'Go to Master Bardo,' Crasto ordered. 'Tell him to come at once. Tell him his brother has not returned empty-handed after all – tell him Master Amisso has brought home a great gift! Make haste and fetch him!'

Enclosed by walls hung with rich tapestries and roofed by a gilded ceiling, five silent figures, dressed in fine clothes, were gathered around an ornate table on which lay four shiny seeds. The Almus seeds glowed with the same lustre as the polished wood on which they rested but Crasto, Bardo and Verna seemed unimpressed with the gift that Amisso had brought home. For some time, silence was their only response to Amisso's tale of the wonderful Almus fruit. Beata squeezed Amisso's hand encouragingly, but even she could find nothing to say.

The silence of each had a different quality: Crasto's expressed deep disappointment; Verna's, incomprehension; Beata's, despair for her friend; Amisso's, a lingering hope; and Bardo's, the self-satisfied scorn of someone whose prejudices have been amply confirmed. The elder brother picked up one of the seeds and weighed it in his hand. It was slightly heavier than he had expected. He held it to the light from the candelabrum, then tossed it into the air and caught it.

'So this is going to pay for your feast, is it?' he sneered.

'It's all I have,' Amisso replied.

'He doesn't need to pay for the feast,' Crasto said wearily.

'But somebody does,' Verna reminded him.

'Exactly!' Bardo said. 'The feast has to be paid for somehow. Our lives have to be paid for... and what has Amisso contributed? A handful of seeds!'

He flicked the Almus seed in the air contemptuously and caught it again. He knew that his anger was destroying his father's happiness, and, much as he resented Amisso, that was something he was loath to do. He heaved an impatient sigh and picked up the other three seeds, laying them in the palm of his hand. He considered them for a moment, then came to a decision and closed his fist on them.

'If they grow as easily as he claims, and if the fruit's so good,' Bardo said, 'then there should be a healthy profit margin. I'll plant them on the north hill and see what happens. The land's good for nothing else but goats – it won't be wasted.'

'No,' Amisso protested.

Everyone looked at him in surprise.

'It's not meant for selling,' he said firmly. 'The mountain people don't sell it. It's free – it just grows and they eat it.'

'Mountain people!' Bardo said. 'What do they know about anything? They're probably too ignorant to know how to trade,' and he slipped the seeds into a pocket at the waist of his doublet.

'They're for Father,' Amisso told him, 'not for you.'

Bardo turned to his father for judgement, and for a moment Crasto glanced from one son to the other with that indecisive look that seemed so strange to Amisso. At last, the senator put his arm round Amisso's shoulder.

'Bardo's right,' he said. 'Your seeds could be a great gift after all if they turn in a great profit. When you stood at the door and refused to come in, you wanted to make amends, Amisso. Perhaps a good crop of this Almus will help you do that – it could help repair our fortunes. You have given the seeds to me, so they are mine to do with as I please, and I give them to Bardo. Not only that – I give him responsibility for their cultivation.' He put his other arm round Bardo now. 'The business has nearly killed you, my son,' he told him. 'You need to get out of the city. You need fresh air and the land. Tomorrow we'll hire some men and you can set them on to clear the north hill. You can manage the estate, Bardo – and Amisso, you can help him. Perhaps your adventures have knocked some sense into you at last; if we can't make a merchant out of you perhaps we can make a farmer. Maybe Bardo can teach you to make a profit from the land. You're brothers – work together as brothers! Be reconciled.'

He took their right hands and brought them together. Amisso looked from Bardo to Crasto and he realised that for the first time in his life he was in a position to make a decision that had significance for the rest of his family. It was a strange feeling, but stranger still was the sense that he was equal to the moment. What he was about to do was his own choice – his own judgement of what was best for them all.

'Very well, Father,' he said.

He squeezed his brother's hand and looked steadily into his face, but he felt no answering warmth in Bardo's grip and saw none in his eyes.

'And tomorrow,' Crasto went on, 'when the Senate session is over and I've seen off Perdo and his friends, I shall return to my office. Our business has been without its captain far too long. There's something for you to celebrate, Bardo: I've got a son back, but you've got a father back too. It's business as usual, my sons – business as usual again!'

7
The Harvest

The north hill was covered in Almus, and it had only taken two months. Bardo was on his way from his father's villa to the plantation and he stopped his horse for a moment to gaze at the hill rising gently before him in the middle distance. Where once there had been only rocks and scrub, there was now a blanket of dark green. The little bushes crowded in on each other and Bardo knew that in the shade of their leaves hung a wealth of the golden yellow Almus fruits, shaped like pears but no bigger than plums. He should have been delighted, and to begin with he had certainly been excited with the phenomenal growth of the crop and the potential for profit. It was so cheap to produce – once the ground had been cleared the plants required little attention, and the few labourers Bardo employed needed no food as they simply ate the fruit and it kept them going for hours. But still Bardo was not happy as he contemplated the hill his father had given him to cultivate. Instead of cheering him, the heat of the morning sun just made him feel uncomfortable and the chirping of the cicadas was an irritation.

'Come on!' Bardo shouted, turning in the saddle. 'We haven't got all morning.'

His brother, Amisso, rode up behind him at a brisk trot.

'I was talking to Beata,' he explained. 'There's still no news.'

'Of course there isn't,' Bardo snapped. 'She won't see her father until all this is over – maybe not even then. I don't know why you even bother asking.'

Amisso didn't reply, and the two trotted on together in silence. Amisso had worked hard on the hill and had shown surprising ability in the practical tasks involved in setting up the plantation, but Bardo had not been able to get rid of his resentment towards his brother. He could talk politely to Amisso as they worked, but he felt no warmth for him anymore. Even when Amisso's story about the miraculous growth of the Almus had been proved correct, Bardo had found he was more annoyed than glad. It seemed that even though they were now physically together again they had taken different roads in their hearts and there was no going back.

As the plantation gate came in sight, Bardo noticed a huddled heap beside it and knew that it would be a beggar. The Mercatorian authorities had periodic campaigns to rid the State of such people, but still they kept on appearing. Bardo swore under his breath and kicked his mount into a canter, hoping his men would see him coming and have the gate open so that he could simply ride past the man. But the labourers were slow to react so that Bardo had to bring his horse to a halt and endure the man's pleading for a moment before he could get safely past him and into his property.

'Please, sir, just a scrap,' the man begged, 'or just a mouthful of water. I'm parched.'

Bardo held his head high, not even looking at the man, and as soon as the gate was open he was away, leaving the beggar to cough in the dust from his horse's hooves.

But Amisso stopped. Once Bardo was safely inside the wall he'd had built round his new plantation, he brought his horse to a halt and turned to watch as Amisso dismounted and gave the man a drink from the leather flask tied to his saddle. The elder brother was furious.

'Don't do that again!' he ordered, as Amisso caught up with him. 'If you do, we'll never get rid of him.'

'Why should we want to?' Amisso said.

Since his return, Amisso seemed to have acquired a habit of answering back. But it wasn't a boy's cheek – there was a quiet assurance about it that unsettled Bardo and further annoyed him.

'We can't support beggars,' Bardo told him sharply. 'We're practically beggars ourselves.'

Amisso looked at the Almus, stretching away to the skyline.

'Are we?' he asked.

Bardo didn't answer. He could have said that the profitability of the Almus remained unknown – that they still had to find out if there was a market for the fruit – but he couldn't deny that since his father had returned to his office, the ducats were flowing back into the House of Crasto. His father's business sense was as acute as ever, and the senator had thrown himself back into work with renewed enthusiasm, like a man waking from a long sleep. Senator Perdo was not pleased – but neither was Bardo.

Crasto's elder son couldn't rid himself of a sense that his father's confident success simply showed up his own failure to keep the business in profit. Bardo felt as if he'd been given the plantation project to keep him out of the way while his father got on with the serious business of reversing their fortunes and it made him bitter.

'People have to work for what they get,' Bardo reminded his brother. 'That's the way we do things in Mercatorius – you know that.'

'Perhaps it isn't always possible,' Amisso pointed out. He looked back at the man by the gate. 'I was just a heap by the roadside once,' he said. 'If someone hadn't been generous enough to help me, for nothing, I'd have died.'

Bardo stared at his brother's face – the clear, blue eyes and golden curls he'd grown up with and loved through their childhood together. The fleeting thought that he might feel happier if his brother had been left to die flashed into his mind, and he hated himself for it. But he also hated the shame that Amisso had brought on their family.

'That part of your life must be forgotten,' Bardo told him firmly.

'Anyway, the man's too weak to work,' Amisso persisted. 'Perhaps if we gave him some Almus—'

'And what is he going to pay for it with?'

'He could come in and work for it,' Amisso suggested, 'after he's eaten.'

'That's the wrong way round,' Bardo replied. 'Work first, then wages, then pay for Almus – that's the way it has to be.'

But Amisso refused to be cowed.

'Almus is a gift,' he said. 'It was given to me, and it ought to be given to anyone who needs it.'

Bardo laughed harshly.

'If you felt like that about it, you should never have given it to a merchant,' he said. 'Get rid of that man at the gate,' he shouted to one of his workmen, 'and make sure he's not there tomorrow.'

Bardo walked his horse on towards the barns that had been built for the Almus crop. So far, Bardo had not stored the Almus fruit, replanting it as fast as it ripened so that they could build up a massive yield before launching the product onto the market. He had realised that anyone could grow the fruit once it was on the market, so he wanted to establish himself immediately as the major supplier throughout the region to make sure that no one else would think it worth their while to compete. Now, at last, the crop was as big as Bardo could get it and he was ready to fill his storehouses. But he was worried. It was this anxiety that was fuelling his bad temper now and it had kept him awake throughout the night.

For half the morning, Bardo had his younger brother holding poles and rope ends while he measured. He measured the dimensions of the barns he'd had built; he measured the dimensions of the plots into which he'd divided the hill; he counted bushes and fruit; he had Amisso pick fruit and lay it in a tray then count the fruit while Bardo measured the tray; and all the time Bardo was scribbling notes at a portable desk that one of the workmen carried round after them. When everything had been measured, Bardo settled in the shade of one of the barns and did the calculations. He did them three times, then called for wine. Bardo drank deeply as he gazed out of the barn door at the spreading acres of Almus. There was no escaping the truth – he'd made a serious mistake.

'There's too much of it,' Bardo told his father. 'I'd no idea the stupid plant would make so much fruit.'

'Surely you must have seen,' Crasto said. 'You've been working with it for two months! Why on earth did you keep on planting?'

'I wanted to have as much of it as I could get,' Bardo told him. And he went on to explain his thoughts about dominating the market.

They were in Crasto's office at the villa. The senator had had a hard day in the city. Sordes was being openly aggressive now in its threats to Mercatorian ships, blockading some ports against them, and all trade had become highly risky. Crasto was only making money because he was better than most at judging when to take a chance, but he was living on his nerves and it was exhausting. He found that his mind kept wandering as his son was talking – these plants of Amisso's seemed a very minor matter to the senator.

'But, son,' he said, when Bardo had finished, 'do you even know if there is a market for Almus? What makes you think there's going to be a fight to produce it? It's only a fruit, after all – the world is full of fruit.'

Bardo had been pacing in front of his father's desk. Now he stood still and looked at Crasto. His white hair was a reminder of the trauma he'd been through during Amisso's absence, but everything else about him seemed restored. His square shoulders and deep chest, his firm chin with its trim, pointed beard: all said that here was a man of power.

'I want the plantation to be a success,' Bardo said. 'I want to show you what I can do – to be worthy of you.'

Crasto was surprised by his son's earnest tone and the pleading look in his eyes.

'But I know what you can do, Bardo,' he said. 'How can anyone who did what you did while I was ill need to prove himself?'

'But I failed, father – now you're back, everything's all right again, but I nearly ruined everything.'

Crasto got up and came round the desk. He took his son by the shoulders and looked him in the eye.

'You did not fail,' he said. 'No young man of your age in the whole of Mercatorius could have done as well as you did. When you're my age – long before you're my age – you'll be able to do what I do – and with ease. It's just experience, son. All you need is experience, and that must come with time.'

He squeezed Bardo's shoulders, then went back to his seat. He felt very tired and rested his head in his hands for a moment.

'As for being worthy of me,' he went on quietly, 'it was me that abandoned you to look after the business on your own. You don't need to do anything to show you're worthy of a man who abandons his son.'

'But you've sent me away,' Bardo insisted. 'You sent me to the plantation. I thought you didn't want me in the office.'

'I put you in charge of the plantation because I trust you,' Crasto told him. 'I want you to set it up for Amisso to take over, then I want you back in the business with me.'

There was silence for a few moments, and Bardo sat in one of the other carved seats in the room. With his head he understood what his father was saying, and he accepted it; but in his heart the pain of seeing the family business decline under his management would not go away. He knew that only a financial triumph with the Almus would wipe the feeling out; he was desperate to achieve something remarkable with the fruit.

'Then the plantation must be a success,' Bardo said. 'A great success.'

'And so it will be,' Crasto assured him. 'Fill your barns, then burn off your surplus crop – that's all you have to do. You'll have ample produce to test the market.'

The thought of all the extra piles of Almus going up in smoke was unbearable to Bardo.

'No,' he said firmly.

His father looked at him in surprise.

'I don't want to burn the surplus,' Bardo explained. 'I want to pull down the barns and build bigger ones.'

Crasto genuinely had a great deal of respect for his son's abilities in business, but this was madness.

'Son, we've only just built them,' he said, 'and they cost a small fortune. Things may be better in the city now, but we can't be throwing money away like this.'

'It'll be worth it,' Bardo insisted. 'An investment – you'll see.'

Crasto put both hands flat on the desktop in a gesture that anyone who did business with him knew to mean that there would be no further discussion.

'Bardo, we don't have the money to spare,' he said. 'It's out of the question.'

Bardo knew that his father was right, but he was in the grip of feelings that wouldn't be swayed by good sense.

'Then I'll use my inheritance,' he said. 'You promised to let me have it whenever I asked. At least I'll have something better to show for the money than Amisso did.'

A holiday had been declared at the plantation now that the harvest was in, and Amisso had gone with Beata to one of their favourite places – the promontory west of the city. It gave a fine view of the seaways in and out of the harbour of Mercatorius. To the east, they could see their family estates, divided by the main road out of the city, and north of Crasto's estate was the dark green carpet of the Almus plantation. Bardo's new barns were so big they could be seen even from the coast. They shone in the summer sun.

'Did he really spend all his inheritance to build them?' Beata asked, throwing herself onto the springy grass that covered the headland.

'Not all of it,' Amisso told her, 'but they did cost an awful lot.'

'What did your father say?'

'Nothing,' Amisso told her. 'Things have been very tense at home. It's not that they've fallen out over it, but neither of them is happy about what's happened. A lot's going to depend on how things go when Bardo starts selling. He's agreed with Father to load up two galleys and do a coastal run. Then there are the markets in Mercatorius and Munius.'

'What about you and Bardo?' Beata asked. 'Are you getting on any better?'

'He seems in a better mood,' Amisso said, 'now that he's got his new barns and the crop's safely in. But I don't think he'll ever forgive me. I've stopped expecting it, or even hoping for it.'

'Did the mountain people have barns to store their Almus?' Beata asked.

'No,' Amisso replied. 'They just ate from the bushes. They didn't cultivate Almus like we're doing. It grows all around them, naturally, and there always seemed to be enough for everyone.'

'Don't they work, then?' Beata enquired.

'Oh, yes,' Amisso told her. 'They work hard. But they only do work that they find valuable – they're not driven by hunger, you see – and they're not frightened that hunger might come in the future.'

'So what kind of things do they value?' Beata asked, sitting up with interest.

'Anything that helps them enjoy the world,' Amisso said. 'At least that's how it seemed to me. They've spent years cutting paths and stairways into the rock so that you can get to the best viewing places – just to look at the mountains. And they've built decorated shelters so that you can sit and watch the mountains for hours, in all weathers. They're brilliant at all kinds of arts and crafts and their homes are beautiful. And they look after each other – they always care for anyone who's old or ill. They've discovered lots about how you can use plants for medicine and they're always hunting in the mountains for more plants to find out about and use. Then there are the celebrations. They take as much care organising a celebration as we do organising a trading trip.'

'What do they celebrate?'

'Just being alive, I think. And being together in their village. They take it in turns to have village celebrations and invite all the people from the nearby villages.'

'Don't they fight with their neighbours?' Beata asked.

'No. They don't even have weapons,' Amisso explained. 'They told me that once, over a thousand years ago, an army from a distant country had struggled through the mountains on its way to a war in some other land, but it never found any of their villages, and it never came back. The mountain people don't even kill animals – they apologise if they even step on an insect, and they use wool, not leather, for their clothes.'

'Don't they need weapons to defend their sheep?' asked Beata. 'What about wild animals?'

'That was the strangest thing of all,' Amisso told her. 'The wild animals eat Almus too. The people leave bowls of it out for them – so they don't have to eat the sheep.'

For some time they watched in silence as the pale green sea washed gently against the rocks 50 metres below them. Beata stole little glances at her friend's thoughtful profile. There seemed to be a new firmness about his features and a focus in his eyes. But there was a distance in him too. So many strange things had happened to him. He'd travelled among the mountain people and seen their ways, but now he seemed to have turned into a farmer, working from dawn to dusk with Bardo in hopes of a huge profit. She didn't know where she was with him. For 16 years she and Amisso had shared their lives but now he almost felt like a stranger to her and he made her a little nervous.

'What about you?' Amisso asked at last, and it sounded like the question of a stranger, making polite conversation. 'How are you coping? I've been so busy on the plantation that I don't seem to have seen you for ages. And Verna doesn't come over now that Father's recovered, so I can't ask her about you.'

'She wouldn't know,' Beata told him. 'We hardly ever speak to each other these days. She's always busy with the house, and I've been out most of the time just lately. We keep ourselves busy – I suppose that's how we cope. It seems disloyal, but sometimes it seems best to try not to think about Father. I just hope they're not mistreating him, even if they won't let him come home just at the moment.'

'What do you mean, you're out most of the time?' Amisso asked. 'You've not been wandering around the estate at all hours again, have you, like you were when I came home?'

'No,' she said. 'There's more to it than just wandering.'

Amisso waited, but she didn't elaborate.

'Well, go on,' he said. 'What are you up to?'

She looked at him, and her dark eyes were troubled.

'I don't know whether I can tell you,' she said, then turned away and started pulling at stalks of grass.

'Why?'

She looked at him again with the same uncertain expression and it made Amisso hurt inside.

'I don't know if you'd understand,' she said.

Just then they heard the boom of a cannon, then another. The sounds seemed to have come from the north and Amisso and Beata scanned the sea stretching out to their right, but it was empty to the horizon. A sharp exchange of cannon fire followed a moment later, and then they noticed smoke drifting over a headland about a kilometre further up the coast. A couple of minutes passed before they saw a large carrack round the headland and make for the open sea. They heard another cannon shot and a spout of water off the carrack's port bow showed where the missile had landed.

'Look,' Amisso shouted, 'I think that went through the mainsail.'

It was difficult to tell at such a distance, but the big square-rigged sail amidships did seem to be flapping strangely.

The carrack wasn't far clear of the headland when another ship came into view under full sail with its banks of oars glinting as the blades left the water in perfect rhythm. It was a galleass of the Mercatorian navy, and now they could tell by the flag flying from the carrack's mizzen mast that it was a Sordesian warship.

The captain of the galleass must have been confident that he could overhaul the carrack as he abandoned a straight line of pursuit and set a course wide and to the north of the Sordesian ship. Amisso and Beata were caught up by the excitement of the chase and they cheered their ship on as it gradually drew alongside the carrack. As soon as the two vessels were neck and neck, there was a barrage of explosions that seemed loud even to the spectators on the cliff, and they realised both ships had fired a broadside. A surprising amount of smoke hung over the vessels, and it was a moment before Amisso and Beata could see clearly what had happened. It seemed that the Sordesians had aimed for the body of the galleass and they could see gaps in the usually tidy ranks of oars where cannon balls had torn into the rowing deck. But the Mercatorians must have elevated their guns, as their shot had ripped the Sordesian sails to shreds and taken down the mainmast. The carrack had virtually come to a dead halt, with the broken mast and the remains of its sail dragging in the water. The young friends could see the tiny figures of the sailors frantically hacking the mast free of its rigging so that it could drop clear into the water. Meanwhile, the galleass was sailing on and turning in front of the carrack. As it crossed the path of the enemy vessel it raked the bows, bringing down the foremast. Amisso knew the Sordesians would only have a couple of light cannons aiming forwards from the forecastle and they could do little damage as the Mercatorian warship sped across in front of them.

Although their ship seemed to be getting the better of the exchange, Amisso and Beata had stopped cheering. The chilling reality of what they were witnessing had begun to strike them.

'This is war,' Amisso said softly. 'They can't pretend this is to do with pirates – that ship's flying the Sordesian flag. I don't know who started it, but this is an act of war.'

'What about Father?' Beata asked.

'He should be safe,' Amisso told her. 'Even in a war, they're not allowed to harm diplomats.'

Beata didn't seem convinced.

'They're Sordesians!' she said. 'You can't expect them to play by the rules.'

The kindly face of Peregrino, his Sordesian rescuer, came into Amisso's mind but he said nothing.

By now the galleass had got well clear of the Sordesian ship and had come about. Its oarsmen were driving it straight back at the carrack and the Mercatorian captain was clearly aiming to come at the port side of his adversary. But this time he didn't stand off to deliver a broadside – he brought his vessel almost bow to bow with the enemy then shipped oars and crashed in alongside the Sordesian warship. Amisso and Beata heard the grinding of timbers, even on the cliff. Then they heard another blast of cannon fire and realised that at least one and probably both vessels had fired a broadside at point-bank range. Immediately, smoke covered the scene. They could hear bugles signalling, the crack of firearms and a distant roar that sounded strangely like a crowd at the racing arena.

Gradually the smoke cleared and they could see that all the action was on the deck of the carrack. The Mercatorians had boarded her. It was impossible to make out individual men and establish which side they were on. They were no bigger than insects and the whole deck of the carrack looked like a broken ant's nest seething with dark creatures swarming all over each other. Even though it was cut off from them by distance, it was a chilling sight. They watched in silence, Beata gripping Amisso's arm, until the turmoil on the fore and aft castles gradually ceased and it became clear that the only resistance remaining was in the waist. Here too the fighting finally came to an end and the friends saw the flag of Sordes being lowered from the mizzen mast – the only mast still standing on the now captured ship. The cries of battle had died away, but there was a ragged cheer that carried over the waters as the hated emblem of their enemy was cut from its rope and cast into the sea.

'Hey, you kids!'

The shout came from behind Amisso and Beata, and they looked over their shoulders to see a squadron of Mercatorian cavalry drawn up in line 100 metres away. Their captain came galloping towards them as they scrambled to their feet.

'Move!' he shouted as he rode. 'Get back to the city! The Sordesians have landed!'

He pointed inland and the friends saw a thick blanket of smoke billowing across the landscape. It was so disorientating that for an instant they didn't take in what they were seeing. Then Amisso realised what it meant and started running in the direction of the distant smoke. The cavalry officer swerved and rode across in front of him.

'No!' he ordered. 'Go home, lad – back to Mercatorius!'

'That is my home!' Amisso shouted, pointing at the smoke.

'Mine too!' Beata added as she caught Amisso up.

The captain called out to his lieutenant, who left the squadron and rode quickly over to them. Amisso lifted Beata up behind the lieutenant then mounted behind the captain and they rode off towards their estates, with the squadron fanning out behind them in line of battle.

When they arrived, there was no battle to be had. The action, such as it was, was over, and the Sordesian raiders gone.

'That way,' one of the plantation labourers told them, pointing to the hills that lay between Mercatorius and Munius. 'About twenty of them – soldiers, not pirates.'

'We were watching a Sordesian carrack fighting one of our ships,' Beata said. 'They must have come ashore from that.'

'Hit-and-run tactics,' the captain replied. 'We've been expecting something like this. That's why we've been mounting extra sea patrols. It doesn't look as if the Sordesians were anticipating that. One up to our spies.'

The air was still thick with smoke, although the fires were dying down now. The captain wiped a smut from his eye and turned to his lieutenant.

'Back to the city,' he ordered. 'Take six men with you and report to the colonel. Ask him to get a column of infantry sent out. We'll need to hunt the raiders down or they'll be back, but those hills are no place for cavalry – we'll leave it to the boys on foot. I'll mount a picket out here until further orders.'

The labourer helped Beata from the lieutenant's horse, and the officer galloped back towards Mercatorius with his escort while the captain surveyed the damage. Neither of the villas had been touched and only the Almus plantation had been set on fire.

'It must have been those big barns that attracted them,' the captain said. 'You could see them for miles – a prime target! And look at them now.'

The fire had been fierce and the great barns were gutted; nothing was left but the charred frames. Everything inside was destroyed and the whole north hill was nothing but a blackened, smoking wasteland. The Almus crop and every last bush had been wiped out. It was a hot summer and everything was powder-dry – the little bushes had been planted so close together that they must have burned as fiercely as a forest of pine trees. Amisso dismounted from the captain's horse and stared at the scene of the disaster, dazed. He started to wander among the smoking remains of the bushes. Then a sudden thought brought him up short and he wheeled towards the labourer.

'Where's Master Bardo?' he asked.

The labourer bowed his head and didn't reply.

'Tell me, man!' Amisso demanded, running up to him and shaking him by the shoulders.

'I'm sorry,' he replied. 'We tried to get him to leave it, but he wouldn't. He was trying to put the fires out. He wouldn't give up. He was in that barn, there – the biggest.'

'He said he had to save his crop,' the labourer explained to the captain. 'I don't know why he bothered, though – it was going rotten anyway. Stunk something awful. I don't think that Almus stuff keeps.'

Amisso set off running in the direction the man had indicated.

8
Changes

Fallax hammered on the door so hard that the frame shifted.

'You should get that fixed,' the sergeant said. 'There'll be a draft blowing through that now.'

'Hold your tongue,' Fallax told him. 'You and your men are here to help me collect my rent, not to advise me on the upkeep of my property.'

He snatched the man's halberd and beat on the door with the butt end of it.

'Come out or I'll have you dragged out,' Fallax bellowed. 'I told you last week I'd be back with the Guard.'

There was discontented muttering among the half dozen guardsmen, and their sergeant did nothing to discipline them. They all detested being assigned to escort the city's taxmen, but they regarded it as outrageous that Fallax had somehow got the commander of the city garrison to assign him an escort for his private rent collection as well. Mercatorius was at war and had been for a month – it seemed unbelievable that any of the City Guard should be used like this at such a time. There had been much discussion at the barracks about how much the commander must owe to Fallax, and for what.

'Ten seconds and I'll have the door broken down!' Fallax shouted.

'That won't take much doing,' the sergeant told him. 'Look at the state of this place. Why don't you ever repair these houses? You charge enough rent for them.'

Fallax glared at the man.

'Your business is getting my money – nothing else,' he said. 'I don't forget faces, sergeant. One day you'll owe me money, and then you'll regret what you've said today. I'll make sure of it.'

There was a cracking sound as the damaged door opened. A small man of about 40 stood in the shadow of the doorway, as if he was frightened of stepping too far into the light. His hair was thin and unkempt, his face pale and he wore a long nightshirt that almost came to his ankles.

'I told you last week,' he said in a shaky voice. 'I've been ill. I can't work. I've nothing to pay you with.'

'I'm not a doctor,' Fallax told him. 'I don't want a medical report. I want my money.'

The man's wife came to stand next to him now. She was carrying a wicker basket.

'He's getting better,' she said. 'We thought he'd die a few days ago, but then he started eating these and he's started getting back his strength.'

She held out the basket and Fallax saw a pile of golden yellow fruit, shaped like small pears.

'They're called Almus,' the woman told him. 'He'll soon be strong eating these, then he can get back to work and pay you your rent.'

'You're a month in arrears,' Fallax said. 'Money today or you're out.'

'We've no money at all,' the woman replied. 'Please, sir – take these instead. It's all we've got.' And she held out the basket.

Fallax took it and picked up one of the fruits. It felt firm, and when he held it to his nose it had a delicate scent like a sweet blossom – very welcome in the stinking streets of the Poor Quarter.

'Eat them fresh,' the man told him. 'They go off if you try and keep them. Plant the seeds and you can grow your own – they grow anywhere. We've got a little bush in the back yard. It's only been in a couple of days and it's already this high.'

He held his hands about thirty centimetres apart.

'Thank you for the gardening tips,' Fallax said, stepping out of the way of the door. 'Do your job, sergeant – them and their belongings on the street, and nail up the door.'

'But, sir!' the woman cried. 'The fruit!'

'A very kind gift,' Fallax replied, 'but I only take cash for rent.'

Ten minutes later, the man, his wife, three children and a pile of their cheap belongings were on the street, the door had planks nailed across it and a notice saying that anyone entering the property would be guilty of housebreaking, and Fallax with his guardsmen was marching back to his office.

'Fruit, Sergeant?' Fallax said, holding out an Almus from the basket.

'I wouldn't touch anything that had been in your hands, sir,' the soldier replied coldly. 'I'd be afraid I might get poisoned.'

'Please yourself,' Fallax said, and took a bite himself.

Nefa's heart sank when word went round the holding cells that the Court of Justice was to be chaired by Senator Crasto that day. She wasn't the only one who rapidly recalculated the chance of getting off the charge brought against them, or at least receiving a lenient sentence.

'It's not fair,' a woman's voice said in the dark. 'It's not our fault his son got killed. Why should he take it out on us?'

There were murmurs of agreement.

'Haven't you never lost a child?' Nefa asked.

'Plenty,' the reply came back.

'How did you feel?'

'Like murdering someone – every time.'

'It don't get any better, no matter how many you lose,' another woman added.

'Senators are still human, like us,' Nefa said. 'It's the same for them as for us, no matter how rich they are.'

'It's still not fair our cases are up today with him in charge,' the first woman complained.

'I'll agree with you there,' Nefa replied. She knew only too well that her only hope was to get a very sympathetic hearing in court.

Senator Crasto methodically put on the special robes of the Chair of the Mercatorian Court of Justice. The rest of the 20 senators who made up the bench shared the same robing room with Crasto, but they kept their distance from him, talking quietly in twos and threes as they put on their embroidered cloaks and silk caps. The white-haired Crasto was an isolated figure at the far end of the room. It was two months since his elder son had died – trapped and incinerated in the barn set alight by the Sordesians – and in that time the senator had withdrawn into himself. Following this loss he hadn't, however, withdrawn from public and business life – much to the disappointment of Senator Perdo and his allies. He had told himself that he'd failed the Senate when Amisso disappeared and he had failed through weakness. He had determined not to let weakness lead him into failure again and so he had proceeded to conduct himself in both business and public duties with a cold ferocity that had startled his colleagues. He was not unfair when he chaired the Court of Justice, but he applied the letter of the law exactly, without compassion or mercy. The Mercatorian Court was not known for kind-heartedness, but its members were beginning to be as unhappy as the prisoners when Crasto presided.

There was a knock at the door of the robing room and a young page entered, looking very nervous. He scanned the room, then approached Senator Crasto with great caution, sweeping a deep bow before him and speaking to the polished wood floor in front of his left toe.

'Senator Crasto, sir,' he said, 'there's a man to see you.'

'Tell him to wait,' Crasto snapped. 'We're about to go into session. Tell him to come back when the Court rises.'

'He says he can't wait, sir,' the boy said, with a wavering voice. 'He says it won't take a moment.'

'Who is he?' Crasto asked.

'He's a taxman, sir,' the boy replied.

The rest of the room fell silent at this.

'This is ridiculous!' Crasto erupted. 'Are my taxes so overdue that he has to pursue me to the Court for them?' He turned to the rest of the senators, who were all now staring at him. 'I shall be back in a moment, gentlemen,' he said coldly. 'Please be kind enough to wait for me.'

The door of the small chamber burst open and Senator Crasto strode through. Fallax was standing in the middle of the room.

'Well?' the senator demanded. 'Have you come like a carrion crow to pick over my rotting body? I know my taxes are overdue, man – I don't need a visit here to tell me that. I've a plantation destroyed, two inheritances ruined, ships stranded in every port you care to name waiting for naval escorts home, and a son dead. I've got other things on my mind. A fair tax demand is more than I'd care to see just at this moment, let alone the barefaced robbery that seems to be your stock-in-trade.'

Crasto's chest swelled and he glared at the tax collector. Fallax was silent, but he seemed unshaken by the tirade. He was holding a small brass-bound casket and now he handed it to Crasto. The senator was puzzled. He opened the casket and stared at the contents, speechless. It was full of gold.

'What's this?' he asked.

'What I owe you,' Fallax told him. 'It's all that I've overcharged you on your taxes since I took up my post. A refund.'

Then he walked out of the room, leaving Crasto still staring at the money.

Fallax didn't know his way around the Palace of Justice and got lost trying to find his way out. He went down rather more flights of steps than he thought he needed to, and the corridors he found himself walking along became increasingly dark, dingy and cold. Then, suddenly, he heard voices approaching. There were shouted orders and the clanking of chains, and round the corner came half a dozen guardsmen with a row of four prisoners between them, chained hand and foot. Fallax stood to one side to let them pass, and as they did so his eyes met those of one of the prisoners. The two recognised each other at once. The last time they'd met, the prisoner had spat in Fallax's face after trying to steal his purse. She let out a moan and sank to her knees, bringing the whole line to a halt, and one of the guards took a step towards her, raising his halberd to strike her with the butt.

'Wait!' Fallax shouted. Then he knelt down beside Nefa. 'What is it?' he asked. 'What's the matter?'

'As if you didn't know,' she said. 'I've been fitted up good and proper now – all they need is for you to tell them how I tried to thieve off you and it's all sewn up. First Crasto, now you – I don't even stand a chance.'

'Come on you,' the sergeant ordered, 'on your feet.' And he yanked her up by the chain attached to her hands. She winced as it bit into her flesh and struggled to her feet.

'I wouldn't mind,' Nefa called as the prisoners were led away, 'But I've given it up.'

'What?' Fallax shouted after her.

'Thieving!' she replied.

Fallax stood thinking for a moment, then he turned and hurried after the prisoners.

Senator Crasto heard scuffling at the back of the court and looked up from the papers that were spread in front of him. Two court guards were struggling to prevent someone coming in. It was Fallax. The senator was still dazed from his earlier meeting with the taxman and instead of ordering the guards to throw him out, he shouted for them to leave him alone.

'What is your business with this Court?' Crasto asked.

'I think I may be of service,' Fallax answered, 'as a witness.'

Crasto glanced at the State Prosecutor, but the lawyer shrugged his shoulders, looking mystified.

'Very well,' Crasto said. 'Show him to a seat, officer.'

Crasto nodded to the court usher, who stepped out into a side corridor and shouted, 'Case number one!'

A moment later, Nefa was brought in and made to stand in a wooden pen, facing the bench. She looked around the courtroom with wide eyes until she caught sight of Fallax, then she bowed her head.

'The case against, if you please,' Crasto said to the Prosecutor.

The man rose and addressed the bench.

'Your Honour, this is a simple matter,' he said, 'and easily dealt with. The woman before you, who goes by the name of Nefa, is a well-known villain. I have witnesses who can tell you the story of her life. She claims to be about 30 years of age and my witnesses can swear that she has supported herself by theft and robbery for 20 of those years, living off the honest people of Mercatorius like a parasite. She has three times been before this Court. The case notes are in front of you, your Honour, recording her convictions and punishments. So far she has been treated lightly: she has been pilloried, whipped and imprisoned. But if she is found guilty today, the laws of our State demand execution.'

'Yes, indeed,' Crasto interrupted. 'You have no need to remind us of our duty, Master Prosecutor. You can be assured that we will carry it out. Now, the particulars of the case in hand?'

'On the fifth of last month, your Honour, this creature robbed Master Mustelo—'

'It is alleged,' Crasto corrected.

'Indeed, your Honour. It is alleged that while Master Mustelo was about his lawful business, collecting payment for his employer, Signor Largo of the Guild of Chandlers, this wretch cut the purse from his belt – a purse containing 20 ducats – and made off with it.'

'It's a lie!' Nefa shouted.

'Silence, woman!' Crasto ordered. 'Or I'll have you whipped for contempt of this Court.' He glared at her, then turned back to her accuser. 'Well, Master Prosecutor, and what is your evidence?'

'There are witnesses, my Lord,' the Prosecutor replied. 'Master Mustelo himself saw the woman running off and is able to identify her; the customer at whose house he was calling also saw her; and a neighbour in the street saw the purse cut and raised the alarm. All are in court and ready to testify, if you require it.'

'And the purse, Master Prosecutor – has it been recovered?'

'It has, your Honour. When the woman was tracked to her hovel the purse was found among her possessions.'

'And the 20 ducats?'

'Gone, your Honour,' the Prosecutor replied.

Senator Crasto called for the witnesses to give their story, and all three gave a description of events that matched the Prosecutor's charge. Crasto was surprised to note that Fallax was not among those called.

'Thank you, Master Prosecutor,' Crasto concluded. 'Now, to the prisoner. What have you to say in your defence, woman? Mercatorius faces dangers enough from without: dangers from an enemy that would tear the heart out of our State, an enemy that has already torn the hearts of our citizens by its unprovoked attacks. Is this the time for enemies to be attacking us from within? If you are guilty, you can expect no mercy at my hands. Now speak, if you have anything to say!'

Nefa was holding the wooden wall of her pen to steady herself. She looked instinctively towards Fallax. She too was surprised he hadn't been called by the Prosecutor and tried to read from his face what might be in store. Perhaps the Prosecutor intended to let her make her defence, then destroy her credibility with this last witness. But what she saw in the taxman's face confused her even more: he was smiling as if he wanted to give her encouragement.

'Your Honour,' Nefa said quietly, 'I didn't do it. These people are telling lies about me. I don't know who cut this man's purse, but it weren't me. It's right that I've done a lot of bad things, like the Prosecutor said, and I've got the scars to show I've been lashed. But I don't do none of that no more, and I didn't do this to Master Mustelo.'

Crasto waited, but she said no more.

'You say you don't steal anymore,' he said. 'Could you tell me why that is? Have you got an honest job?'

'Maybe she's claiming that she's stolen enough to retire on,' the Prosecutor joked.

Several of the senators, seated on either side of Crasto, laughed at this.

'Perhaps an inheritance from a wealthy relative – a gift?' the Prosecutor went on.

Crasto scowled as the senators laughed again. 'Enough, sir,' he ordered.

'It was a gift,' Nefa said.

'What was?' Crasto asked.

'The food, your Honour – the fruit. One of my neighbours gave it to me. You can grow it anywhere. I've got a bush growing in my room, in a bucket. You eat the fruit and you don't need nothing else. It's food and drink and everything. So I don't need to thieve no more, your Honour. I don't feel as if I need nothing but this fruit, so I've given the thieving up. It's called Almus, your Honour – it's Almus fruit.'

There was a hum of conversation in the court and Crasto let it run unchecked for several moments. It was the Court Usher who eventually called for silence.

'I grew Almus,' Crasto said. 'My son grew it on my estate.'

'Then you know,' Nefa replied excitedly, not noticing the heaviness in Crasto's tone. 'If you've eaten it, you know what I'm saying's true.'

'Why should I eat such a pathetic little thing?' Crasto said. 'The best fruit the world has to offer is served at my table, woman. Do you expect a senator of Mercatorius to bother himself with something that grows like a common weed?' There was anger in his voice now, and Nefa was taken aback. 'What I know is that your story can't be true. Every last Almus bush and fruit was destroyed when my estate was attacked and my son was murdered. You have been extremely unwise to remind me of it with your lying tale. You are clearly guilty—'

'Wait!' Fallax shouted, jumping up. 'It's true... What she's saying is true.'

Crasto stared at him. 'Am I to understand that you are a witness for this woman's defence?' he asked.

'If it please your Honour,' he replied.

'Very well then,' Crasto said. 'Speak.'

'I can't tell you how it got there, sir,' Fallax told him, 'but there is Almus in the Poor Quarter of the city. I've seen it there. I own property in the Poor Quarter and one of my tenants gave me a basket of the fruit. I've grown it myself and I eat it all the time now. She's right: you don't need anything else, and you don't want anything else once you've had Almus. Gentlemen, you know me – you know that I was as much of a thief as this woman was, except that I robbed people without breaking the law.'

There was muttered agreement from many in the room who had had to pay their taxes to Fallax in the past. 'But I'm here to tell you that I've given all that up,' he continued, 'and there's someone in this room who has the proof of that.' He looked clearly at Crasto, and his fellow senators whispered among themselves, reminding each other of the visit Crasto had received before they came into court. 'If Almus can change me, your Honours,' Fallax concluded, 'then it can change this woman too, or anyone in the world.'

Once more, conversation broke out around the room, but this time it was Crasto who called for order.

'This is all very well,' he said, 'but how can you explain the Prosecutor's witnesses and Master Mustelo's purse.' Crasto scanned the court. 'Has the woman a witness who can explain that to the Bench?'

'Simple,' Fallax replied. 'I think you'll find, if you ask him, that those 20 lost ducats didn't belong to Master Mustelo but to his employer. We've heard that Master Mustelo was collecting payment for Signor Largo and I would suggest that he decided to keep the money for himself. What better way of doing it than to pocket it, pretend it's been stolen and put the blame on a known thief? It would have been easy for Mustelo to plant the empty purse in Nefa's room when he visited with the guards. But I think you'll need to look for the contents of the purse in Master Mustelo's rooms – 18 ducats of it, at any rate. I should think at least a ducat each has found its way into the two other witnesses' pockets.'

'How do you know this?' Crasto asked.

'Thieves know the ways of thieves, your Honour,' Fallax replied. 'It's a common practice. Mercatorius is the home of enterprise, after all.'

When the senators had withdrawn to their chamber to deliberate, they waited for Crasto to begin the discussion, but he sat silently at the head of the table for some moments.

'Is it true?' he asked, at last. 'Is this kind of deception common in Mercatorius?'

Several of the senators who felt confident they wouldn't be observed exchanged smiles. Crasto's sharp understanding of trade was legendary, but in some things he seemed as naive as the one son who was left to him.

'Only among the lower classes,' one of the other senators replied reassuringly.

'Very well, then,' Crasto said wearily. 'Can we accept her defence?'

There was a long list of cases to get through that morning, and it only took the senators a few moments to return to the court.

'Prisoner, rise!' the Usher instructed, and Nefa struggled up from the bench where she had slumped.

'This Court finds you not guilty of the charge brought against you,' Crasto informed her. 'You are free to go.' Then he turned to the guards at the door. 'And this Court orders the arrest of Master Mustelo,' he continued. 'Take him to the cells and have a search made of his home.'

The guards took Mustelo away, and Fallax helped a stunned Nefa out of the dark courtroom into the brightness of Senate Square as the Usher's voice was heard shouting, 'Case number two!'

9
Emergency Meeting

The Audience Chamber was one of the smallest rooms in the Senate House, but still it shone with gold, and bright paintings by the city's greatest artists decorated the ceiling and walls. However, no one was paying any attention to the beautiful surroundings when the joint delegation from the city's traders, farmers and employers started to present its case. The room was supposed to be a quiet place where a small group of leading senators could hear petitions from the people of the city and decide whether to take their issues to a full Senate meeting. But there was no quiet on this occasion. The Audience Chamber was in uproar.

'Nobody's buying anything!' a market trader shouted.

'The food's rotting on our stalls!' another added.

'We can't get rid of our harvest!' a farmer complained. 'None of the traders will buy! They're ruining us!'

'How can we buy stock when we can't sell it?' one of the traders yelled back, angrily.

Several farmers demanded that the market traders be made to pay for their usual orders of produce – some suggested that agreements for supplies had been made and then cancelled by the traders. A furious argument raged between the traders and farmers and it was no longer possible for the six senators to make any sense of what was being said.

'Silence!' Crasto bellowed.

He was the Chair of the Committee of Audience, and it was his job to guide his five fellow senators to a decision on the case before them. He was on his feet now and his powerful voice made the little chamber ring. The senators' carved seats were on a raised platform at the end of the room, and all the members of the delegation turned from their squabbling to face the Committee.

'Citizens,' Crasto told them, 'this Committee will dismiss your petition unless you can behave in a civilised manner and make your case clearly. Now, you,' Crasto pointed to one of the market traders who looked least red in the face, 'explain yourself. Why are the stallholders unable to sell?'

'It's the Almus, sir,' the man replied.

Crasto stared at him for a moment, then sank back into his seat. It was three weeks since Nefa had used Almus in her defence against the charge of theft, and Crasto had been struggling to put the word out of his mind. He couldn't help blaming the fruit for what had happened to Bardo. And he couldn't stop blaming himself for having let his son's obsession with it run out of control.

'Almus,' Crasto repeated.

'It's a fruit, sir,' the man began.

'Yes, yes – I know what Almus is,' Crasto interrupted. 'Just tell us what it's got to do with your loss of trade.'

'Everyone's eating it, sir,' the man explained. 'It's all over the city.'

'Not on my table,' Senator Gannio remarked.

'Among the poorer people, sir,' the trader told him. 'They don't want to eat anything else, so they don't buy our food.'

'Then sell Almus instead!' Senator Mero suggested.

'What are we to do?' a farmer shouted.

'Grow Almus!' Mero told him.

Crasto shifted uncomfortably in his seat.

'It can't be done,' the trader told him. 'You can't farm it because you can't store it for market; it goes rotten straight away if you don't eat it fresh from the bush. And there's no point in trying to sell something that everyone can grow for free. You can grow a bush anywhere, and a bush is all you need to feed a family for ever; it just keeps making fruit as fast as you eat it – day after day, without fail.'

The trader stopped and there was a tense silence in the room. The man had done his job well – the exact nature of the problem was immediately clear to the senators and they each stared into space with mounting concern as they digested the implications of what had been said. Finally Crasto roused himself and searched out one of the employers in the delegation whom he knew and could trust to be level-headed.

'We have heard nothing from the various men of business represented in your delegation,' Crasto said to the man he had selected. 'Tell us what your interest is in the Almus affair.'

'I'll tell you what happened to me, Senator,' the man replied. 'And that will illustrate the problem. As you know,

I run a printing business – one of the most successful in the city—'

'Spare us the sales talk,' Senator Tundax interrupted.

'I only mention it,' the printer replied, 'to remind you that anyone in my employment can expect to do well, very well indeed – especially my top people. Which was why I was surprised when one of my most skilled employees started taking days off – not sick, you understand, just failing to turn up for work. After a couple of weeks I had the man into my office and demanded an explanation and the explanation was Almus. He said that thanks to Almus he didn't need money to feed his family any more, so he didn't need to work so much. I tried to reason with him; I told him that not buying food would mean he could save more money from his wages if he kept on working regularly. He could build up his capital more quickly and start a business of his own – something I know he'd been planning for years. But he said he didn't want to do that anymore. As I talked to him it became clear that he'd lost all material ambition. When I pointed this out, he simply said that since he'd been eating Almus, he'd started to look at things differently. In the end I had no option but to threaten him with losing his job if he continued to behave in this irresponsible way. Then to my astonishment, he apologised for putting me out and told me that in that case he would give his job up there and then; he could do without the money.'

'But that's ridiculous,' Senator Gannio burst out. 'Almus might feed him but it can't clothe him and keep a roof over his head!'

'Exactly what I told him. Believe me, Senator, I had no wish to lose this man; he was one of my best. I found myself using every argument I could think of – almost pleading with him in the end – but he would have none of it. He said he had money saved for the other necessities and that there were other jobs he could do casually, when he needed. He even had the cheek to suggest that I might employ him from time to time for the odd few days if he needed a little cash. He seemed as confident as a man with a million ducats in the bank. "Tomorrow will look after itself," was all he had to say, and he bid me good day. And that, your Honours, is our difficulty. It's the same story throughout the city. Our workers can no longer be relied upon to work when we require them. When they turn up they work hard and well – harder than they did before if anything – but they only work when they want to. They work for the pleasure of working; if there's no satisfaction in a job, or they don't think it's worthwhile, they won't do it. And the threat of losing their employment seems to mean nothing to them anymore.'

Crasto dismissed the delegation and the six senators considered their response. For a moment, Crasto gazed at the pictures that decorated the room – scenes of the triumphs of Mercatorius, paintings of its great buildings, fleets and heroes, every one set in a thick, elaborately carved, gilded frame.

'All of this,' Crasto said at last, gesturing to the paintings, 'is under threat – threatened with destruction by a wretched plant!'

'You're exaggerating, Crasto,' Senator Lenex replied, but without much conviction.

'Am I? If what we've heard is true, the whole system on which we depend, and the very drive that has made this city the greatest in the world, could be destroyed.'

'Perhaps we should eat some of this Almus. By the sound of it, we'd end up not caring what happened,' Senator Mero suggested.

'Don't be ridiculous!' Tundax snapped.

'We can beat this surely,' Senator Lenex said. 'We can use it. If it's such a wonder, let's export it.'

'Are you mad?' Crasto responded. 'It would destroy the economy of any city we sent it to; our overseas markets would collapse if no one felt the need to buy or had the drive to generate any wealth to pay for our produce.'

'Anyway,' Gannio reminded them, 'we couldn't trade it; they say it won't keep.'

'All we can export are the seeds,' Crasto said bitterly, remembering the cursed day Amisso had placed four of them on his table.

'Why don't we send them to Sordes?' Tundax urged. 'If the plant can destroy a city, what better city to destroy?'

'Perhaps they sent it here,' Senator Mero suggested.

'Where did it come from?' Gannio asked.

'Never mind where it came from,' Crasto snapped. 'It's here, and unless something's done about it, it'll cause more damage to this city than Sordes ever could. I move that the issue of Almus be put on the agenda of the Senate as a matter of absolute urgency – this is a State emergency, gentlemen.'

Crasto's proposal was agreed unanimously.

In fact, when he heard the details from Crasto, the Dux decided the question of Almus was so urgent that he called an emergency session of the Senate later that day. An emergency session was an unusual event, and when word of it leaked out across the city, the crowds began to gather in Senate Square. The subject of the emergency debate wasn't known at that stage and many assumed that it was to do with hostilities against Sordes. War might have been formally declared after the attack on Crasto's estate, but that had been nearly three months ago and little had happened since, apart from a series of similar hit-and-run raids on both sides. The rumour spread that the Senate was meeting to plan a proper offensive. But there were several in the growing crowd who knew of the delegation about the Almus that morning and suspected the mysterious fruit might be on the agenda.

Those who had been in the Square longest were nearest to the Senate House building, and foremost among them was Fallax the taxman. If others were having trouble getting their employees to work, that was not the case with Fallax, and this was entirely due to the work he was asking them to do. After giving tax refunds to all the people he had robbed, he still had a considerable amount of money left and he had used some of this to hire workmen to repair his properties in the Poor Quarter. The builders and carpenters had thought that this was good work to do and so they had done it gladly and to a very high standard. This was how it was among the Almus eaters: because they worked for the pleasure and satisfaction in a job, they worked cheerfully and with pride. The atmosphere in the Poor Quarter had become very positive as a result; it felt good to live there despite the lack of luxury, and Fallax himself had taken rooms in the Quarter, in one of his own properties. It was all due to the Almus, and when Fallax had heard that a delegation was going to complain to the Senate about the fruit, he had immediately become anxious. News of the emergency session had sent him to the Square at once.

A detachment of guards in full ceremonial uniform kept the crowd at a safe distance from the arcade of gleaming white pillars that formed the base of the Senate House wall. There was no way the people would know what was going on until the session was ended, but still Fallax and the rest stayed in the Square throughout the afternoon. From time to time someone would find a box or cart or mounting block to stand on and would make a speech to the section of the crowd that could hear. Most speakers poured insults on the heads of the Sordesian dogs, calling all true Mercatorians to support an all-out attack on their neighbours, but occasionally one would denounce those who were complaining about Almus. It was a lively and excited gathering.

As dusk was beginning to gather, there was a sudden flurry of activity at the Great Gate, a huge pair of wooden doors in a highly decorated porch, which was the entrance that only senators could use. An honour guard formed up. Coaches came rattling over the flagstones. The crowd caught glimpses of the fur-trimmed cloaks of famous senators hurrying away to their suppers. And then the army of clerks and minor officials began to pour out of the less important doors, flitting among the pillars on their way to have orders printed and distributed and to carry news of the Senate's business to those who needed to know. It was from this buzzing group that word of the Senate's decisions leaked out to the crowd. It was not welcome news.

'They've banned Almus! They're going to confiscate it all! It's going to be destroyed!' These were the rumours that passed rapidly round the Square. And then came more startling information: 'They've arrested Senator Crasto. They're saying it's his fault the Almus is here. They say he's a traitor, a Sordesian agent.' Long before finer details of the session had started to spread among the crowd, such as the fact that it was Senator Perdo who'd led the move to have Crasto arrested, Fallax had gone. He was hurrying back to the Poor Quarter, intent on saving Almus from destruction.

As he muscled his way through the narrow alleys, another figure, wrapped in a dark blue, hooded cloak, was struggling free of the crowd on the northern edge of Senate Square. The cloak and hood completely hid the owner's identity, but the size and movement of the figure showed it to be female. Once out of the Square, she took the broad road that cut through the Poor Quarter and led to the Northern Gate.

Amisso's eyes were red. He was trying hard not to cry. The page of the heavy ledger that was open in front of him was a mess. There was so much crossing out that he was having trouble working out which tiny, rewritten entry went in which column. His father wouldn't be able to make any sense of it at all – so it would have to be written out again. But Amisso couldn't copy it until he was sure the figures were right, and at the moment he was sure they were wrong. Somehow, 58 ducats had gone missing in the accounts sheet he was working on and he couldn't find out why. It was this that was bringing tears to his eyes – they were tears of anger and frustration. He was also exhausted. He had worked a full day in his father's office in the city and now he had had to bring this ledger home to try and get it right. The figures danced before his tired eyes.

The only way that Amisso and his father had been able to cope with Bardo's death was to work. Two days after the nightmare of the attack, Crasto had woken his remaining son and told him simply, 'You must take Bardo's place now.' There had seemed no possibility of arguing, and Amisso hadn't wanted to. Ever since that morning he had gone to the city with his father and done his best to learn the business. His best had barely been enough to make him a passable clerk, let alone a partner in the business, but neither father nor son had complained. They had simply gritted their teeth and got on with it. It felt to both of them as if they were doing penance. They each felt guilty about Almus – Crasto for allowing its cultivation without finding out more about it, and Amisso for bringing it to Mercatorius in the first place.

It was nearly ten months since Amisso's master had given him the seeds in their leather bag and now the excitement he'd felt about bringing the miracle fruit back to his father seemed a long way away. He'd hoped so much that Almus would make his father happy and proud of him, and even when the plant had been grown for sale Amisso had been able to overcome his unease by looking forward to the time when the fruit would make a contribution to his father's business recovery. But when the plantation had been reduced to ashes, Amisso had felt no grief for the loss of his plant. All he'd been able to think about had been the death of his brother, and his only feeling about Almus had been that it was to blame. Despite their different characters, despite Amisso's jealousy of Bardo's achievements, and despite Bardo's unforgiving attitude after Amisso's return, it was still his brother who had died in the blazing barn. Amisso continued to have nightmares about it almost every night.

Amisso stared blankly and hopelessly at the page of accounts, and the endless debate that distracted so many of his waking hours started to run once again in his mind. On the one hand a voice argued that Bardo had only himself to blame – that his huge barns had attracted disaster and his greed had prevented him from escaping the flames – but relentlessly the opposing voice replied that if only Amisso had not brought the Almus seeds, Bardo would still have been alive.

The internal argument was only brought to an end by an urgent hammering at the door.

'Come,' Amisso called wearily.

The servant opened the door and started to speak, but before he could get two words out a small figure in a dark blue cloak pushed him aside. She pulled back her hood and the flickering light caught dark, urgent eyes and a tangle of black hair.

'Beata!' Amisso said, struggling to his feet.

'Come quickly!' she told him, 'there's no time to waste.'

She grabbed his hand and hauled him round the desk to her.

'Wait! What is it?' he asked.

'Talk as we walk,' she said. 'Trust me. Get a cloak and come with me now.' Then she turned to the servant. 'I was never here and you don't know where Master Amisso's gone,' she said. 'Do you understand?'

The man looked to Amisso and his young master nodded.

'Yes, Mistress Beata,' the man replied, and stood aside as Beata whisked Amisso out of the room.

By the time they reached the safety of Beata's home, she had explained to Amisso about the Senate session and his father's arrest.

'But what were you doing there?' Amisso asked, as they stood in the starlight on the balcony of Beata's family villa.

'Never mind that,' she said. 'You must stay here for the time being.'

'Why?'

'Don't you see? Your father didn't bring Almus here, you did.'

'Father would never tell them that,' Amisso said shocked.

'Of course not, but there must be other people – servants – in your household who know,' Beata explained. 'It wasn't a secret, after all. Perdo and his gang will find out. They've got eyes and ears everywhere.'

'So you think I'm in danger?'

'Of course you are. There's nothing much happening in the war so the people want a victory, and if arresting Sordesian agents will give them one, then that's what the Senate will do; the more they can arrest, the better.'

'But how can they think Father is working for Sordes?' Amisso protested. 'It was his estate that was attacked, his son that died.'

'The rumour in the Square was that it was all a cover-up – all your father wanted was to get Almus into the city, and the burning of his estate was to hide his tracks. People were saying Bardo's death was just an unlucky accident. That much is true, at any rate.'

Amisso gripped the balustrade that ran round the balcony.

'That's madness,' he said. 'None of it makes sense.'

'We're in a war,' she told him. 'What do you expect?'

There was movement on the road out of Mercatorius. From Beata's balcony they could see a coach with a cavalry escort heading in their direction at speed. Outriders carrying flaming torches lit the way.

'That's my father's coach,' Amisso said minutes later, as it drew close enough to make out its shape.

'At least that's something to be thankful for,' Beata muttered.

'What do you mean?' Amisso asked.

'They've spared him a prison cell,' she explained. 'They must be putting him under house arrest.'

Sure enough, once the coach had passed through the gateway to Crasto's estate, two of the troopers dismounted, tethered their horses and stood to attention on sentry duty. Then the sound of tramping feet on cobblestones travelled through the still night air to Amisso and Beata and they saw that a small detachment of infantry was following the cavalry. A quarter of an hour later they too entered the gates of Crasto's estate, and no doubt deployed themselves in the house and grounds. Amisso watched it all with a mounting feeling of desperation. At last he turned back towards the house.

'I'm going,' he said with determination.

'Where?'

'To be with my father,' he said. 'I can't leave him to face this on his own. What's the point in me being free? If he has to be locked up I might as well be locked up with him.'

'No!' said Beata, grabbing his arm. 'You're needed.'

He turned to her in surprise.

'What do you mean?' he asked.

'For Almus,' she told him. 'Almus needs protecting.'

'What have you got to do with that cursed plant?' Amisso asked.

She looked him in the eyes for a moment.

'Have you forgotten?' she said. 'You gave me two of the seeds.'

The sound of footsteps on the path to the villa from the gate of Beata's estate sent the pair back to the edge of the balcony, where they saw a sergeant and half a dozen soldiers marching towards the house.

'I suppose that was only to be expected,' Beata said. 'They'll want to know where you are, even if they're not arresting you yet – and the first place they'd look would be here. Come on. We'd better disappear.'

As the sound of the sergeant's fist on the door boomed out, Amisso and Beata were already creeping through the olive groves, making for open country.

~

Beata had always been a strong character, and throughout their growing up, Amisso had tended to let her take the lead in their games and exploits, but he'd thought of it as just humouring her bossiness. Now, however, there was a new purposefulness and assurance about her. Something seemed to have given her an authority that Amisso instinctively accepted and he entrusted himself to her judgement entirely as she led the way through the darkness – even when, to his surprise, she turned towards the city rather than the hills.

They didn't follow the main road but, cutting through fields and groves, she eventually brought them to the Northern Gate.

'Pull your hood up,' she told Amisso. 'Lean on my arm and limp. And don't say anything.'

He did as instructed, but Beata drew her hood back to show her face. The sentry seemed to be expecting her.

'Evening, miss,' he said in a kindly voice. 'Found another one?'

'Soon have him fit again,' she said and she steered Amisso through the fortified gateway.

'Goodnight, miss,' one of the other sentries called after her.

'Don't say anything,' Beata whispered to Amisso as they moved away from the gatehouse. 'And keep your hood up: that golden hair of yours will get you recognised anywhere.'

Amisso soon realised that they were heading into the Poor Quarter. When he had last been among its twisting passageways, 11 months ago, he had felt lost, like a foreigner, but Beata seemed to know exactly where to go. She didn't hide her face and there were some people in the narrow alleys who, like the sentries, seemed to know her and called out greetings. At last she knocked on the door of a dingy-looking house in the middle of a long gloomy row. It seemed to be leaning out over the street as if its front wall might one day give up the effort of standing and fall forward to rest against the house opposite. Beata and Amisso waited for a few moments, then the door creaked open and an alarming face appeared in the moonlight – staring eyes and a grin that showed a missing front tooth.

'Let us in, Nefa,' Beata said. 'We need to hide.'

10
Neighbours

'I've no room for another down-and-out,' Nefa said as she led them up her damp, narrow staircase. 'No room for visitors, hardly. I've already had one tonight; he's still here.'

They reached her room and found two men there. One, perched anxiously on the edge of a wooden stool, Amisso recognised at once. He was Fallax the taxman, who had often visited his father's offices. The other man was half reclining on a little bed that had been made up against the wall and he too seemed familiar, although Amisso couldn't immediately place the face. The man seemed to recognise Amisso, however. When Beata explained who Amisso was and why she had brought him, the man patted the mattress.

'I'll vouch for him,' he said. 'Come and sit by me, Master. I owe you something for your kindness.'

Amisso accepted the offer, while Nefa gave Beata the only proper chair in the room, and pulled up another stool for herself. It was a small room, barely a quarter of the size of Amisso's bedroom at home, and it clearly served as a kitchen and dining room as well as sleeping quarters for the man he was sitting beside. It was dark, lit by a single tallow candle on the table, but what surprised Amisso was the fact that, although the whole house was clearly damp, the room didn't smell bad. In fact, there was a sweet perfume in the air like some kind of blossom. It was a familiar smell and Amisso glanced round the room, looking for its source. Then he saw it. Sprouting from a wooden bucket in a corner of the room was the shadowy shape of an Almus bush.

Beata saw him looking at the plant.

'It wasn't all destroyed when your plantation was burned,' she said. 'I brought it here.'

Amisso had very mixed feelings seeing an Almus bush again. Just the scent of it lifted his spirits for a moment, but the pleasure was immediately followed by the memory of all the suffering that had come to his family as a result of the plant.

'I didn't mean to give you those seeds, you know,' Amisso told her. 'They were supposed to be all for Father.'

'Well, whatever made you give them to me saved the Almus,' she replied.

'And saved my life,' the man on the bed added. 'When your brother had me driven away, I was on my last legs,' he told Amisso. 'Then Mistress Beata took me in and fed me some Almus, and it turned me round.'

The man introduced himself as Ebrio and now Amisso realised who he was – the beggar to whom he'd once given a drink of water at the gate of the Almus plantation.

'Verna wouldn't let me feed him with any food from the house,' Beata explained, 'but I'd grown your seeds and I told myself the Almus fruit was mine to do as I liked with, so I gave him some of that and it started making him better almost straight away. When I saw what it was doing for Ebrio, it made me think what it could do for the poor people in the city. So I brought it here.'

'And she brought me in the end,' Ebrio added.

'I was hiding him in an outhouse,' Beata explained, 'but I thought it'd be safer for him in the city as Verna pokes her nose in everywhere. When I asked around, Nefa said she could take him in.'

'Asked around?' Amisso asked. 'Do you mean you know more people in this place?'

'She's been all over the Quarter,' Nefa said, 'spreading Almus and bringing in beggars she's found out on the roads – to find them a bed and give them the Almus treatment.'

'So this is what you were doing, that you didn't know if you could tell me about,' Amisso said. 'Why on earth did you think you couldn't tell me?'

'You seemed so involved with Bardo,' she said, 'growing Almus for profit. I didn't know if you'd approve. Eating Almus and sharing it with other people seems to have changed the way I think about things and I didn't know if you'd understand.'

'I've eaten it too, you know,' Amisso reminded her.

But he realised as he said this how long it was since he had last eaten the fruit – not since they'd started the plantation in fact. Somehow, the only way he'd been able to come to terms with growing the plant for profit had been to stop eating it. The life-changing power of Almus had certainly faded in him during the months that had passed. Beata looked at him for a moment with a seriousness he'd never seen in her eyes before, and he began to understand where her strength and authority were coming from.

'When I look at what Mercatorius has done,' she said, 'how it's wrecked your family, this stupid trade war with Sordes, my father a prisoner, how it treats the poor – I hate all that our city stands for. But maybe by spreading Almus around we can make it a place to be proud of after all. Do you understand that?'

'I'd forgotten,' he said. 'But I did – I do understand.'

'We all do,' Fallax butted in impatiently. 'But we can't spend the whole night discussing it. We have to move fast: Almus is in great danger.'

'I know,' Beata replied. 'I was in the Senate Square.'

'Fallax came to find me,' Nefa explained. 'We've been trying to think how to save the Almus.'

'And not getting very far,' Ebrio commented. 'All we seem to have worked out up to now is that there's not much hope of getting the Senate to change its mind. That's after we'd spent an hour planning a campaign to get the senators to vote again,' he explained to Beata and Amisso, 'and then another hour working out how to sneak Almus into the senators' food.'

'I thought that was a good idea,' Nefa interrupted. 'If we can get them to taste it, they're bound to change their minds.'

'I told you,' Fallax replied, with annoyance, 'you'll never get anything into the kitchens that's not been tested and approved three times over; with this war on, they're all too scared of poison.'

'We've got to get it out of the city,' said Beata. 'If they're determined to destroy the only thing in the whole city that's any good, we'll have to take it out of their reach.'

'I thought you didn't like running away,' Amisso reminded her.

Beata looked at him steadily and he realised with a shock that she had found something else to care about in life apart from him – maybe apart from her father too, he suddenly thought.

'That was different,' she said. 'You didn't have a plan – it was pointless. This is to save Almus, to make sure it's not lost to the world. Anyway, it shouldn't just stay in Mercatorius; it was a free gift – it should be given to everyone everywhere.'

'I said that to Bardo,' Amisso told her, 'when he wouldn't let me give some to Ebrio!'

He felt excited, as if he had rediscovered the long-lost solution to a puzzle.

'We haven't got time for this,' Fallax broke in again. 'If we're going to get the Almus out, how are we going to do it? Take a pocketful of seeds each and make for the hills with it?'

'Too many patrols,' Beata told him. 'There's no one moving in the countryside except soldiers these days. There haven't even been any beggars on the roads these last few weeks. The Guard's on full alert for Sordesian landing parties.'

Amisso had gone to the corner of the room and was eating an Almus fruit, feeling its sweet, refreshing juice trickle down his throat.

'The sea,' he said suddenly.

They all turned to look at him. The dream that he'd thought was gone for ever had returned to him like sunshine breaking through clouds, and they could see it lighting up his face. Although he hadn't been to his father's map room since his return, he saw again in his imagination the whole world set out on its walls.

'We have to take Almus far away from anywhere that Mercatorius has ever been before,' he explained. 'We have to find places it hasn't spoiled.'

'If you sign on for a ship's crew again, you'll have to go where the captain takes you,' Beata said cautiously. 'That'll just take you to another trading port.'

'No, no,' Amisso told her. 'This time I need a ship of my own. We need a ship. Then we can go where we want.'

There was a moment's silence, followed by one or two cautious comments, then a burst of excited talk as his vision caught fire in everyone's imagination. Amisso watched for a moment, astonished by the way that these adults, twice his age and more, were taking on his suggestion. It was the same with the way they seemed to accept Beata's authority, young though she was. Wealth and status automatically gave the children of the gentry a certain power from an early age, but this seemed to be something more than that. Looking at their faces as they talked to each other – a taxman, a beggar, a pauper and an ambassador's daughter – he realised that eating Almus and serving it appeared to have given them a strange equality. Class, profession and age didn't seem to matter any more; all that was important was how best to serve the precious fruit.

'But how would we pay for it?' Nefa asked, bringing them to practicalities at last. 'It's alright living off Almus here in the Quarter, but Almus won't pay to fit out a ship. We haven't got any money.'

'I have,' Fallax said. 'I've still got enough to take care of this.'

They looked at him in disbelief.

'You'd be surprised how much I made,' he muttered. 'We'd need a captain, though,' he pointed out. 'Someone we could trust. And someone who was prepared to take the risk of sailing into a war zone.'

There was silence for a moment, then Ebrio cleared his throat.

'I know someone,' he said.

'Who?' they all asked.

He looked down at the rough material covering his bed, seeming embarrassed.

'Me,' he said softly.

Ebrio explained that for years he had been a captain working for Senator Perdo until the day he had lost a head start and had failed to beat one of Crasto's vessels to a distant port with a shipment of wine. This failure had meant that Crasto had got all the business and Perdo had lost a substantial amount of money.

'Perdo said I'd been beaten because I was drunk in charge of the ship,' Ebrio explained, 'but it wasn't that at all – we stopped to help a carrack that had had its rudder blown away in a storm. We had to tow it to the nearest port and that lost us two days – and the race to deliver Perdo's wine. He was so furious he didn't just sack me; he put the word about in Mercatorius and every port you can think of that I was a drunk. I couldn't get work anywhere, even as a deckhand. I was so miserable I did become a drunkard in the end, until I had no savings left and all I could do was beg.'

'Can you still—?' Beata began hesitantly.

'Command a ship?' Ebrio asked. 'Of course I can – now my head's clear and Almus has given me back my health.'

'Then you're a captain again,' Beata declared. 'If only we can find you a ship.'

Here, finally, they ran out of ideas. The only possibility seemed to be one of Crasto's vessels, but they were certain that the three which were in port at the moment would be under guard by now, and if Amisso went anywhere near them he was sure to be detained.

'You're not even safe to be out in the streets till we can get you a disguise,' Nefa warned. 'And you'd better change your clothes too, Mistress,' she told Beata. 'If the two of you's disappeared, it won't take much brains to work out you're together. They'll be looking for both of you now.'

Nefa didn't have any spare clothes, but she said she'd visit her neighbours and see what she could come up with. Amisso offered some coins, but she waved them away.

'If it's to do with saving Almus, no one's going to want that,' she told him.

It was an hour before Nefa returned with a bundle of clothes under her arm, but she didn't look pleased.

'More trouble,' she said. 'There's a dead Sordesian in the doorway. We'll have to shift the animal. If anyone finds him, they'll call the Guard for sure, and we don't want them poking around our door. I can't work out how he got here – I thought all their traders were thrown out of the city months ago.'

'And the port's been closed to their shipping since the war started,' Fallax added.

'Well, wherever he came from, he's not staying to rot on our doorstep,' Nefa told them. 'Get changed, Master, then you and Fallax can drag him off and dump him in an alley somewhere. See if you can find a rubbish pile to throw him on – it's where he belongs.'

So, for the second time in a year, Amisso found himself in simple workman's clothes, although this time he was spared having his hair sheared. Nefa had nothing to cut it with, so his golden curls were twisted up inside the greasy cap she had found for him. He and Fallax looked up and down the narrow street outside Nefa's door. No one was about, and there was no clue as to how the body slumped across the threshold might have got there. The baggy trousers and loose shirt showed the man to be a Sordesian, as Nefa had said, but they also showed something else: he was not a poor man. As Amisso took hold of the body by the arm to drag it, he could feel the quality of the material. Fallax gripped the other arm and they began to haul. They looked anxiously from side to side, sure that at any moment the scraping sound on the cobbles would bring a neighbour to their window or door. Then the man groaned.

'Wait,' said Amisso. 'He's alive.'

'So?' Fallax replied. 'Let's get him dumped and get out of it, quick.'

They dragged him for a few more paces, then Amisso stopped.

'No,' he said. 'The man needs attention.'

'Are you mad?' Fallax replied. 'He's a dog. Leave him to die; he deserves it.'

'You don't know anything about him,' Amisso answered.

'I know he's a Sordesian,' Fallax snapped back. 'That's all I need to know. You of all people shouldn't think twice about throwing one of these animals on the rubbish heap. They killed your brother.'

Amisso looked down at the unconscious face and all he saw was a strong-featured man in his thirties with short, dark hair and blood oozing from his forehead. He could find no anger in himself towards the Sordesian.

'This man didn't kill Bardo,' he said.

'They destroyed your precious Almus crop,' Fallax persisted.

'How could they know what they were destroying?' Amisso replied.

The man groaned again as they argued over his body.

'Look,' Amisso said at last. 'All I know is that I was once in as bad a state as this man, and it was a Sordesian that saved my life.'

'I bet he didn't know you were a Mercatorian,' Fallax said.

'He did, as it happens, but I don't think he cared what I was,' Amisso replied. 'I was just someone who needed help.'

Five minutes later, Fallax was sweating and swearing as he helped Amisso drag the injured Sordesian up the stairs to Nefa's room.

'What do you think you're up to?' Nefa shouted as they struggled through the door and dropped the body in the middle of the room.

'He made me,' Fallax told her angrily. 'He said if I didn't help bring the dog in he'd give himself up to the Guard.'

The look on Nefa's face said she wished Fallax had let Amisso do just that.

'Then who knows what he might have told them about our plans,' Fallax went on.

'I didn't say anything about that,' Amisso replied angrily.

Beata glared at her friend. 'What are you thinking about?' she said. 'These animals have got my father.'

'I wonder what's happened to the Sordesian ambassador to Mercatorius,' Amisso commented quietly. 'He hasn't been seen in public for months.'

Beata turned away. No one spoke and it seemed as if the intrusion of this wounded foreigner might break their fellowship, or at least exclude Amisso from it.

Amisso went very deliberately to the Almus bush in the corner of the room and plucked one of the little golden-yellow fruits. He knelt down over the injured man and crushed the fruit in his fist until the juice ran out and dripped onto the Sordesian's mouth. The man licked his lips and Amisso dribbled more juice onto them. Then, as the man's mouth began to work, he scraped some of the fruit pulp out of his palm and pushed it between his lips with his finger. The others watched in silence as Amisso passed his wet hands gently over the man's forehead, and wiped away the blood from a nasty-looking gash. Then he dragged the man to the bed by the wall. None of the others lifted a finger to help him.

'Let me tell you a story,' Amisso said. 'Helping your neighbours out when they're in trouble is a good thing, we all know that. But we think that our neighbours are just the people next door, the people in our Quarter, the people in our city, at best. A lot of things happened to me when I was away, and one of them taught me a lesson about who my neighbours are.'

Then he told them all about what Peregrino the Sordesian had done for him – the risks he'd taken and the money he'd spent to make sure that Amisso got safely home.

'So please don't call this man a dog anymore,' Amisso concluded. 'If Peregrino treated me like a neighbour, how can I not treat this Sordesian as my neighbour too?'

'But they're our enemies,' Beata protested weakly.

'We might have fallen out with them for the time being,' Amisso told her, 'but they're still our neighbours. You said yourself it was a "stupid trade war". It's not about anything important.'

'None of this gets us any nearer to what's important to us right now,' Fallax reminded them with obvious irritation. 'We still don't know where to get the ship we need.'

There was a stirring on the bed and they turned to see that the Sordesian had raised his head slightly and was looking at them with unfocused eyes.

'I've got a ship,' he croaked.

For the next twenty-four hours, they fed the man Almus until he was well enough to tell them his story. His injuries were the result of a severe beating, but the only dangerous one was the gash across his head, which had caused concussion and considerable loss of blood. His name was Gemmax and the ship he had mentioned was a Sordesian merchant vessel – a caravel called the Oryx – that had been captured by a Mercatorian naval patrol. Now that war had been declared, all shipping was counted as fair game, and both sides were attacking any vessels from the enemy state that they came across, whether they were warships or not.

'We were travelling in a convoy, with a naval escort,' Gemmax told them, 'but your patrol drove straight though our formation and my captain couldn't manoeuvre well enough to rejoin the group so we found ourselves cut off on our own. We weren't a fighting vessel, so we surrendered straight away and were escorted back to Mercatorius by one of your warships. My captain and crew were taken away in chains when we docked, but your commander must have guessed I was a merchant of some consequence in Sordes, because I was led to the Palace of your Dux to arrange a ransom demand. But while I was waiting to see the Dux something very strange happened. One of your senators dismissed the guard from the room where I was being held and asked if I wanted to do a private deal with him: all the gold and jewels I had on me in return for my freedom then and there. I expected him to organise some safe passage out of the city for me and so I agreed; it seemed a much cheaper and quicker arrangement. But once he had my treasure, he simply took me to a back door of the Palace, pushed me out and told me to run. I didn't know where to go or what to do but somehow I'd wandered into these narrow streets before I was recognised as a Sordesian. A group of men from one of the taverns set on me and beat me and kicked me until I was unconscious. I suppose they must have left me for dead. The next thing I knew, I was being dragged up the stairs here.'

'So where is your ship?' Nefa asked.

'When we were taken off her, she was at anchor in the harbour here,' Gemmax replied.

'With a guard aboard her, I should think,' Fallax said.

'What do you want a ship for?' Gemmax asked.

Amisso explained about their mission to save Almus from the city authorities.

'And this is the fruit you've been feeding me on?' Gemmax said. 'You say they want to destroy it? But it's a miracle plant – how could they want to do such a thing? My bruises and pains are gone, and this cut on my head is healed as if it was a week old, not just a day. You can have my ship with pleasure if it will prevent such madness.'

Amisso looked at the others. They were still far from convinced about taking Gemmax in and continued to be very grudging in their hospitality towards him.

'Don't you feel as if we've all been drawn together for this?' Amisso asked. 'Every one of us has a purpose in serving Almus, and now Gemmax has come to give Almus a ship. He's part of it – part of the plan. He belongs with us.'

'That's all very well,' Fallax put in, 'but he's giving us something that's not even his to give anymore. How are we going to get our hands on his ship if it's under guard? And how are we going to sail it if the crew are in chains?'

'The last part's easy,' Beata said. 'Nefa can ask round the taverns – she'll be able to raise a crew.'

'I wondered what I had to do in the plan,' Nefa said. 'Any other time you wouldn't stand a chance getting a crew for a Sordesian ship, but if it's for Almus, there won't be no trouble.'

'And we wouldn't need many, would we?' Amisso asked Ebrio.

'That's right, Master,' the captain replied. 'A galley would be a different matter, but we'd only need a handful of men to get a caravel under sail and out of port. Then if we've got the money, we can hire a full crew further down the coast once we're out of Mercatorian waters.'

'But we still need to get the ship,' Fallax insisted. 'It's a prize of war; it belongs to the Senate now.'

'In that case, we need a senator's permission to take it,' Amisso said.

'And which senator's going to do that for us?' Fallax asked scornfully.

'My father,' Amisso replied.

'But he's under house arrest,' Beata said.

'Which is why he can help us,' Amisso explained. 'If he was in prison it would be a different matter, but if we can just get into the house and explain to him, he'll be able to find a way of making the order without the guards knowing.'

'But what makes you think he'd help us even if you could get to him?' Fallax asked. 'He led the attack on Almus in the Senate. It was his committee that called the meeting.'

'And what's his say-so going to be worth even if he agrees?' Nefa put in. 'He's supposed to be a traitor.'

'It's his seal that'll do it,' Amisso explained. 'All the senators' seals are the same – you can't read my father's signature anyway. The Harbour Master won't care who the order's from as long as it has the Senate seal. We'll get Father to write that the bearer of the order is to take the ship out to sea and sink her, then we'll just sail her out of harbour and keep going.'

'But Fallax is right: will he want to help us in the first place?' Beata asked.

'Let's see if we can get to him,' Amisso said. 'Trust me, Beata. It just feels like the right thing to do.'

They looked at each other, and she sensed the determination in him. She also remembered that he had given her the two seeds in the first place because of a feeling.

'All right,' she said. 'We'll try.'

'Let's getting moving then,' Fallax told them. 'Nefa, get us a crew. I'll fetch the money. You youngsters get the order. We'll meet back here as soon as we can.' Then he looked at Gemmax. 'Keep eating Almus and get strong, Sordesian,' he said. 'You're coming with us. We want you where we can see you!'

11

Under Cover of Darkness

The house was in chaos. Beata couldn't believe that her sister was doing nothing about it, but Verna was simply sitting in the midst of the mess with her long, elegant neck bowed, staring at the marble floor. What's more, she was actually sitting on the floor - something neither Beata nor Amisso could remember having seen her do since she was a girl, supervising them in the playroom. Beata and Amisso stood still in the reception lobby of Ambassador Capax's villa and looked around them at the wreckage. They'd come here to gather any information they could about how things stood at Senator Crasto's villa, and to plan their mission - they hadn't expected to find a new crisis at Beata's home.

Several moments passed as the two friends took in the extent of the damage. Every ornament had been thrown onto the floor. Delicate jars and urns had been smashed. Hangings had been torn from the walls. Drawers had been pulled out and lay with their scattered contents on the marble. There was a deep stillness in the room and when Verna eventually looked up it startled them, as if one of the fallen statues had moved. But her expression startled them even more. There were no tears on her cheeks, just rage. Her naturally pale face looked completely white and her expression was rigid. It seemed as if she might shatter with the force of her anger, like a cool glass suddenly filled with boiling water.

'I sent the servants to bed,' she said. 'This must stay as it is. The Dux will have to see this for himself. All Mercatorius is going to hear of it. Our father's lost his freedom in the service of the State, and this is how the State rewards him.'

'What happened?' Beata asked.

'They were searching for Almus,' Verna explained. 'When the guards came looking here for Amisso, the sergeant asked whether we had any Almus on the estate, since Senator Crasto had grown it on his, and I said no. I thought I'd told you to destroy the ones you grew. But when they took their torches into the grounds to look for Amisso, they found two Almus bushes and came storming back to the house. They thought I'd lied and that I must be hiding more Almus, so they turned everything upside down.'

She got up and led them through the villa. Every room had been given the same treatment. It looked as if wild animals had been loose in the place. The only room they didn't look in was the one belonging to Sera, the girls' mother.

'She wouldn't come out,' Verna explained as they passed the splintered door, 'so they broke it down. I put her things back for her when they'd gone and put her to bed. She's sleeping now.'

They ended their tour of the house in the kitchens. Every pan was on the stone flags of the floor. Every cutlery drawer had been emptied. Fine gold and silver vessels lay jumbled with the servants' pewter dishes.

Beata and Amisso realised that for Verna this was the worst atrocity. To her, the kitchen was the heart of the house – the heart of her life – and it had been desecrated. Beata and Amisso also began to realise just how seriously the authorities were taking the threat of Almus.

'If they've done this here, just think what they'll do in the Poor Quarter,' Amisso said.

'They must be really frightened,' Beata replied.

Verna made a strange gulping sound and they turned to look at her. Her face was still set hard, but a single tear was running slowly down her cheek. Its trail glistened in the candlelight.

'Surely we can clear the kitchen up,' Amisso said. 'The Dux doesn't have to see this.'

He and Beata began to pick things off the floor and Verna didn't stop them.

'It will all have to be washed,' she said after a moment. 'We can put the drawers back, but pile everything else on the tables and work benches. Every last thing will have to be scrubbed.'

So the three of them set to work, painstakingly collecting all the pieces of Verna's world and arranging them under her supervision in strict order on every available surface.

'We'll boil water in the morning,' Verna said. 'There's a day's work for the scullery maids to clean all these.'

As they cleared the mess, Beata and Amisso began the task they'd really come to do. They started to talk over the possibility of getting into Amisso's home and out again without being detected. They were sure that Verna would dismiss the whole idea as just another one of Beata's foolish escapades, so they didn't bother to include her in the discussion. But after a few minutes, Beata's sister surprised them by asking what they were planning.

Amisso looked at Beata for a moment. With Sera hidden away in her room, Verna was effectively the head of the household and Amisso realised that she could forbid Beata to involve herself in the plan. But their world was changing. Perhaps it was eating Almus, or perhaps it was the work Beata had been doing, but Amisso could sense a strength in his friend which had not been there before. He knew that she would continue to serve Almus, whatever her sister said. Beata gave him a slight nod and, as they continued to tidy up, Amisso began to explain the whole story to Verna. Soon Beata joined in, describing the effect of Almus and the secret work she had been doing with it in the Poor Quarter, while Verna had been too busy running their household, tending Sera and keeping an eye on Crasto's domestic arrangements to wonder where her sister was spending her time.

The clearing up was having a reviving effect on Verna and she felt a growing determination to do more than simply report the conduct of the guards to the Dux. The anxieties about their father's safety had been eating away at her too throughout the months of tension and now of war. In her heart, she blamed the Senate for letting matters get to this state and she blamed them for abandoning her father in Sordes.

'I don't know anything about Almus,' Verna said, when Amisso and Beata had finished, 'but after what the Senate's done to us – if they're against it, I'm for it.'

The friends looked at her in surprise.

'If you want to get into Amisso's house without being noticed,' Verna went on, 'I'll show you how.'

Amisso was anxious to start straight away when she had explained her plan, but Verna put a hand on his arm to stop him.

'Do you know what time it is?' she asked.

It had been a long night, and Amisso realised that it must now be the early hours of the morning.

'I can't think of any better way of alerting the sentries than creeping around the house when everyone's supposed to be asleep,' Verna said. 'You need sleep yourselves. Leave it till tomorrow evening. Hide here during the day – you'll need the time to work out how you're going to persuade Amisso's father to write that order.'

Because Verna had helped so much with the running of Crasto's household since his wife had died, she had a detailed knowledge of domestic arrangements in the senator's villa, and this was the key to her plan. Next day, as soon as the light began to fail, she led Amisso and Beata on a wide looping route that took them north of both villas, well out of the sight of prying sentries, across the highway and into Crasto's estate, then down behind the senator's villa to a little walled enclosure beyond the stable yard.

'They won't be guarding this,' Verna whispered as the three of them crouched behind the brick wall.

'I'll make sure,' Amisso whispered back, and he crept away from them in search of the door into the enclosure.

He disappeared round a corner of the wall, then moments later, his head re-emerged and he beckoned to the sisters. Together, the three of them slipped through the wooden door and immediately they were engulfed in an invisible cloud of the most wonderful fragrances. Beata gasped. Verna breathed deeply and smiled.

'This is the best herb garden south of the hills,' she told them with pride. 'I made it for Bardo, to soothe him after his work.'

'Oh Verna,' Beata said, 'It really is beautiful.'

Verna put a finger on her sister's lips. 'Hush now,' she instructed. 'All we have to do is wait and make sure the maid doesn't scream when she comes.'

It wasn't more than five minutes before they heard the sound of light footsteps on the path from the house, and a girl's voice, humming softly to herself. The latch clicked and one of Crasto's kitchen maids came though the door. At once a hand clamped over her mouth and an arm fastened itself round her waist. Amisso held her tight. For an instant she froze – her eyes bulging with fright – then she exploded into action. She bit hard into Amisso's fingers, kicked at his shin and twisted sharply, driving her right elbow into his solar plexus. Amisso groaned and his grip slackened, but before the girl could writhe herself free and start yelling Verna stepped out in front of her.

'It's all right!' she hissed. 'Don't make a noise.'

Then Beata appeared beside her sister, and the maid stopped struggling as she recognised her master's neighbours.

'Let her go,' Verna ordered.

Amisso did as instructed and stood where the maid could see him, the bitten hand in his mouth and his other massaging his stomach.

'Oh sir!' the maid said in horror. 'Master Amisso, I'm so sorry!'

'It's all right, Florea,' Amisso muttered, struggling for breath. 'Not your fault.'

'We didn't want you to shout and give the alarm,' Beata explained.

A few moments of whispered conversation were enough to establish that Florea and the rest of the servants were sufficiently incensed about their master's arrest to be more than willing to help in Verna's plan. Florea had come, as Verna knew she would, to pick fresh herbs for the evening meal, so her little trug was quickly filled. And some minutes later the sentry who had idly watched Florea go out of the kitchen door on her errand watched the dim shape of a girl in a maid's smock come back through the gloom and re-enter the kitchen with a trug full of herbs.

Senator Crasto stood at the window of his private chamber staring out into the gathering dark. Bats were flitting past – twisting, black shapes only just visible against the navy blue of the evening sky. He didn't envy them their freedom. Even if there had not been a guardsman outside his chamber door, a detachment of guards surrounding his villa and a sergeant holding court in his dining room as if the place belonged to him, Crasto would not have wanted to leave his home. He had been accused of treason and just the accusation was enough to make him hide in shame. His life had been dedicated to the service of Mercatorius and now he had been accused of betraying all that he held most dear. What made it so much harder to bear was that no one had leapt to his defence in the Senate Chamber.

It was only to be expected that Perdo would find any excuse to attack his business rival, but the rest of the senators were not so dishonest. They were fine, noble citizens yet the Senate had accepted the charge against him without argument. As he watched the bats swoop and flutter across the dark rectangle of his window, Crasto couldn't help feeling that if that was the case then he must, indeed, be guilty. Treason implied an intention to cause harm, and he had certainly never meant to damage Mercatorius, but the fact remained that by allowing the strange crop to grow on his land he had put the whole Mercatorian way of life in danger. The Senate had accused him of treason; he accused himself of stupidity. Either way, the result was the same: he had endangered his beloved city and he felt shamed forever.

There was a knock at the chamber door.

Crasto called out, 'Come!'

The door opened and, reflected in the glass of the window, he saw a maid bringing in his food. He could have dined downstairs with the sergeant, but for the last twenty-four hours he had not felt inclined to leave his chamber. The girl set out the food and cutlery, and a wine flagon and goblet on the large, polished table in the middle of the room. The senator waited for her to leave, but when everything was prepared she simply stood by the table.

'Well?' Crasto asked impatiently, without turning.

'Uncle,' the girl said, 'it's me.'

Crasto wasn't Beata's uncle, but as she and Verna had practically grown up in his household it was what they always called him. He recognised her voice at once and swung round to see Beata dressed in one of his maids' smocks, holding the chair for him to sit and eat.

'Have your supper, Uncle,' she said, 'and I'll explain.'

He recovered from his surprise and motioned for her to draw a chair up to join him, then she told him everything.

He listened without interruption and when she had finished he was silent for some time.

'I still have my seal,' he said at last. 'They haven't taken that from me yet. And the sentries are not watching my every move, so I can certainly do what you ask. But I can't imagine why you should think that I'd want to. The plant is a curse. It killed my son, it will destroy Mercatorius, and it's destroyed me – and you want me to take part in a plot to save it! You must be mad, Beata. Why on earth should I want to save Almus?'

She looked him squarely in the eyes and said, 'For Amisso.'

'What?' he replied.

Mention of his son seemed to shake Crasto more than the unexpected appearance of Beata had done. His face stuck in a strange, undecided expression like someone startled out of sleep, and Beata realised that he was looking old. The last year seemed to have aged him ten.

'Almus was his gift to you,' she explained. 'He's so desperate to please you – he always has been. He wants to be a success for you, but he just can't seem to do it in your way. He has to find his own way to do something great, and maybe Almus is it.'

Crasto shook his head, more in confusion than denial.

'How can it be great to destroy a city?' he asked.

'But it won't, don't you see?' Beata told him. 'Our plan is to take it away from Mercatorius – far away from anywhere Mercatorius has ever been or is ever likely to go. We've tried to give it to the city, and the city has decided it doesn't want it, so we'll take it somewhere else.'

There was a long silence before Crasto spoke again.

'You'll really take it away?' he asked. 'That's what you want to do? You won't spread it in Mercatorius?'

'It seems such a shame to leave the Poor Quarter without it,' she said, 'but if that's what it takes to save Almus for the world, then yes.'

Crasto had eaten as much as he had the appetite for, which wasn't a great deal, and he began to push the scraps around his plate like a child playing with food. Time was passing, and Beata thought of Amisso and Verna hiding with Florea in the dark. She had to push things to a conclusion.

'Remember, it's for Amisso, Uncle,' she said. 'Your son needs your help.'

Amisso heard the clunk of a bucket handle. Someone was approaching the piggeries, where he was now hiding with Verna and Florea. Night had fallen, and the light from the moon and stars was only sufficient to show him a silhouette, opening the gate to the pigs' enclosure and moving towards the trough. The size and movement of the figure suggested it was a girl. Amisso watched her tip the contents of her bucket into the trough. Then, instead of turning back to the gate, she continued towards the corner where the three were hiding.

'Are you there?' the girl hissed.

'We're over here, Beata,' Amisso replied.

In a few moments, Florea had taken her maid's smock back from Beata and was making the return journey to the house, carrying the empty slops bucket. The plan was completed.

'Well?' Amisso asked.

Beata groped for his hand in the dark and pressed a packet of folded paper into it. He could feel the ribbon round the paper and the hard disk of sealing wax that made it an official Senate document.

'He did it for Almus?' Amisso asked, passing it back to her.

'For Mercatorius,' she said, 'and for you. Come on. It's time to get out of here.'

Their intention was to retrace their roundabout path back to Verna's villa and leave Beata's sister there, then for Amisso and Beata to return to the city. However, they had just reached the point, north of the two estates, where they meant to cross the highway when they heard shouts from the direction of Crasto's villa. They had the unmistakeable sound of barked orders. The three froze. A moment later, the flickering lights of torches could be seen, moving away from the entrance to Crasto's villa, and fanning out in the grounds. A detachment headed to the left, in the direction of Verna's villa.

'That's torn it,' Amisso muttered.

'What are they looking for?' Beata said. 'It can't be us.'

'Unless Florea's given us away,' Verna suggested.

Judging by the torches, a large number of soldiers – probably most of those guarding Crasto – had now turned out. They soon left the grounds and started working their way north in a line abreast across the fields.

'Whatever they're looking for, they're making a thorough job of it,' Amisso said.

'They're cutting us off from the city,' Beata pointed out. 'And our villa, Verna.'

'We'll have to head for open country,' Verna replied.

'We?' Amisso said.

'I'm coming with you,' Verna told him. 'If Florea's given us away, then I'm in this too now.'

'I'm sorry, Verna,' Beata said. 'I didn't mean to get you mixed up in what we're doing.'

They could hear the voices of the soldiers calling to each other as they paced steadily towards them.

'We'd better move,' Verna replied.

An hour later, the three were on the rising ground that would soon turn into the hills that separated Mercatorius from Munius. Their slight elevation gave them a good view of the men they assumed were their pursuers and they were relieved to see that the line of soldiers appeared to have stopped. The three had been moving faster than the guards and had put quite a distance between them, so they couldn't hear what orders were being given, but after a few moments it seemed that the line was retreating. Five minutes later, there was no doubt about it. The fugitives were gasping after their rapid climb and they rested for a while, watching with satisfaction as the soldiers headed back to Crasto's villa.

'Now what?' Amisso asked when his breathing had steadied.

Beata linked his arm and clung to him fiercely. She tilted her head to gaze at the millions of stars scattered across the darkness.

'It's as if the richest person in the universe had taken diamonds and thrown them all over the sky for everyone to have,' she said.

They were safe now that the guards had turned back and they took their time to survey the wealth of the heavens. The distant lights of Mercatorius looked very poor in comparison.

'I wish we could scatter Almus like the stars,' Beata went on. 'Do you think we can?'

'It would be a different world if we did,' Amisso said.

'I think that's what Almus is about,' she told him. 'I think you've found the secret of a new kind of world. We've got to save it, Amisso – we've just got to.'

Amisso squeezed her arm against his side and despite their desperate situation, he felt himself fill with happiness. After Bardo's death, he'd lost confidence in Almus – even cursed it for the pain it seemed to have caused. But since she had whisked him away from his home, Beata had given him back his faith in the plant and what it could do. They'd all eaten Almus together at Nefa's before setting out on their tasks, and he could still feel its energy in him now, filling him with hope.

They continued to watch the stars for some minutes before Amisso suddenly turned and peered into the darkness to left and right.

'Where's Verna?' he asked.

Beata screwed her eyes up but could see no shadowy shape that might be her sister.

'Verna?' she called, as loudly as she dared.

Amisso took a step away, calling out Verna's name too, but Beata grabbed his arm again.

'Don't leave me,' she said, 'or we'll all be lost.'

So they held hands and started walking on up the sloping ground in the direction of the hills, calling softly as they went.

It was several minutes before their calling got a reply. Verna's voice carried through the darkness from 100 metres away.

'I'm here – to your left,' she told them.

The ground was starting to become rocky underfoot and the two picked their way carefully towards the sound, feeling with their feet before they put their weight down. This was goat-grazing terrain and when they found Verna she was sitting on a small boulder outside a dilapidated goatherd's shelter.

'I thought I'd better find us somewhere to stay for the night,' she said.

12
Disguise

At first, Amisso thought that it was the cold, dewy air of dawn or the hardness of the earth floor that had woken him. But after a moment he realised that it was a sound: the crunch of footsteps approaching across rocky ground. He heard the clack of stones knocking together as they were scuffed. It sounded to Amisso as if there was only one person out there. He looked quickly at the sisters. They were both awake too. There was nowhere to hide in the simple hut and nothing that would make an improvised weapon, so Amisso motioned the sisters to stand behind the rickety wooden door, while he stood on the other side of the doorway, ready to strike with his fists.

A moment later, the door creaked open and a man stepped into the hut. The sun was on the point of rising, and he was just a silhouette against the first light of day. Amisso lashed out at once with a swinging right to the jaw. He was an excellent boxer and the man's head snapped back. He crashed into the open door and crumpled in a heap on the floor. Amisso turned away for a moment, shaking his hand and rubbing his knuckles, while Verna and Beata peered round the door to examine the intruder.

'Look!' Beata cried.

Amisso spun round and stared at the man. He was dressed in the clothes of a servant, but the white hair and stern face were very familiar. It was Crasto. Verna was on her knees beside him at once, cradling his head in her lap, and Amisso crouched down by his side.

'Father,' he said urgently. 'Are you all right?'

The senator struggled into a sitting position and shook his head; then he gaped at the three people surrounding him as he realised who they were.

'I hope it wasn't either of you that hit me,' he said to the sisters.

'No, Father, it was me,' Amisso admitted. 'I didn't know who you were. Please forgive me.'

'You did the right thing,' the senator told him. 'I should have called out before I opened the door.'

Crasto looked at Amisso for a moment, rubbing his jaw.

'You struck well, son,' he said. 'I couldn't have done it better myself.'

'I didn't know you boxed, Uncle,' Beata remarked, dusting him down.

'When I was young,' he told her, 'I was almost as good as Amisso.'

He held his hands out and Amisso pulled him to his feet.

'It's usual for a gentleman to give warning, though, before he starts a bout,' Crasto added.

'I don't think this is the time for being a gentleman, Father,' Amisso replied.

Crasto looked down at the rough clothes he was wearing and a grim smile flickered over his face.

'No, son,' he said. 'I don't suppose it is.'

Verna came forward and took his hands.

'Are you really all right, Uncle?' she said earnestly.

He smiled properly then.

'Yes, my dear,' he said. 'And all the better for being among friends. Although it's a surprise to see you in such a place, dressed like ruffians!'

'We might say the same of you,' Beata replied, and he laughed.

'What's happened, Father?' Amisso asked. 'How have you escaped?'

'Simple,' Crasto told him. 'There's a secret passage from my private office. I had it made when the villa was built. It seemed a sensible precaution for a man in my position – although I hardly thought I would have to use it to escape the officers of my own State.'

'I never knew,' Amisso said. 'Did Bardo know?'

'No, son,' he answered. 'No one knew – except your mother. It seemed safer that way when you were children.'

'Why didn't you escape straight away?' Verna asked.

'I had no reason to,' he told her. 'Until Beata's visit last night.'

'How has that changed things?' Amisso asked.

'I want to come with you,' he said.

There was an astonished silence. The sun was just up now and it penetrated through dozens of chinks in the roughly made stone walls, dappling the occupants of the hut. The hillside seemed suddenly alive with birdsong.

'You want to save Almus?' Beata said.

'No,' Crasto replied, bowing his head as if he was embarrassed. 'Please don't talk to me about that.'

'Then why?' Amisso asked.

'Beata said you're going far away from anywhere that Mercatorius is known,' he explained. 'After what I've done, that's where I want to go.'

'But you're not a traitor,' Verna said. 'The charge is ridiculous. Once it comes to court—'

'The court verdict isn't the point, my dear,' he said. 'I've passed my own judgement. I've failed the greatest city in the world and I can't bear to live here anymore.'

'How have you failed—?' Amisso began, but his father cut him short.

'Please don't ask me anymore,' he said. 'Tell me your plans and then we must go. The search parties will be out again now that the sun is up.'

Crasto approved when he heard that they intended returning to the city.

'Good,' he said. 'That's what I'd planned myself. It's the last thing they'll be anticipating and the safest thing to do - the countryside's full of military patrols. I didn't expect to find you in this hut. I was looking for food. Sometimes the goatherds leave a little. I was intending to double back to the city and see if I could find you skulking round this Sordesian ship you were so concerned about.'

As they set out, Amisso asked his father how he knew about goatherds and what they did, and Crasto told them he had spent a lot of time in the hills when he was young. The senator surprised them all with his knowledge of the countryside as they crept slowly along hidden gullies and behind screens of ancient trees, on their roundabout route back to Mercatorius.

'I explored every last scrap of this territory when I was a boy,' Crasto explained.

Amisso was astonished.

'And did you know the flowers and the animals, Father?' he asked excitedly.

'Yes, I suppose I did,' Crasto replied.

'And what songs the different birds make, and what scents the flowers have?' Amisso went on.

Crasto was puzzled by his son's sudden enthusiasm.

'What's a flower without its scent?' he said.

They were relieved to see that the search parties sent out from the villa later that morning, and the extra troops who were brought up from the city, all set out to comb the hills to the north. But still the fugitives were very cautious as they headed back towards the city gates. When they were still some distance away, Beata called a halt.

'I've been thinking,' she said. 'The search parties last night were looking for you, Uncle, not us.'

'Yes,' Crasto replied, 'of course. It can't have taken the guards long to realise that I'd gone into my office and hadn't come out again. I didn't get much of a start on them.'

'So Florea didn't betray us,' Beata continued.

'Of course not,' Crasto said. 'I'd trust that girl with my life.'

'Then there's no reason for you to come with us anymore, Verna,' Beata pointed out. 'It was only because we thought Florea might have said something about you that you didn't go home last night.'

Verna looked shocked at the suggestion.

'Don't be silly,' she said. 'You all need someone to look after you.'

'But what about Mother?' Beata asked. 'Who's going to look after her?'

'We have servants for that,' Verna replied, a little coldly. 'Or maybe she can learn to look after herself.'

Half an hour later the sentry at the Northern Gate greeted Mistress Beata with another of the beggars she kept finding on the highway. This one looked in a bad way. He was staggering and had a cloak wrapped completely round his head. The cloak had been provided by Verna. She was the only one who'd had the sense to take one with her the previous night. It was the gardener's, and she'd been wearing a kitchen maid's clothes beneath it. Under the cloak now was hidden the distinctive white hair of Senator Crasto. A few minutes later the sentry had to let another party through the gate – a wagon of produce with half a dozen peasants in attendance. One was a teenager with a cap crammed tightly on his head. He was accompanied by a young woman with a long, graceful neck who looked vaguely familiar. She seemed rather out of place in her drab working dress, but the sentry didn't pay them any more attention as he waved them through. Once inside the gates, Amisso and Verna detached themselves from the group of peasants as silently as they had joined them and slipped away from the main road into the back streets of the Poor Quarter.

The Poor Quarter was usually bustling in the middle of the day, but it had a strange stillness as Amisso and Verna entered it. They soon caught up with Beata and Crasto who had waited for them by the public well. The shady little square where people would gather to gossip as they drew their buckets of water was empty and silent.

'I don't like this,' Beata said. 'Something's wrong.'

They hurried on, following Beata as she led them to Nefa's home. The door was ajar, and Amisso raced up the stairs. He burst into the little room to find their four friends gathered there.

'We got it!' Amisso cried, gesturing towards Beata.

She had come into the room behind him and was holding the precious Senate Order in her hand, but she wasn't sharing in Amisso's high spirits. She saw that Nefa and her guests had hardly reacted to their arrival and were staring at them with troubled faces. Even the fact that a senator wearing servant's clothes had just stepped into her room didn't seem to raise any interest from Nefa.

'Have you got the money, Fallax?' Amisso asked.

Nefa pointed unenthusiastically at a wooden chest in the middle of her table.

'The crew?' Amisso enquired.

'There's plenty willing,' Nefa said in a gloomy voice.

'Then we have all we need,' Amisso announced, 'ship, money, crew.'

'Just one thing missing,' Nefa told him and she nodded to the corner where her Almus bush had been growing in its bucket.

The bucket was still there, but it was on its side, and the earth it had contained was scattered on the uneven floorboards. Of the Almus bush there was not a sign.

'What happened?' Beata asked, but she already knew the answer. She'd seen what had taken place in her own home.

'They went through the whole Quarter,' Nefa told her.

'It was an army,' Ebrio added. 'They sent an army. You'd have thought the Sordesians were here.'

'They must think Almus is even more dangerous than Sordesians,' Nefa said. 'They took the bush and left him.'

She gestured to Gemmax. 'No offence, meant,' she added grudgingly.

'They came back again this morning,' Fallax said, 'to catch anyone who'd managed to keep some Almus hidden and thought they were safe to bring it out again. They're taking no chances.'

'Is there none left?' Amisso asked.

'Not even a seed,' Nefa said. 'I've asked round. They've got every last bit. People were too frightened to hide any. It's all gone.'

As they'd been talking, they'd been aware of a noise in the street. It began to build up until eventually it was like a dull roar and Nefa stuck her head out of the window to see what was going on.

'Here, look at this!' she cried.

It was a small window – the only one in the room – and Nefa was nearly pushed out as the others crowded in behind her. The narrow thoroughfare directly beneath was a solid mass of moving people.

'Oi!' Nefa shouted. 'What's going on?'

A medley of voices called back from the shuffling crowd. It appeared that now people had had time to get over their shock and think about what they'd lost, the whole Quarter was on the move in protest at the confiscation of their Almus. They were on their way to Senate Square. Nefa elbowed her way back into the room.

'Come on!' she cried. 'Let's get out there!'

She set off down the stairs, and Fallax – who seemed to have appointed himself as her protector – started after her. Nefa had organised a change of clothes for Gemmax after the scare of the soldiers' visit the previous night, so he had no worries about joining the crowd. He and Ebrio helped each other down the stairs. Beata grabbed Amisso's arm and dragged him after them. Verna looked at Crasto.

'I can't remember such a thing ever happening before in Mercatorius,' he said in a puzzled tone. 'The world's falling apart.' He went to the window and watched the surging mass for a moment longer, then he turned decisively. 'The State is in danger,' he said. 'I must go. Perhaps I can do something.'

'I'll come with you, Uncle,' Verna said.

'No, Verna,' he said. 'This is no business for a gentlewoman to be involved in.'

'Beata's gone,' Verna pointed out.

Crasto sighed deeply.

'While your father's away, I count myself as your guardian,' he said.

'I'm 21 years old, Uncle,' she said, gently but firmly. 'I don't need a guardian. But Beata does – she's only a teenager. We must follow her. And anyway, is it safe to leave me on my own in a strange building in this Quarter?'

'Come then,' he said, offering her his arm. 'But stay close.'

The sides of Senate Square were formed by palaces. The most magnificent was the Senate House taking up half of the southern side, with the Palace of the Dux next to it and to the west. To the east of the Square was the Palace of Justice. The western side was taken up with the palaces of the Grand Admiral and the General-in-Chief. To the north was the Palace of the Guilds. And over everything loomed the City Watchtower, soaring into the sky from the south-west corner of the Square – providing security to the City and a warning of Mercatorian might to enemies far out at sea. Senate Square was a huge space, the largest square in the whole city. Several regiments could parade in it. But today there was not a soldier in sight, and this perplexed Senator Crasto. The people of the Poor Quarter had been allowed to swarm unchecked from their streets and to pour into Senate Square until they completely filled its vast area. Crasto had had no idea that so many people actually lived in the Poor Quarter. Verna was locked to his arm and they were now crushed in the centre of the crowd with no hope of escape. Crasto had had no clear idea what he might do in defence of his city, but now he was swallowed up in this huge assembly it seemed impossible that, on his own, he could do anything.

'I can't understand what's happened to the Guard,' Crasto shouted to Verna above the hubbub of the crowd. 'They should have stopped this. They should have defended the Square.'

'Come out and answer us!' a big man yelled a few metres ahead of them.

There were shouts of approval and, heavy though the man must have been, he was hoisted onto the shoulders of his neighbours.

'Come out and answer us!' he bellowed again, brandishing his fist at the Senate House.

'They've all run away!' someone else shouted.

This suggestion was met with cheers, and soon it was being shouted through the crowd as a fact.

'We've driven them out!' came the cry, and everywhere people started shaking hands and embracing. Constant waves of cheering surged through the crowd.

'What are you talking about?' Crasto shouted at the top of his voice. 'If the Senate's gone, then so has your safety.

This is madness. Sordes is at the door and you're cheering the loss of your protectors!'

But no one took any notice. There were no arms to lift him onto willing shoulders so that he could address the crowd. The cheering drowned his words.

The enthusiastic shouting was only brought to an end by a powerful blast of clarions. The crowd fell silent at this, and as they looked around there was a simultaneous gasp from thousands of throats. The Guard had at last made an appearance. Every balcony of every palace was lined with guardsmen and each was pointing a heavy harquebus, supported on its stand, at the crowd below. There was an instinctive move towards the exits from the Square but this was checked at once. Every exit was blocked by guardsmen drawn up in ranks ten deep, the front rank also armed with harquebuses and protected by pikes 6 metres long, thrusting through from the rank behind. There was another clarion blast and the Square seemed to explode as the harquebuses were discharged.

The roaring of the firearms was followed by a cacophony of screaming. The crowd surged to and fro, and many people lost their footing, only the pressure of bodies preventing them from falling and being trampled underfoot. Once more the clarions sounded, but there was no further firing, and the screams gradually subsided as the crowd began to realise that there were no injuries among them. The smoke was clearing from the balconies and they could see that at the last minute the harquebuses had been angled up at the sky. Their shot had pattered, spent and harmless, onto the city roofs. A frightened silence and stillness fell over the crowd, and then those in the southern half of the Square saw a magnificent sight. The Dux in all his golden robes, his head crowned with his pointed cap of office, stepped out onto the balcony of the Senate House. Kettledrums started to beat a solemn march and the other senators came to join him in a stately procession, each in their crimson state robes and wearing a white, domed cap. The whole Square turned to face the Senate House. Crasto had been clutching Verna in an attempt to protect her. He let go of her now, and his arms hung limply at his sides. No one in the crowd would notice that a senator was absent, just as surely as none of them realised that the missing senator was stranded in their midst, dressed not in a crimson robe but in the clothes of a working man.

'Citizens of Mercatorius,' the Dux proclaimed, 'you have nothing to fear from your Senate!' He had a deep, strong voice, which carried far, and his words were repeated through the crowd until they reached those out of earshot of their Head of State. 'The Senate exists for no other reason than to protect you,' he continued. 'This has always been the case. This will always be the case until the end of time. As leader of your Senate it was my personal order that the Guard should fire a warning above your heads. But I must tell you, fellow citizens of Mercatorius, that if you need to be protected from yourselves then next time the Guard will fire into your ranks until you see sense.'

There was a low murmur, and when the protestors glanced at the balconies of the surrounding palaces, they saw that the soldiers had now reloaded and were indeed levelling their weapons at the crowd.

'We know the cause of your complaint,' the Dux declared. 'But I am here to tell you that Almus has been taken from you for your own good and to save our city from a Sordesian act of war. It is Sordes that has sent Almus into our city, and the dogs have sent it here because it is poisonous!'

A murmur of confusion and disbelief rolled through the crowd as this startling news was passed back. It was followed by horrified gasps as a group of half a dozen men was brought out onto the balcony to be exhibited. They seemed to stagger uncertainly as if they were very drunk, and when they reached the front of the balcony they clung to the marble balustrade, swaying with stooped shoulders and lolling heads. Every now and again, one of them would gaze out across the Square, his eyes rolling as if he could barely see. But those at the front of the crowd could see them well enough – they could see that the men's faces were grey as slate. They were stripped to the waist and their bodies were the same unnatural colour and horribly blotched with yellow and green patches that looked like pus-filled sores. Someone shrieked at the front of the crowd and soon the Square was filled with hysterical wailing which only died away when the Dux stepped to the front of the balcony and raised his arms for silence.

'These men were among the first in our city to eat Almus,' the Senate Leader explained. 'They've eaten nothing but Almus for many months and this is what it has done to them. Some others like them have already died. You can see that it is for your own safety that we have prevented you eating any more of this poisonous fruit. The Physician General has been studying the case and he is hopeful that if the consumption of Almus ceases at once, only those who have been eating it continually for as long as these men have will die. But if you are allowed to keep on eating Almus you will all undoubtedly meet their terrible end.'

There were moans, and cries of misery rose from the Square. Some of this was mourning for the loss of their seemingly miraculous Almus – 'I told you it was too good to be true,' was muttered by many people to their neighbours – but mostly it was fear that they might have been eating the fruit for as long as the victims on the balcony and would soon suffer their fate.

'Do not despair!' the voice of the Dux boomed out.

He held his arms wide and the crowd fell silent again.

'The Physician General has saved you!' he announced. 'He has discovered a way of preparing your beloved Almus that will destroy its poisonous properties and render it safe for you to eat. The evil plans of Sordes have been thwarted! From now on, therefore, Almus will be grown and prepared only by the State – and provided to you, its citizens, without cost or danger! The first distribution will take place here in Senate Square at noon tomorrow!'

The clarions sounded once more and after a few moments of their triumphant sound the Dux and the other senators withdrew to an accompaniment of drums and prolonged cheers. The guards had disappeared from the exits to the Square and the people began to disperse in better spirits, feeling that somehow they had scored a victory. As the crowd thinned, Crasto remained, staring at the now empty balcony of the Senate House.

'That is a great man,' he said to Verna. 'And a great Mercatorian. It has been one of the greatest privileges of my life to be able to call him a friend and to serve him as my Dux. While ever we have such men and such a Senate, Mercatorius can never fail.'

Elsewhere in the emptying square, Beata was trying to reassure Amisso.

'How can you have brought poison to Mercatorius?' she was saying. 'It didn't come from Sordes – it came from the man who bought you, your "master".'

'But what if he was a Sordesian?' Amisso asked. 'What if it was a trick?'

'And what about the people you met in the mountains?' she reminded him. 'You told me they always ate Almus. Were they poisoned?'

'Maybe they were allies of Sordes,' he said miserably. 'Maybe they were lying.'

'And what about you?' Beata persisted, 'You were the first to eat Almus - long before those men on the balcony could have got hold of it - and you're all right.'

'The Dux said those men had been eating Almus continually - I stopped months ago. Maybe I didn't eat it long enough for it to take hold,' he answered. 'None of us ate it while we were growing it. Bardo seemed to despise the stuff. I used to think it was because I'd brought it - he couldn't bring himself to think it was any good if it came from me, even though he wanted to make money out of it. Father was the same; they both refused to eat such a poor-looking fruit and they said it was beneath any of the rest of the household to eat it too - it was only fit for the workers.'

'Verna wouldn't have any either,' Beata told him. 'She said that it wasn't in any of her cookbooks and that I had to destroy it in case it wasn't safe.'

'Perhaps she was right,' Amisso replied.

13
Accusations

In contrast to the previous day, the City Guard were very much in evidence and in control when the State-prepared Almus was to be distributed. They were regulating access to Senate Square, with the result that many hundreds of citizens were kept waiting in the adjoining streets. Once in the Square, the people were marshalled into blocks, each surrounded by soldiers, and told that one at a time these blocks would be brought forward to receive their Almus. They were also told that they would receive Almus supplies for a week, which surprised them as they knew that Almus must be eaten fresh from the bush.

Before the first citizens received their Almus, however, those who were mustered in the Square were treated to a lavish ceremony. The balconies of the palaces were lined not with soldiers and their harquebuses but with musicians and choristers, dressed in brilliant white and gold uniforms. The composers and orchestras of Mercatorius were renowned throughout the world. It was the State musicians who now occupied the palace balconies and began the ceremony with a song in praise of Mercatorius. The soaring voices, the rich harmonies, the autumn sun on the bright uniforms and shining buildings of the Square, and most of all the stirring words of the song filled the hearts of the people with pride and confidence in their great city. They seemed to feel themselves swell and grow in stature with every deep breath they took.

A song of thanksgiving followed – thanksgiving for the preservation of the people from the evil plots of Sordes and for the wisdom of the Senate. Next came a song calling destruction down on the heads of all enemies of Mercatorius, all traitors who would betray the Glorious City, and particularly the dogs of Sordes. Bass voices, bassoons and drums featured strongly and a mood of stern determination came over the crowd. Finally, a stunning new composition set the air sparkling above the Square. The Master of the Mercatorian Music had been up all night composing it, and the orchestra and choir had been hard at work throughout the morning practising. It was a song in praise of Almus – the Almus provided by the State.

As this final song was sung, the Dux appeared once more on the balcony of the Senate House, this time wearing the special robes used only on occasions of State thanksgiving. They were pure white silk, and shimmered in the bright light. On his head he wore a special headdress consisting of a senator's white cap with a golden disc, half a metre across, secured to the back. It looked as if the sun itself was shining behind the head of the Dux. It was a sight none of the crowd had seen before – the poor of Mercatorius were not invited to State celebrations. The inhabitants of the Poor Quarter were overawed by the sounds and sights in a much deeper way than they had been by the guns of the soldiers the previous day. They felt themselves to be in the presence of powers beyond any human being to withstand. The Dux was carrying a golden bowl, and as the last notes of the song died away, he raised it high in both hands. Clarions sounded, and the Dux declaimed to the assembled company that in the bowl was the blessed Almus – transformed by the good offices of the Glorious State from the food of death to the food of life – to be received from this day forward as a reminder of the power of the Senate and its love for the people.

The Dux lowered the bowl and handed it to a white-robed attendant who carried it into the shadows of the room that opened onto the balcony. A few moments later he reappeared on the broad marble staircase leading up to the main entrance of the Senate House where the distribution was to take place. The Dux remained on the balcony with his arms outstretched towards the crowd as music played again and the guards formed the first block of citizens into a queue to receive their Almus. The long line of people made their way up the left-hand side of the staircase. At the top was a marble pedestal on which the golden bowl had been placed. The citizens formed lines of ten across the top step and as they stood with heads bowed a team of white-robed servers placed seven Almus fruits in their outstretched hands. They then filed down the right-hand side of the staircase and were directed out of the Square.

Many lines of citizens had received their Almus and the golden bowl had been replenished several times from the stores held ready in the Senate House, before strange rumours began to spread first among those who were waiting in the queue, then among the blocks of citizens formed up around the Square, and finally out into the neighbouring streets. Whatever the Senate had done to the Almus had changed it. Instead of seven, glowing, yellow fruits, people were being given a handful of hard, dry, shapeless lumps – so the story went. The lumps were dark brown and they had no seed in them. Not long after that tale had started to spread, another even worse rumour began. This new Almus tasted of ashes. The people had been told to wait until they got home before eating the precious fruit, but many had been too impatient and had started to chew on the brown morsels as they walked away from the Square. They were leathery and bitter, and apparently the majority of people had spat them out. Those who had chewed and swallowed had instantly been gripped by stomach cramps and had staggered home, white-faced and nauseous.

Although the guards were discouraging them, several people eventually got back into the Square and started passing the vile brown lumps around among those still waiting. Just sniffing this treated Almus was enough to convince people that the Senate had destroyed anything beneficial in it. It didn't smell like a fruit at all – it had a faint odour of rancid meat. Horrified, the citizens looked up to the Senate House balcony, but the reassuring sight of their Dux had been replaced by something more grizzly. Where the Dux had been standing, six bodies were now on display. Word spread that they were the victims of Almus poisoning who had been exhibited the day before, but now they were hanging from the balcony by ropes passed under their arms, stripped to the waist, blotched all over their grey skin, and clearly dead. Gradually people began to slip out of the waiting groups in the Square, and the guards didn't try to stop them. The people queuing in the streets were already melting away. In the end the grand Almus distribution which had looked as if it would last the rest of the day was over in little more than an hour, and all those who had received it swore that they would not be coming back again next week.

Amisso, Beata and their friends had come early to Senate Square, and they had come with high hopes. If the Senate really was going to give out Almus, then their failure to save the fruit could be ignored and all would be well. Crasto had come with them, but with rather less reason for elation. Even if Almus had been rendered harmless, it might still destroy the city's economy, and he would count himself responsible for that. Nonetheless, the senator was anxious to assure himself that the citizens were not going to fall victim to Sordesian poisoning. If that could be achieved, he still had faith that the wisdom of the Dux and the Senate could save the city. Verna was there too, with no other motive than to look after her neighbour.

The eight of them were in one of the blocks of people waiting in the Square when news of the tainted Almus began to spread. They were unsure what to do - unwilling to give up and leave, but increasingly reluctant to take their turn in the queue as the evidence of the catastrophe grew. Crasto found himself drifting away from Amisso and his friends as they discussed the situation. The senator was aware that his perspective was rather different from theirs.

If the people couldn't stomach this treated Almus, then his fears for the city were gone. If they couldn't eat Almus, they would be forced to go back to buying and working to order, and all would be well again. As the rumours grew, so did Crasto's satisfaction.

Two other members had separated from the group as people began to drain out of the Square. Gemmax had had his suspicions about the poison victims who had been exhibited the previous day, although he hadn't shared them with anyone. But now the bodies were on show he wanted to make sure. He whispered his thoughts to Ebrio, and the pair of them slipped away into the shadowy cover formed by the arcade beneath the balcony of the Palace of Justice. They strolled casually round the outside of the Square, keeping in the shadows all the way, until they reached the southern side and found themselves below the Senate House balcony. They could see the six bodies hanging down a little to their left – gruesome silhouettes against the daylight in the Square.

'We can't see from here,' Gemmax said. 'We'll have to go out into the open.'

'I'm game,' Ebrio told him. 'There's no reason we shouldn't have a look, anyway. That's what they're there for.'

'Maybe,' Gemmax replied. 'But if I'm right, they won't want people looking too closely.'

There were still people going up the great staircase to receive their Almus and all attention seemed to be on that, so Gemmax and Ebrio were able to step out into the Square and saunter up to the bodies without attracting notice from the guards. Now he was close to them, Gemmax didn't need to look for more than a moment.

'It's them,' he told his companion, turning to go.

'Just a minute,' Ebrio said.

Gemmax watched in astonishment as Ebrio went up to one of the pillars supporting the balcony and put his arms round it.

'What are you doing?' he hissed.

'If what you've said is true, I've got some suspicions of my own,' Ebrio explained. 'This won't take a minute. It's nothing to what I've had to do aboard ship.'

To Gemmax's horror, the former sea captain clamped his arms and legs round the pillar and began to shin his way up. The first of the bodies was less than a metre from the pillar and hanging only 4 metres from the ground. In seconds Ebrio was on a level with it and he reached out to its torso.

By the time Gemmax and Ebrio returned to them, Amisso and the others were on their own in the Square. The remainder of those who had been waiting with them had dispersed, and the military presence had melted away.

'Where have you been?' Amisso asked Gemmax. 'They were all for leaving you until they saw Ebrio was missing too.'

'Still not sure if a Sordesian's worth bothering about?' Gemmax said calmly.

No one answered.

'Well you might give my people some credit,' Gemmax continued. 'We've just performed a great service to your State. Six Sordesians have just helped your Senate stage the biggest piece of deception I've ever seen in my life. Although I don't suppose they did it willingly.'

Crasto had returned to the group when the crowd around them had gone and had been one of the most outspoken in favour of abandoning the missing Sordesian.

Now he looked ready to demonstrate the boxing skills of his youth.

'Take that back, dog!' he snapped. 'The Senate of Mercatorius sets the standard of honesty for the whole world.'

'That's sad for the world then,' Gemmax replied, 'because those six citizens of Mercatorius, poisoned by an evil Sordesian plot, aren't Mercatorian citizens at all. They're members of my crew.'

'And they weren't poisoned either,' Ebrio added.

He held out his hand. The palm was smudged with a mixture of grey, green and yellow.

'That's greasepaint from the theatre – what the actors use,' Ebrio explained. 'All those blotches were painted on them.'

'And the captain tells me that to judge from the marks round their necks, it wasn't Almus that killed them but a strong pair of hands,' Gemmax concluded. 'My men were strangled and your people have been cheated.'

Frantic discussion broke out in the group, but Amisso didn't join in. He was watching his father. The Square was completely empty now and Crasto stood facing the Senate House, the symbol of all he stood for, defiled by the six deceiving bodies hanging from its balcony. Amisso could see tears welling up in the senator's eyes. His father looked very small and vulnerable, standing on the edge of this huge, deserted square. Amisso took a step towards him and put a hand on his shoulder.

'I've devoted my life to this city,' Crasto said angrily. 'The greatest city in the world – or it was until this. To think that the Senate could stoop to such things: deception and murder.' He heaved a deep sigh. 'Take me away from here, Amisso,' he said. 'Take me far away.'

'You're going nowhere,' a harsh voice cut in behind him. 'You're a fool, old man, and always have been. I might also remind you, you're under arrest.'

Crasto turned slowly to confront Senator Perdo, backed by a detachment of guards.

'Take him,' Perdo ordered. 'And his good-for-nothing son.'

Crasto sprang towards his fellow senator, and Perdo took a hasty step back, but two guards had Crasto in their grip before he could land a blow. Amisso's father strained towards Perdo, his face dark with rage.

'Good-for-nothing? My son's worth a hundred of you, Perdo,' he declared. 'You're a disgrace to your city.'

'Strange that it's you and not me who stands accused of treason then,' Perdo replied coolly. He turned to the sergeant of the guards. 'Take them all in for questioning,' he said. 'If they're with this traitor, they're probably all part of his plot.'

The Department for State Security was located on the ground floor of the General-in-Chief's palace and this was where Crasto and the others were taken and held. That evening they were interviewed by a major of the City Guard, in recognition of Crasto's position in society. But there were no concessions to his status when it came to the room in which he and the others were interrogated. It was small, with tiny windows set high up in its bare, stone walls, and it was cold. The eight were made to stand in a line facing the wooden desk at which the major was seated. A secretary was sitting at his side ready to take notes, six guards were drawn up along the back wall, and Perdo stood to one side of the desk.

'Senator Perdo,' the major began, 'you have had my men arrest these people on suspicion of various treasonous acts. Before I authorise a prosecution, you must explain the details of the charges.'

'Gladly, Major,' Perdo replied and turned to stare at his old business rival. 'Senator Crasto already stands charged with treason, by authority of the Senate,' he said. 'In his case, he is simply being returned to custody, having escaped from his house arrest. I would suggest that to the charge of treason be added the charge of contempt for the Court of Mercatorius, since he clearly did not intend to present himself for trial. I also suggest that he be kept under lock and key in the cells until his trial, as he cannot be trusted in his own house.'

'Granted,' the major agreed. 'Add the new charge.'

His secretary's quill pen squeaked on the heavy charge book for a few moments, as he carefully wrote up the details.

'As for Senator Crasto's son, Master Amisso,' Perdo continued, 'I have information which links him with the growing of Almus on the senator's estate – the basis of the charge of treason against his father.'

Perdo dropped a document onto the major's desk, which the officer began to read.

'Let me see that!' Crasto demanded. 'No one in my household would give evidence against my son.'

The major ignored him, but Perdo gave him a triumphant smile.

'Your servants were stubborn, Crasto, that's true,' he said, 'but think of all those men your unfortunate son Bardo hired to build his great barns. They had plenty to say about how hard Amisso worked on the plantation. They also reported overhearing conversations between your sons that seem to indicate it was Amisso who first brought the poisonous weed to our city.'

Crasto glared at his rival in silence as the major finished reading the testimony.

'Record a charge of treason against Master Amisso,' the officer instructed his secretary, 'and enter this document in the list of evidence.'

The quill squeaked again.

'I have another document,' Perdo reported, when the secretary had finished, and he dropped an Order of Senate on the table. The seal was broken.

The major raised his eyebrows.

'The prisoners have been searched,' Perdo explained, 'and this was found in the possession of Mistress Beata. It is an order for the release of the Oryx, a Sordesian ship at present held by us as a prize of war.'

'It says the Oryx is to be sunk,' the major observed.

'It also says the order was made by Senator Crasto,' Perdo pointed out, 'and the date shows he was under arrest at the time. Why would a senator under charge of treason be making orders for the release of a Sordesian ship? Why would the order be in the possession of his neighbour's daughter – a known friend of Master Amisso, who is now himself charged with treason? And why is she disguised as a commoner? I suggest this is all evidence of a treasonous plot to assist our enemy by liberating a prize of war. That is the charge I bring against Mistress Beata, and I add it to the charges against Senator Crasto, together with the charge of misusing Senate authority, since his name is on the Order.'

'Record the charges, and enter the evidence,' the major instructed, passing the Senate Order to his secretary.

'And this,' Perdo continued, pointing to Gemmax, 'is none other than the owner of the Sordesian ship in question. He escaped—'

'You let me escape!' Gemmax broke in indignantly. He had recognised Perdo at once in Senate Square and had been waiting for this moment ever since they were arrested. 'This senator took money from me,' he told the major. 'He took everything I had and said in return he'd organise my escape from the Palace of your Dux. I accuse him of treason!'

The friends looked at each other in amazement, but Perdo seemed unruffled.

'Is the accusation of a dog acceptable in Mercatorius?' he asked the major.

'Maybe not,' Crasto said, 'but the accusation of a citizen is, even one under charge of treason himself. I accuse you, Perdo, on his behalf.'

Perdo turned to his enemy with a smile.

'Your evidence?' he asked politely.

Crasto looked at Gemmax.

'Find the sentries who were on duty when I escaped,' he said. 'They'll tell you – he personally dismissed them all so that he could let me out of the Palace.'

'Send for the sentry rota,' the major ordered one of the guards.

'No need,' said Perdo, placing another document on the table. 'The men are listed here. You can check them against the rota later, Major. They testify that this dog used a potion to drug them. He opened a glass vial and the fumes overcame them. He must have taken a counter-potion beforehand to make himself immune to the effects. Such evil sorcery is common in Sordes, as we all know.'

'You have been busy this afternoon,' Crasto said. 'How much did you pay them to sign their names to that pack of lies?'

Perdo smiled again. He was clearly enjoying himself.

'I'm shocked, Senator,' he replied. 'Mercatorius is the home of honesty. Would you believe the testimony of a Sordesian dog, rather than the sworn statement of men who have taken an oath of loyalty to our State?'

There was silence in the room. The secretary's quill hung above the great book, ready to write.

'I charge the Sordesian with the practice of sorcery,' Perdo announced.

'Record the charge and enter the evidence,' the major ordered once more.

'Shall the signatories' names be checked with the rota, sir?' the secretary asked, tapping the statement with his quill.

'No need,' the major replied. 'We can accept the word of a Mercatorian senator.'

Perdo bowed slightly. 'As for these two,' he said, 'they have identified themselves as the taxman Fallax and Nefa who is a well-known thief. I have had investigations made, and it appears the records of the Court of Justice show that both are enthusiastic supporters of this Almus weed. The woman made wild claims about its properties as part of a ludicrous defence against the charge of robbery, and the taxman spoke in support of her. They were obviously part of the Sordesian plot to get our people to eat this poison. Unbelievably, the Court acquitted her, and you may be interested to know, Major, that it was chaired on that occasion by none other than Senator Crasto – clear evidence of collusion. The charge against both Fallax and Nefa is that they are accomplices in Crasto's treason.'

'Record the charge and enter the Court records as evidence,' the major instructed.

'This man, a former sea captain by the name of Ebrio,' Perdo continued, 'stands accused of slander against the good name of the Mercatorian Senate, which in the current climate amounts to an incitement to rebellion – an act designed to assist our enemies during a time of war. The guards who accompanied me to re-arrest Senator Crasto can testify that he claimed the bodies of our poor unfortunate fellow citizens, killed by the poison of Almus, were actually Sordesian sailors, covered in greasepaint.'

'They were!' Ebrio burst out. 'Look – I've still got it on my hand!'

He held out his hand to the major. Much of the paint had rubbed off during the afternoon, but the colour was still visible.

Perdo looked at the outstretched hand for a moment, then rummaged under his cloak and brought out some small jars.

'Theatrical greasepaint,' he said, placing them on the major's table, 'found in the possession of the accused when he was taken into custody.'

'That's a lie,' Ebrio shouted. 'I never had those on me!'

'The colour on the hand of the accused is indeed greasepaint, but not from the bodies of our poisoned citizens: he put it there himself.'

'Those were my sailors hanging there!' Gemmax protested. 'They weren't Mercatorians at all. Bring out the bodies and I'll identify them.'

Perdo turned to the officer.

'That will not be possible, I'm afraid,' he said. 'They were beginning to rot, Major, and the Senate was fearful that the Almus poison might be rising in the foul vapours they were giving off. The bodies have been burned on the orders of the Dux.'

'And suggested by you, no doubt!' Ebrio shouted.

'Be silent!' the major ordered, and one of the guards struck the captain in the small of the back with the butt of his halberd.

'The charge against Ebrio,' Perdo stated, 'is of treasonously plotting to aid the enemies of the State during time of war. I myself am prepared to give testimony against him in Court as he is a former employee of mine, and I know him to be a drunkard and an untrustworthy liar.'

The major's voice sounded weary as he ordered the recording of the charge against Ebrio, and the entering of the paints as evidence.

'And what have you to say about Mistress Verna?' he asked Perdo. 'I must say that I'm most surprised to see so respected a member of Mercatorian society under accusation here.'

'This treasonous plot stretches to the highest in Mercatorius,' Perdo declared. 'She is clearly involved with her sister and her neighbour. Why else would she be with them in the Square, disguised as a servant? Besides, the soldiers who were sent to guard Senator Crasto at his villa report that when they performed a routine check at Mistress Verna's villa she deliberately concealed two Almus bushes from them. Their testimony—'

And once again he reached in his pocket for a piece of paper, but Verna cut him short.

'No!' she cried. 'It was my sister who planted them! I told her to destroy them long ago. That was why I told the soldiers we had no Almus. But she disobeyed me and preserved the bush; I didn't know it was still there! Have mercy on me, Major, I beg of you! I was only in the Square trying to bring my sister home. I've been so worried about her lately; she'd been spending so much time with undesirables. I was pleading with her to leave these people and come back with me. It's been so hard on us, with my father a prisoner in Sordes. I dress like a servant because that's what I've become, sir. My mother's a broken woman, and I have to work every hour of the day to keep the estate from collapse. I beg of you, have mercy!' and she threw herself in an ungainly heap in front of the major's table.

The friends looked down at her in astonishment, and Perdo gave a short, scoffing laugh.

'Come, come, Mistress,' the major said in some alarm. 'Don't concern yourself, please. Yours is clearly a different case from the others. Your honesty and integrity are known throughout the city. In my judgement you are an unfortunate victim here – caught up by accident in a treacherous plot that you knew nothing about.' He sat up straight in his seat, squared his shoulders and looked Perdo firmly in the eye for a moment. 'I shall have no charge recorded against you, Mistress Verna,' he announced.

Then he turned to the sergeant.

'Help Mistress Verna up,' he said, 'and provide her with an escort home. But take these others to the cells.'

14
Mercatorian Justice

Beata had managed to control her feelings throughout the ordeal of their arrest and the hearing before the major, but as the door of the dungeon cell slammed shut behind her and the heavy lock clanked into place she let out a sob. She was standing in complete darkness, and the cold, damp air made her shiver. Then a hand was laid on her arm. It was Nefa.

'Don't you worry, Mistress,' she said, 'I've had plenty of this before. I'll look after you.'

Beata groped blindly for Nefa and clung to her.

'You'll be all right,' Nefa told her. 'You're gentry. They'll probably just send you into exile – set you up on some little island somewhere till everyone's forgotten what you're there for. Then they'll let you come home again.'

'What about you?' Beata asked.

'Don't worry about me,' Nefa said.

'Oi! Is that you, Nefa?' a woman's voice called out.

Beata jumped. She hadn't realised there was anyone else in the cell

'It's all right, Mistress,' Nefa said. 'I know that voice. She won't do you no harm. That's Fura. How many have we got in here, Fura?'

'Six before you came,' the woman replied.

Amisso and the other male prisoners had been taken off elsewhere in the dungeon. This was a female-only cell. The rest of the women now said their names and Nefa knew most of them.

'Where's there some room?' she asked.

'The pair of you can squat down here by me,' Fura told her.

Nefa took a firm hold of Beata's hand.

'Go carefully,' she said, 'and watch out for the slops bucket. Where is it, Fura?'

'Left-hand corner,' Fura replied. 'Come straight towards me and you'll be all right.'

Cautiously the two newcomers edged their way in the direction of Fura's voice. It was a small cell, and in a moment Nefa was guiding Beata's hand until it touched the stone wall at the back. Instinctively, Beata pulled her hand away. The wall was cold, wet and slimy.

'I know,' Nefa said, 'not quite your fine plaster and tapestries, but it'll help you find your way around until you get a feel for the place. Give it a few days and you'll be able to move round as if it was broad daylight. But for now, you hang on to that wall then you'll know where you are. Just slide down it, then you can sit next to Fura.'

Beata did as she was told and found herself sitting on an earthen floor. It was rock hard, but the dampness in the cell made the surface slightly muddy and sticky. She leaned back against the wall and the coldness of the stone struck right through her clothes. She shivered again. She closed her eyes and found that it made no difference to the darkness, but she kept them closed because it helped her make pictures in her imagination. She was picturing her sister Verna, being taken home by the escort that had been ordered for her. During their interrogation, Beata had been furious when Verna had turned against the rest and begged for mercy. But now she just found herself feeling thankful that her sister wasn't having to suffer. Next, Beata held a picture of Amisso's face in her mind and wondered what conditions he would be held in. If this was a women's cell, what on earth would the men's be like? Perhaps the men wouldn't even have a slop bucket to relieve themselves in. Perhaps they were chained to the walls. Beata could almost feel the pain she imagined Amisso might be suffering and she took a sharp breath that caught in her throat in another dry sob.

'Don't upset yourself, Lady,' Fura said gently. 'Here – have something to eat. This'll cheer you up and no mistake.'

Beata could feel Fura's hand against her arm and she fumbled to take hold of the food that was being offered. It was something smooth and firm, about the size of a plum. Beata bit into it and the texture and taste were such a surprise that she almost choked.

'Nefa,' she spluttered, 'it's Almus!'

'What?' Nefa exclaimed.

'Here you are, old girl,' Fura said, 'have some yourself,' and she leaned across Beata to give Nefa one of the fruits.

'How did this get here?' Nefa asked, her mouth full of Almus.

'I had one on me when I was taken,' another prisoner explained. 'I'd robbed it off a bush in this house I was doing over.'

'But you don't have to steal Almus,' Beata said.

'I didn't know that, did I?' the woman explained. 'I'd never even seen it before. Thought it looked like a nice treat for when I'd done the job. But I never got the chance to find out before I got caught. Not till I got down here that is. Then I just ate it to cheer myself up and spat the stone out on the floor.'

'And it grew,' said one of the other women. 'Next day, I was going for the bucket and my foot kicked into this thing, and when I felt down to see what it was, it was this little bush - really tough little thing. I hadn't kicked it out of the ground - it'd got itself really rooted, even in this hard earth.'

'But that's amazing,' Beata said. 'How can a plant grow without light?'

'You tell me, Lady,' the woman answered. 'But it did. And now it's big enough to feed us all.'

'I knew there was something wrong about this place,' Nefa said.

'What do you mean, "wrong"?' Beata asked.

'Smell it,' Nefa told her.

'It smells all right,' Beata said.

'Well it shouldn't,' Nefa explained. 'It should smell of the slop bucket and mould and filthy bodies. The Almus bush must be taking it all away.'

'It is,' Fura told her enthusiastically. 'And I'll tell you something else: it's making us feel better than we've ever felt in our lives before. No one's been sick in here since we started eating it.'

'We're saving the seeds,' said the woman who'd brought the Almus in. 'We all reckon that if we ever get out of here all we need to do is just grow this stuff and eat it and we'll never need to go thieving again.'

'We've been slipping the seeds to other prisoners when we get out on exercise,' Fura went on. 'There must be a bush in half the cells in the prison by now.'

With the sweet taste of Almus in her mouth, Beata felt the horror of the dungeon fade a little. She was still cold and uncomfortable, but her mind was working fast and she felt hope begin to stir and grow inside her.

'You must keep the bushes a secret,' she said.

'You don't need to give an old lag lessons on keeping things hidden in this place, Lady,' Fura told her.

'I mean outside as well,' Beata said. 'When you take the seeds out, you must make sure you keep the bushes you grow a secret from the State. And don't listen to anything anyone might tell you about them.'

Then Beata explained what had been going on in Mercatorius and how the senators had destroyed all the Almus in the city – or so they thought.

'You're the only hope for Almus,' Beata told them. 'You have to save it for the people.'

'If we ever get out,' one of the women muttered.

'*When* you get out!' Beata said. 'Everyone carry seeds hidden in your clothes all the time, then you'll have them with you wherever you find yourself. Give some to Nefa and me. If you're right, Nefa, and I end up on some island, I might still be able to get Almus out to the world. We can't trust it just to Mercatorius now.'

The women could tell how young Beata was by her voice and they laughed at the way she was giving them orders, but Nefa stayed silent.

'I don't think I'll be needing to carry any,' Nefa said quietly when Fura tried to press some Almus seeds into her hand, and Beata realised that with her record, and her place at the bottom of Mercatorian society, Nefa's prospect of ever leaving the prison alive was probably non-existent. The thought of losing Nefa made Beata realise just how important her friend had become to her during the past three months. She'd been Beata's key contact in the Poor Quarter and she felt like another mother and sister to Beata, all rolled into one.

'Take some anyway,' Beata said softly. 'You never know.'

Beata heard Crasto long before she saw him. She and Nefa were being led under guard along a dim passageway in the Palace of Justice and the senator's voice echoed back to them from somewhere up ahead. It was the first contact Beata and Nefa had had with any of their friends in the three days since they'd been locked up in the city dungeon.

'Where are you taking us?' Beata heard Crasto demand. 'This isn't the way to the Court Room. We were informed our case was to be heard this afternoon. I insist that you tell us where we are being taken.'

There was clearly no reply, as the senator repeated his demands several times before Beata and Nefa rounded a bend in the seemingly endless network of corridors and saw Crasto, together with Amisso and the other men, being escorted by a squad of guards.

'Amisso!' Beata cried out, and her friend looked over his shoulder.

They couldn't wave to each other – their wrists had been chained before they'd been taken from their cells so had their ankles. Beata saw one of Amisso's guards strike him with the butt of his halberd, and in the same instant a guard slapped Beata round the head with such force that she staggered and saw stars. As Beata and Nefa drew closer to the men, Beata saw blood in Crasto's white hair. This must have been the response he received to his demands.

Eventually all seven prisoners were marshalled outside the gilded door of one of the chambers in the palace. Beata and Amisso exchanged glances, but did not dare speak. Beata was desperate to let Amisso know that she had Almus seeds with her – that all was not lost. She was certain they would be found guilty, but she took comfort in picturing the island to which Nefa had said she would be exiled. Surely Amisso and Crasto would be sent there too. They'd be together and they would cover the island with Almus. Soon there would be a whole cargo of Almus seeds ready to put on board a ship that they would somehow get hold of. She was sure that this could be achieved and smiled at Amisso, willing him to understand that all would be well. He smiled back, but the look in his eyes told her at once that no Almus had found its way to the men's cells. Crasto was staring straight ahead with an expression of grim determination on his face. Ebrio, Fallax and Gemmax had their heads bowed, and Gemmax looked as if he had been beaten – a prison cell was probably the least safe place of any in Mercatorius for a Sordesian in time of war.

The door opened, orders were given and the prisoners were marched into a small room. There was nowhere to sit and all seven stood in line, facing a raised platform at the far end. On this platform were seated the Dux himself, the General-in-Chief, the Grand Admiral and four senior senators who served in the Court of Justice. One of the senators was Perdo. Another was Tundax, the man who had backed Perdo so strongly when the deputation had called on Crasto to demand his resignation. The other two were known supporters of Perdo. It was clear to Crasto straight away that they could expect little understanding or justice from such a gathering.

'I demand—,' Crasto began.

'You demand nothing in the presence of the Dux!' Perdo snapped.

But the Dux raised his hand.

'Peace, Senator Perdo,' he said. 'Crasto has not yet been found guilty of treason – and unless or until he is, he remains a senator of Mercatorius.'

It was only at this point that Amisso fully appreciated the implications of a guilty verdict against his father. Crasto would be stripped of his place in the Senate – the thing that seemed to mean more to him than anything in the world. Amisso looked at Crasto, standing with squared shoulders and chin held high, and he was suddenly filled with admiration for a man who could face the destruction of his dreams with such fierce determination. Amisso felt proud that Crasto was his father and would have given anything to tell him so.

'As a senator of high standing, Crasto has a right to be heard,' the Dux continued.

'But not to demand!' Perdo insisted.

'Let that be,' the Dux told him firmly. Then he turned to Crasto. 'Speak, Senator,' he said. 'The Dux will hear you.'

'I demand,' Crasto repeated, glaring defiantly at Perdo, 'to know why our cases are being heard – if that is what is to take place here – in a private chamber and not in public in open court. I demand to know why charges of treason against the State are not being heard before the full Court of the State. And I demand to know why such serious charges are not being heard before a Senate jury.'

The Dux had a heavy ring of office on each hand – the left symbolised the power of the Senate; the right the armed power of the State. They seemed to weigh his hands down in his lap. The leader of the State of Mercatorius examined his rings for a moment in silence, but when he finally looked up, his expression was impersonal and every bit as determined as Crasto's.

'We are at war, Senator,' he said, 'and war brings rules of its own. The recent attempt by Sordes to poison our citizens—'

'That's a lie!' Gemmax broke in.

'Silence, dog!' the Dux shouted. 'A senator may exercise certain rights before the Dux, but a Sordesian dog has none. Speak again and I'll have you taken to execution at once.'

Two guards hauled Gemmax out of the line and pinned him against the back wall, with a dagger held to his ribs.

'The recent attempt by Sordes to poison our citizens,' the Dux repeated, 'has shown us the seriousness of our situation and yesterday the Senate agreed a set of emergency wartime measures.'

'One of which,' Perdo put in, unable to restrain himself, 'is that for reasons of security, all charges of treason and charges against enemy aliens should not be heard in public but by a tribunal made up of—'

'Yes, I can see how it's made up,' Crasto interrupted. 'How very convenient for dealing with our cases – I won't say hearing them, because a hearing is clearly not what we're going to get.'

'The Dux presides over this tribunal. Do you not trust the Dux?' Perdo asked with a smile.

Crasto glared at his enemy and was silent.

'Exactly the response I would expect from a traitor,' Perdo remarked.

The Dux then called for the charges to be read and when a clerk had recited them from the major's ledger the Dux invited the prisoners to make their defence and enter their plea. They all looked to Crasto and after a moment's silence, he addressed the Dux.

'My escape and the matter of the ship we must accept as plainly proven,' he conceded, 'but the threat of Almus has nothing to do with poison, as you well know. You see before you neither poisoners, nor sorcerers, nor traitors, but rather the victims of a campaign of persecution. And the man responsible for this campaign is sitting with his friends on the tribunal chosen to pass judgement upon us. If this is what Mercatorian justice has become, then my city has already been captured by a power far more evil than Sordes. That is all I have to say.'

None of the others had any more to add, and the members of the tribunal withdrew for less than five minutes before returning with a verdict. The Dux declared that every one of them had been found guilty on all counts brought against them.

'Now at last we can get out of here,' Beata thought, with a surprising sense of relief, 'Away to our island exile until this war and all its madness is over.'

The Dux stood and removed his white cap to pronounce sentence. He stared over their heads at a curling piece of gilded decoration above the door to the chamber.

'The sentence passed upon you all by this tribunal,' he told them, 'is death. Long life to the State of Mercatorius, and destruction to her enemies.'

The Dux had turned to leave before the prisoners reacted.

'Death for all?' Nefa gasped.

'Mercy, my Lord!' Crasto cried. 'Not for myself, but for the children! Punish me as you will, but surely you can see these children are innocent!'

The Dux did not flinch, but neither did he look directly at Crasto as he turned back.

'We are at war, Signor,' he said. 'There is no mercy for anyone now.'

With that, the Dux left the chamber followed by the rest of the tribunal – all except Perdo.

'Are you staying behind to gloat?' Crasto asked.

'Not at all,' Perdo said mildly. 'Merely doing my duty. Under the Emergency Measures, I have been given responsibility for the execution of all those convicted by this tribunal. I thought you might like to hear the arrangements.'

Beata swayed a little, and Nefa leaned against her for support, but none of the prisoners said a word.

'Such lack of interest!' Perdo said. 'Well, your guards will need to know what to do at any rate.'

The items that had been entered as evidence in the major's charge book were displayed on a table at the front of the room and Perdo went over to them.

'They're actually going to carry out an order of yours, Senator – or rather Signor Crasto, should I say now?' He picked up the Senate Order bearing Crasto's signature from the table. 'They're going to sink this dog's ship,' he said. 'And since you were all so anxious that it should happen, you'd better all be on board to make sure the job is done properly.' He took the order to the sergeant. 'Make sure the prisoners are all tied up below decks so they can accompany their precious ship safely to the bottom,' he said.

'This is a good day for you, Perdo,' the Dux commented.

The two men were standing on the lower viewing balcony of the City Watchtower. At the very top of the tower lookouts kept watch night and day for attack, but this lower balcony was richly decorated and was the place from which the Dux, senior senators, high-ranking officers of the armed forces and the grand masters of the guilds would gather to watch sea pageants, or races or the return of victorious fleets. On this occasion Perdo and the Dux were alone and they were watching Gemmax's ship being prepared for sea. It was the morning after the Tribunal hearing and the Oryx was due to leave at any moment.

'Meaning?' Perdo asked innocently.

'Meaning, your business prospects are about to improve beyond reckoning,' the Dux replied. 'When that ship goes down, your greatest rival goes down with it.'

Perdo leaned easily on the parapet of the balcony and breathed deeply. The sea air had never smelled better to him.

'Are you suggesting that I've pursued this prosecution against Crasto for my own ends?' Perdo asked.

'If I thought that, my dear Senator, I should have set the man free at once,' the Dux told him coldly. 'I have no doubt that what we've done during these past days has been in the best interests of Mercatorius in the long run – even if the methods have been, shall we say, unorthodox. The fact that the outcome has also been in your best interest has merely added an extra enthusiasm to your conduct, Perdo. And I'm sure all Mercatorius is grateful for enthusiasm in its senators.'

They watched as the skeleton crew, half a dozen sailors from one of the naval galleys, hoisted sail on the Sordesian caravel – just enough canvas to get her out of port and clear of the shipping lanes. Their orders were then to explode gunpowder bombs below the water line, blowing holes in the hull, and row back to shore in the small boat that was tied to the stern of the Oryx.

'Not the most civilised end for a senator of Mercatorius,' the Dux remarked.

'Former senator,' Perdo reminded him. 'Uncivilised, perhaps, but it does avoid the difficulties of a public execution.'

'Yes. In spite of everything, he was still well respected,' the Dux said. 'He was a faithful servant to this city all his life – and his fathers before him.'

'Exactly,' Perdo replied. 'Yesterday's man – coming from a long line of yesterday's men. You say this is a good day for me; I say that if it is, then it's also a good day for Mercatorius. If our great city is to remain great in the modern world we need men who aren't afraid of "unorthodox methods".'

'You mean men who aren't afraid to lie and cheat.'

'If that's what it takes, my Lord.'

The Oryx had weighed anchor and was now well clear of the twin lighthouses that marked the harbour entrance. It was obviously important not to sink the vessel anywhere near to the shipping lanes, but as time passed the caravel seemed to be sailing further out than either the Dux or Senator Perdo had expected.

'They're giving themselves a long row back,' Perdo remarked.

'Admirable dedication to duty,' the Dux replied.

Then Perdo suddenly leaned forward over the parapet, shading his eyes with one hand and pointing with the other.

'Look!' he said.

The Dux screwed up his eyes against the glinting of the morning sun on the water. The ship was so far away now that the crew seemed no bigger than insects, but he could make out that some of them appeared to be tussling at the gunwale. Then one of the tiny figures fell over the side.

15
The Crew of the Oryx

'They're throwing them overboard,' the Dux said as another body fell into the sea. 'I thought you gave orders for them to sink the prisoners in the ship.'

'Exactly,' Perdo replied.

'Perhaps your executioners have more humanity than their master,' the Dux suggested.

'Or they're too stupid to read an order,' Perdo snapped. 'Either way they can expect a whipping when they get back.'

The two continued to watch from the balcony of the Watchtower with increasing bewilderment. The distance and the flashing of the sun on the water made it very difficult to see clearly what was going on, but there seemed to be a group of tiny dots on the surface of the sea, in the wake of the Sordesian ship.

'They don't appear to be sinking,' the Dux said at last.

'Those people are swimming,' Perdo muttered, almost to himself.

'People who are tied up don't swim,' the Dux pointed out. 'Something's gone wrong.'

'We should have heard the bombs go off by now,' said Perdo. 'The guards should be rowing back, and that dog's ship should be sinking.'

But the empty rowing boat continued to bob on its rope behind the Oryx, which maintained its course away from Mercatorius. It was impossible to see any figures on the vessel now, but clearly there were still people aboard because suddenly the main and mizzen sails unfurled, bellying out in the breeze. The caravel now had all her canvas spread.

'What are they doing?' Perdo burst out. 'Do they think they have to take it to the other side of the world before they can sink it?'

'Never mind them,' the Dux replied. 'We need to get our prisoners back out of the water. They've clearly escaped. Send a pair of gigs out to pick them up – the fastest oarsmen we've got. And make sure they're armed.'

Perdo thumped the stone parapet with his fist, then hurried away to give the orders.

The Dux remained where he was for some minutes longer – until he saw the two light rowing boats leave the naval dock to the west of the harbour and turn towards the distant group of black dots in the water. He'd often stood at this balcony watching the sailors race their gigs – it was a standard part of any Mercatorian festival – and he could tell that these were crack crews. The prisoners would soon be recaptured. The Dux heaved a sigh and withdrew into the tower, calling out to the officer of his personal bodyguard. He intended to go down to the harbour and see Perdo greet the prisoners. It was not at all necessary for him to do so, but he had a strong urge to see Perdo face the consequence of his bungling. He hoped Crasto would be suitably scornful. The Dux was not surprised that Perdo had so frequently come a poor second to Crasto in business matters – a sure instinct and meticulous attention to detail had always been Crasto's great strengths. If you gave him a job to do, Crasto didn't botch it. Maybe Mercatorius did need a new style of senator in the modern world, the Dux thought to himself, but Crasto would still be a sad loss to the State. The Dux remembered the former senator as a fine swimmer and sportsman in his youth and he hoped that Crasto would not be too exhausted by his ordeal in the water to give Perdo a defiant greeting.

Half an hour later the gigs were pulling into the harbour with strong, determined strokes of the oars, but at considerably less speed than the sprinting pace they'd set as they raced out to sea. Senator Perdo and a detachment of soldiers, together with the Dux and his bodyguard, were waiting on the harbour side. The boats glided in towards the quay, the oars were shipped and mooring ropes were securely tied. The exhausted figures who had been pulled from the sea now climbed unsteadily out of the gigs and lined up on the harbour side. Blankets had been wrapped round them and draped over their heads to keep them warm but now, one by one, they let these coverings slip to their shoulders, revealing their white faces and sodden hair.

There was a moment's stunned silence as the reception party realised that they were looking not at Crasto and his companions, but at the sailors who had been sent to execute them. Perdo was the first to react.

'Where are the prisoners?' he shouted.

One of the sailors pointed a shaky hand out to sea.

'They're still on the ship, your Honour,' he said.

All eyes turned to the west to see that the Oryx had now disappeared over the horizon.

The State of Mercatorius should not be mocked and the Dux was a man who took the dignity of his position as its leader with great seriousness, so he bowed his head for a moment to hide the smile that flickered over his face. Perdo, beside himself with rage, began to bellow orders.

'Make ready the Fulmina,' he commanded.

The Fulmina was the most formidable of all the Mercatorian galleasses and the flagship of the fleet.

'It will need the Grand Admiral's order for the Fulmina to put to sea, your Honour,' the Guard's officer reminded Perdo tactfully.

'You have my order, Lieutenant,' the Dux interrupted, 'and the order of the Dux is the highest in the State.'

'Thank you, my Lord,' Perdo replied, with a slight bow. Then he turned back to the officer. 'There is to be a full complement of marines,' he barked, 'and inform the Captain of the Fulmina that I shall be joining him. I intend to make sure that there are no more mistakes.'

'Kindly inform the Captain that I too shall be joining his company for this expedition,' the Dux added. 'This is clearly a matter of great importance to the State.'

Perdo began to protest, but the Dux raised a hand to silence him. This new turn of events had added a glimmer of pleasure to an otherwise grim affair and he intended to see the fascinating confrontation out to the end.

As men went running to carry the necessary orders and drums struck up to summon the Fulmina's crew, Perdo interrogated the miserable sailors who had failed in the first attempt to do away with Crasto and the others. A young ensign had been in charge of the execution party and he explained what had happened as best he could.

'They were waiting for us, your Honour,' he said.

'Who were waiting for you?' Perdo demanded.

'I don't know, sir – men. There must have been a dozen at least. We'd stowed the prisoners, as you'd ordered, then when we were well clear of the harbour we went below to set the bombs, and that's when they jumped us. They were hiding down in the bilges. When they'd got the better of us and had us roped up fast, they set the prisoners free. Then they manhandled us onto the decks.'

'We thought we were going to die, your Honour!' one of the other sailors put in.

'But they didn't mean us any harm, sir,' the ensign went on. 'They untied us one by one and pitched us overboard to swim as best we could.'

'So we saw,' Perdo commented coldly. 'But who were they – these people who ambushed you?'

'I can't tell you, sir,' the young man repeated. 'They didn't give anything away.'

'More evidence of Crasto's plotting, if we needed any,' Perdo told the Dux.

'Quite so, Senator,' the Dux replied. 'May I offer you a passage to the Fulmina?'

His gilded state barge had just made an appearance from its dock behind his Palace, ready to take the Dux out to the flagship. The war meant that the fleet was on constant alert and they could see that a galley had already begun towing the mighty Fulmina out of harbour, ready for the chase.

'But how did you know they'd bring us to the Oryx?' Beata asked.

'Perdo's only reason for wanting to do away with us like this was secrecy,' Crasto added. 'No one was supposed to know about it until after it was over and done with.'

'There are ways of finding things out,' Verna explained.

The freed prisoners were gathered on the poop deck of the Oryx, and their liberator leaned on the rail, looking back at the horizon. The last glinting spires of Mercatorius had just slipped below it like the mastheads of a sinking ship. Verna took a deep breath of fresh sea air and had to admit to herself that, now it was over, she was taking great pleasure in retelling the adventure – almost as much pleasure as her sister was taking in hearing it.

'What ways, Verna?' Beata asked eagerly.

'Florea is engaged to one of the prison guards,' Verna explained, turning back to her friends. 'One of the advantages of spending so much time with kitchen staff is that you hear a lot of useful things. As soon as I got out of custody myself, I knew I'd have to find out what was going to happen to you before I could plan a rescue, so I asked Florea to discover when your case was going to be heard, and what the outcome was. She didn't have to push her young man too hard to get him to help; he was disgusted at Uncle Crasto's treatment and was only too glad to pass on the information.'

'So did you mean to rescue us all the time when you begged that major for mercy and said you had nothing to do with us?' Beata asked.

'It was obvious we weren't going to get any justice,' Verna explained, 'so one of us had to get out of there and make alternative arrangements.'

They all fell silent then and joined Verna leaning on the taffrail, watching the sun play on the water. They were enjoying the sense of freedom and victory, and going over once more in their minds the story that Verna had told them.

After talking her way out of Perdo's clutches, Verna had returned to the Poor Quarter. Although she'd only been there once before, she'd found her way back to Nefa's house and had loitered on the street, watching the passers-by and wondering how to achieve the next part of her plan. After only a few minutes she'd spotted one of the market tradesmen she often did business with. He'd agreed to help and had asked in the neighbourhood taverns until he'd found one of the men that Nefa had persuaded to crew the Oryx. This man had been able to lead Verna to more of Nefa's volunteers, and by the following evening she'd rounded up everyone who'd promised to help. She'd originally intended using them to capture the Oryx before rescuing Beata and her friends and taking them to the caravel as a means of escape. But when she'd heard that Perdo was actually going to have his victims brought to the vessel for execution, all she'd had to do was get there beforehand and wait for the prisoners to come to her. She and the volunteers had swum out to the Oryx the previous night under cover of darkness, overpowered the single sentry, posted one of their own number in the sentry's uniform to welcome the execution party next morning, and simply lain in wait in the hold.

The fugitives had not been at sea long before Captain Ebrio decided it was time he got to work organising the volunteer crew, and Gemmax set about checking his ship's stores to see how much had been left aboard. Fallax began to feel seasick so he went to lie down in the captain's cabin, and Nefa kept him company. Crasto eventually wandered off alone to the bows, leaving only Amisso and the two sisters on the poop deck, still gazing astern at the place where Mercatorius had been. There was quite a stiff breeze now they were clear of the land. It was filling the sails, driving the ship along at a good speed, and it made Verna's hair stream out behind her. Verna was a little apart from Amisso and Beata, and they found themselves stealing occasional glances at her stern profile. She was still wearing a working woman's clothes but, with her chin held high and proud and her long, curving neck, she continued to look every inch an aristocrat. Beata and Amisso both felt confused and in awe of this person they'd known all their lives as nothing more than a steady, sensible woman of the house.

'I didn't even know she could swim,' Beata whispered to Amisso after a while.

They looked at each other and Amisso smiled, but then his face fell again into the strange disappointed expression it had had since their escape. Beata knew it was time to reveal the surprise she had been saving for him.

'What's the matter?' she asked. 'Anyone would think you were still on your way to execution.'

'Don't you know?' he replied, without looking at her. 'Surely you, of all people, ought to realise.'

'Tell me,' she said.

'We've failed,' he told her. 'We've got away. We've got the ship we needed. But we haven't got the Almus.'

'Oh,' she said and she wriggled her arm free from his.

He continued to lean on the rail, lost in thought and paid her no attention as she rummaged in her clothes. Then she prodded him, and he turned to see her holding out her hand.

'What about this?' she said.

In her palm were six shiny Almus seeds.

'Here,' she said, putting two of them into his hand. 'A present for you.'

Just then, Fallax came staggering up from the captain's cabin. His face was still pale green, but it wore a determined expression.

'We've done it!' he shouted. 'We've saved Almus after all!'

He held his fist clenched above his head in a sign of triumph, gripping the seeds that Nefa had just given to him. Then his face twitched and he swallowed hard. Nefa had come up from the cabin behind him and he hurriedly thrust the contents of his fist back into her hand then dashed, groaning, to the taffrail. Everyone came running to gather round Nefa and Beata as they showed the seeds and told the story of how Almus was growing secretly in the State Dungeon.

'Well,' said Verna, 'when we get to some place where we can grow them, I think I might finally try one these fruits of yours. It seems a shame not to, after what we've just been through!'

They were all so taken up with celebrating the reappearance of Almus that Fallax was the only one looking out to sea when a dark shape appeared over the western horizon. His sickness made him feel dizzy and retching had blurred his vision with tears, so he was uncertain what it was for some moments, but eventually there could be no doubt. With an effort, he turned round and summoned enough energy to shout.

'Ship!' he cried.

At once the excited talking died away and everyone looked astern. There was silence for an instant before Amisso, who knew every vessel in the Mercatorian navy, identified their pursuer.

'It's the Fulmina,' he told them. 'We're finished.'

Everyone started talking at once, but Crasto's firm voice rose above them all. 'Not necessarily,' he said. 'This is Perdo's doing, and Perdo's a fool. He's let pride get the better of sound judgement. If he'd sent a galley after us, he'd have caught us in a couple of hours. But a humble galley's not good enough for him so he's sent out the most powerful galleass in the fleet. The Fulmina might have more canvas than us and a bank of oars, but she's broader and heavier – that evens things up a little. We can give her a run for most of the day by my reckoning, if Captain Ebrio's still as good a sailor as he was when he used to race my ships across the seas.'

'I hope I am, sir,' said Ebrio.

'You know, you only used to lose to my captains because Perdo insisted on overloading your ships till they nearly sank,' Crasto told him.

'That's true enough, sir,' Ebrio replied. 'Every trip I told him he'd put too much cargo aboard, but he wouldn't listen.'

'Greed and stupidity,' Crasto said. 'The man's always been the same.'

'We may be able to give them a race for several hours,' Gemmax put in, 'but they'll still catch us in the end, and what then? My ship's only lightly armed and we've not enough crew to stand and fight if we're boarded.'

Crasto scowled. He still found it hard to speak to a Sordesian on equal terms. But there was no doubt that Gemmax had spoken the truth.

'Do you have a suggestion?' Crasto asked.

'Sordes,' Gemmax said.

There was silence. Fallax retched again.

'Are you mad?' Crasto asked.

'Not at all,' Gemmax replied. 'We'll never outrun the Fulmina if we head on out to sea, but if we turn north and follow the coast we might just beat her to Sordesian waters.'

'And then what?' Crasto persisted.

'We're at war. Our patrols will pick up your Fulmina and engage her, and that will leave us free—'

'To be prisoners of Sordes,' said Crasto.

'To sail where we please,' Gemmax told him. 'You're aboard a Sordesian ship, don't forget. The only vessels likely to attack us are Mercatorian. We can follow Master Amisso's original plan and sail with our Almus seeds to a land that has never heard of Sordes and Mercatorius and their endless rivalry.'

'How do I know I can trust you?' Crasto asked. 'I've never trusted a Sordesian in my life before.'

There were murmurs of agreement from the crew.

'Father,' Amisso broke in, 'it was a Sordesian who saved my life and brought me back home to you. And this Sordesian has given us his ship to escape in.'

'Whose ship?' Crasto asked. 'As it's a Mercatorian prize of war, crewed by Mercatorians, I think the ownership of this vessel is open to question at the moment.'

'Perhaps the person who's paying for our voyage is the owner,' Verna suggested quietly. 'Perhaps he ought to decide which way we go.'

'And who might that be?' Crasto asked.

'Fallax,' Verna told him.

'But his gold's all in my house still, under the bed,' Nefa said.

'I think you'll find it's all safely stowed in the captain's cabin,' Verna replied.

'How on earth did you manage that?' Amisso asked. 'You couldn't have swum out with a casket of gold.'

'Very true,' Verna said. 'A box of gold will sink anyone, but if you share it around you can manage. We took a little each, so we were able to bring it all aboard.'

There were murmurs of astonishment, but Crasto kept silent.

'Father,' Amisso said, 'we need to make a decision – the Fulmina's closing on us every minute.'

'Well then,' his father conceded, 'let the man with the money decide. Fallax?'

'It's a decision for us all to make,' he said weakly, still hanging on to the rail. 'I've had enough of money giving the orders.'

'I suggest we forget the word Sordes,' Verna told them. 'Think of it like this: if we go north we might stand a chance; if we go west we'll certainly be killed. Shall we vote? North or west?'

The result was unanimous.

'Very good,' said Captain Ebrio, rubbing his hands together. 'Haul in that jolly boat and lash her to the deck; she's dragging us back. Rig up a spritsail if you can. Dig out every shred of canvas in the lockers and we'll see if we can't square-rig some topsails.' He strode to the stern and seized the taffrail, leaning over it to hurl his challenge at the ever-growing shape of their pursuer. 'Come on then, you great tub,' he shouted. 'We'll race you to Sordes!'

16
A Crosswind from the Coast

I f Almus had saved Ebrio's life and set him on the road to recovery, the sea chase to Sordes appeared to be completing the job. He grew in strength and vigour by the moment as he bellowed his orders and strode about the ship. Despite the danger of their situation, Amisso couldn't help feeling a thrill of excitement as the Oryx leapt through the water. The timbers came alive, and the ship seemed to answer to Ebrio's every command as a horse responds to an expert rider. Amisso knew that the captain of the Fulmina was said to be one of the finest sailors in Mercatorius, but as the hours passed, he was making slow progress in overhauling the fugitives.

'Are we going to beat them?' Amisso asked, as Ebrio stood at the taffrail, eyeing the Fulmina's manoeuvres.

The magnificent galleass was only half a kilometre astern now, but Amisso's studies in his father's map room told him that Sordesian waters were not far ahead. A Sordesian patrol was sure to spot them soon.

'We'll beat the Fulmina – just,' Ebrio replied, 'but I'm not sure we're going to beat that,' and he turned to point ahead.

They were running along the coast and to starboard the shoreline and inland hills were visible. Ahead, on the starboard bow, Amisso could just make out the bare, towering, limestone mountains that rose behind the city of Sordes and told him how close they were to their goal. It was to these mountains that Ebrio was pointing.

'What is it?' Amisso asked.

'Look at the sky,' Ebrio said.

Amisso had been concentrating on the rocky masses themselves, and seeing them as markers of hope, but now he realised what was taking Ebrio's attention. The sky above the mountains was darkening, and ominous grey shapes were gathering.

'What does it mean?' Amisso asked.

'Trouble,' was Ebrio's terse reply.

He stomped away, shouting orders, and the caravel shifted course, heading out to sea. Amisso was left alone at the taffrail, glancing anxiously from the gathering storm clouds to the doggedly pursuing Fulmina and back again. He felt a crosswind come in from the coast and the rush of air against his cheeks was unsettling.

An hour later there was no need for anyone aboard the Oryx to ask an expert opinion about the change of circumstances. From their gathering point above the mountains of Sordes the thick grey clouds had overrun the sky, and the wind that drove them was now sweeping across the deck of the caravel. The extra canvas that had been rigged up at the beginning of the chase was now rapidly being taken in.

'Why are we doing that?' Amisso called above the wind.

'If we don't do it, the storm'll do it for us!' Ebrio shouted back.

Amisso glanced astern. The Fulmina was close enough now to make out the figures of her crew. They were swarming aloft because the galleass too was taking in sail.

'At least it's the same for both of us,' Amisso commented.

'I wish it was,' Ebrio replied. 'But this is where their weight's going to count. They'll ride the storm better than us, and they've still got their oars. The only good thing is that they'll be more interested in dealing with the weather than with us for a while.'

But that hope proved to be unfounded. Moments later an explosion was heard through the blustering of the wind, followed by a whistling sound and a violent ripping overhead. In the next instant, a spout of water rose no more than twenty metres in front of the caravel's bows. A ball from one of the Fulmina's forward-mounted cannons had passed through the mainsail – the only canvas the Oryx still had set – and plunged into the sea ahead.

'The fools,' Ebrio shouted. 'Someone aboard that tub must be desperate for our blood!'

'My blood!' said Crasto, who had joined them on the poop. 'Perdo's waited the best part of 20 years to see the end of me and he's not going to lose his opportunity.'

'I'm surprised he's being allowed to risk the Fulmina to do it, though,' Ebrio called back.

'What do you mean?' Amisso asked.

'They've come a long way from safety already,' Ebrio replied. 'And if they don't finish us before this storm breaks, even a ship like the Fulmina could be in trouble.'

Now that he was watching the flagship, Amisso saw the light before he heard the sound of the next cannonade – a soft pink blossoming from the forecastle and the two side platforms that were built out over the oars. The crump of the explosions followed at once.

'Get down!' Ebrio shouted.

All hands threw themselves on the deck as the whistle of the cannon balls was immediately followed by the splintering of timber. The gunners aboard the Fulmina were excellent, and now that they had their range, their shot had raked the deck of the Oryx. There was a moment's silence, then a terrible drawn-out groaning that seemed to come from the ship itself, followed by the sound of tearing timber and a thunderous crack as the mainmast parted 4 metres above the deck and fell crashing onto the forecastle. There was a cheer from the Fulmina.

'Finest gunners in the world,' Crasto muttered bitterly, his face resting on the planking of the poop deck.

But Ebrio didn't lie still for more than a moment. He was on his feet at once.

'Cut her free!' he shouted, 'heave her overboard and set the foresail!'

As soon as they saw what was required, Amisso and Crasto scrambled up and joined the men hacking away the rigging from the fallen mast. Before long the useless timber was in the water, and another sail was being set. But the captain of the Fulmina had used the time to draw alongside his prey. Now the whole length of the Fulmina's port side lit up and the roar of her guns, the crashing of balls into timber and the screams of an injured sailor made Amisso reel in shock.

The Oryx managed to fire her guns once, but they were only designed to warn off pirates, not to engage a powerful warship. There were few of them, they were much lighter than those of the Fulmina, and there were no trained gunners in the Oryx's skeleton crew of volunteers. The caravel's guns did little damage, and another broadside from the Fulmina silenced them. The Oryx's gun deck was shattered, the cannon smashed, more of the crew were injured, and in the confusion a fire had started. The storm was on them in earnest now, but despite this and the damage to the Oryx, Ebrio managed to manoeuvre his vessel away from the Fulmina until she was presenting the much smaller target of her stern to the galleass's broadside. But it was only a matter of time before the warship finished them off.

Of the dozen men who had swum across with Verna to the Oryx, four were now injured and beyond being of assistance, Fallax was too weak and sick to help, and although Amisso, Crasto and the women were willing to lend a hand, none of them had the skills to make them any use. When smoke began to rise from the hatches and those below decks came up choking and crying, 'Fire!' Ebrio knew it was all over. The Fulmina shipped oars and crashed against the side of the crippled caravel. Stout lines with grappling hooks were thrown across to bind the two vessels together as they heaved and ground against each other, buffeted by the howling wind. The sky was dark with towering thunderclouds, and rain now lashed the decks so that Crasto and the others could only just see the ranks of marines drawn up on the deck of the Fulmina, bows at the ready. But they could see Senator Perdo clearly enough. He was standing high above them at the very edge of the aft fighting platform. His hands were firmly planted on his hips and rain was pouring from his hair and beard. He swayed dangerously as the elements threw the two ships about in their grip, and glared down at the defiant handful of fugitives huddled together on the deck of the Oryx. His eyes found the sodden white hair of his rival in the miserable group.

'Signor Crasto!' he shouted above the storm. 'Have you put the State of Mercatorius to sufficient trouble? Perhaps now you'll be kind enough to allow me the privilege of killing you!'

He raised his arm as if he might have been going to give some order or signal, but at that moment there was a terrific roar that shook both ships and sent Perdo toppling to the deck. Another roar followed, then two more, and within moments the Fulmina began to list towards the Oryx as if the ship she was bound to were hanging on her like a dead weight.

'Cut her loose!' came the order, and dozens of sailors from the Fulmina's crew sank axes into the ropes that held the two ships together.

The Fulmina sprang back up as the Oryx foundered, but only for a few moments. Soon, the Fulmina resumed her list and started to settle heavily in the storm-lashed sea. The captain of the Fulmina could be seen grasping the front of Perdo's coat, beside himself with rage. 'I told you we shouldn't grapple her!' he shouted. 'Only a madman would order us to tie up to a burning ship!'

The Fulmina's oarsmen began to stream on deck, throwing the marines into confusion, shouting, 'We're holed! We're sinking!'

Aboard the Oryx, Verna was the first to realise what had happened.

'The bombs!' she said. 'The fire must have set them off!'

Sure enough, the fire raging unchecked below decks in the Oryx had reached the bombs that had been abandoned there when the execution party had been overpowered. Now they had finally done their job – blowing the bottom out of the Sordesian ship. But as the Oryx had been bound tightly to the Fulmina at the time, they had also blown a great hole in the Mercatorian flagship. With water pouring into her, the mighty galleass too was doomed. Now that they were no longer roped together, the raging storm battered the sinking vessels against each other and as their crews threw themselves into the water the two shattered ships began to smash each other to pieces.

Verna opened her eyes then quickly closed them again, dazzled by the daylight. She felt the faint warmth of the autumn sun on her face. It was soothing and life-giving. She tried to breathe deeply, but her lungs felt raw. She knew that she had been in the sea and realised that now she was not. She knew that she was lying on her back and feeling with her hands she found that she was on some kind of wooden pallet. It was shifting gently and rhythmically beneath her, and she guessed that she was on board a ship. She became aware of voices and, as she struggled further towards consciousness, she realised with a shock that the voices were Sordesian. Then, as memory returned, she realised that this should not be a surprise. No doubt the Mercatorian flagship had been spotted by Sordesian lookouts or patrols. Once the storm had blown out they would have sent their own warships to investigate. But when the Sordesian ships had arrived they would have found nothing but half-drowned survivors clinging to fragments of wreckage. She remembered holding on to a hatch cover with such force that she thought her fingers would break. She remembered alternately swallowing and spewing salt water – fighting for each breath in between. She remembered being lifted from the water and the pain as her hands were wrenched from the hatch cover.

Once more Verna opened her eyes, but carefully this time, slowly letting the light through her lashes. She turned her head to one side and saw planking, the foot of a mast and a length of wooden gunwale. After a moment, she tried to raise herself on her elbow. Her body was exhausted and the effort required seemed to be immense, but at last she managed it. She saw the sailors then, none of them paying any attention to her. They were going about their duties, chatting calmly, smiling and laughing from time to time. It all seemed so pleasant and ordinary, and yet their accents were Sordesian.

Slowly and painfully, Verna rolled over onto all fours, knelt up, steadied herself and forced herself to her feet. The men took notice then. They stopped their work and stared. One of them smiled and called out 'Good morning' to her and another asked how she was feeling. She understood them well enough – Sordesian was only a different dialect not a different language, after all – but she did not reply. She scanned the deck for other pallets with other survivors, but there were none. So she was alone among the enemies of Mercatorius. She was close to the gunwale and after two shaky steps she was clinging to the top of it. One of the sailors called, 'Well done!' but she ignored him and stared steadfastly out over the water.

The sea was calm now and twinkled in the sunshine. It seemed to be morning, so perhaps she had been in the water throughout the night. She saw that they were sailing across a wide bay. The distant mountains where the storm had gathered the previous day were very close now, towering towards a pale blue sky on the starboard side of the ship, and between the ship and the shore was a long, low island, covered in greenery. It looked beautiful, like something in a fairy story. Being careful to keep her balance, Verna turned so that she could see where the ship was making for. There were more lovely green islands scattered in their path, and beyond them in the distance she saw a sight that took her breath away. A lofty wall of glittering marble had been built right across the head of the bay. It had a narrow opening guarded by massive gun batteries, which must give access to the harbour within. Behind the wall she could see the tops of half a dozen elegant towers, thin as a lady's fingers, shining in the morning sun, and beyond them the huge cylinder of a gleaming citadel that looked as if it could outlast the mountains themselves.

'Sordes,' she muttered to herself.

A dark, all-enveloping wave of horror, loneliness and loss closed around her. She saw the bleached, staring face of her drowned sister floating in front of her for a second, then Amisso, Crasto and the others swirling around her as if they were being sucked down in a whirlpool – then nothing, as she crumpled in a heap on the deck.

Verna had a dim memory of being carried ashore, of crowds and noise, the bumping of a wagon, then some time later the peace and quiet of a cool, fragrant room. She was aware that people had come from time to time to trickle wine or thin broth between her lips. But this was all she knew of her arrival in Sordes and the days that followed. And then one morning she heard music – heard it properly. She realised she'd often been aware of musicians playing in the background since she'd first been brought to the room where she was lying, but this morning she found herself listening intently to the instrument. It was a harp, being played with extraordinary skill. The notes sparkled like sunlight on rippling water and Verna felt her heart swell with delight. But then as consciousness returned more fully and with it memory, the brightness and the pleasure drained away. She remembered where she was and why – that she was alone in the land of her enemy, the sole survivor of a disaster.

Her eyes were still closed and the music together with her loneliness brought a picture of home to Verna's mind: a chamber orchestra playing as her mother and father entertained. And there was Beata, sitting on the floor despite everyone's protests, hugging her knees and staring in wonder at the musicians with her powerful, brown eyes. Tears formed in Verna's own eyes as she pictured her sister. Verna had always seen it as her duty to try and curb Beata's wildness, and she supposed that had meant that she'd never really shown her sister how much she admired her. What an astonishing person she'd been turning into – a girl who could launch a single-handed mercy mission to the whole Poor Quarter of Mercatorius. But now they would never know what Beata might have become, and Verna would never tell her sister how she felt about her. The silence of the seabed had swallowed her for ever.

Other lost figures passed through the vision in Verna's mind: golden-haired Amisso, drifting vaguely in the background of the party, seeming to float on the flow of the music, his blue eyes forever slightly unfocused as if they were waiting to fasten on something just over the horizon, just out of sight. Verna had always envied him his questing, seeking nature – that ability to stand apart from everything the city and their fathers' houses represented, the ability to wait until a better way became clear. The only thing she had not envied him had been his insecurity. But it was too late now to tell him how much she'd thought he was worth – little silver fishes would be swimming among his golden hair, slick ribbons of seaweed plaiting with his tresses.

Then there was Crasto himself. She saw him standing with her father, discussing some weighty business of state, oblivious to the beauties of the music. She saw Crasto as he'd been at his best: barrel-chested and strong, with hair the colour of iron and a beard as sharp as a spearhead. She'd admired him since she'd been a little girl. Next to her father, he was the man she loved most of that generation. While Crasto had been in the Senate, she'd felt as if she lived in the best and safest place in the world. The thought of that powerful body buried beneath the sands of the deep made her feel as if the whole of Mercatorius was wrecked and lost for ever, that there was nothing worth going back to, even if she could ever get out of Sordes alive.

The faces of her sister and her dead friends were too painful to picture, and Verna suddenly opened her eyes. Tears spilled onto her cheeks and she struggled to sit upright, sniffing and shaking her head. The bed was soft and luxurious, and it took her some time but she did not give up. When she'd succeeded, she saw that there was a marble table beside her bed and on it were a porcelain bowl of fragrant dried flowers and a crystal goblet full of a pale pink liquid. She took the goblet and sipped to ease her aching throat. It was the most delicious sherbet she had ever tasted. Sip by sip she drained the glass as she gazed out of the big open window to her right. It reached from floor to ceiling and gave a magnificent view out to the sea and the mountains. A fig tree was growing outside, and its leafy branches framed one half of the window. Birds were perched in it, and their song mingled with the music of the harp. The beautiful sounds seemed to give her strength. Carefully, she turned so that her legs hung over the side of the bed. She pushed against the mattress with her hands and found to her satisfaction that she could stand.

A great weight of sorrow seemed to press down on her. But Verna responded to it as she did to all the burdens of life – by determined action. She took a moment to get her balance, then forced herself to walk towards the open window. It led onto a broad balcony and she leaned on the ornate balustrade to regain her breath and take in the view. From her bed, Verna had only been able to see the distant outlook, but now she had a clear sight of what lay directly below the house – spread out in a gentle slope, stretching for an incredible distance, were the neat and ordered streets of Sordes. Verna was astonished. Over the years, her upbringing in Mercatorius had led her to think of Sordes as a place of earth tracks and filthy mud huts, inhabited by animal-like people who had barely progressed beyond sewing skins together for clothes. It was what everybody thought. How Sordes could ever be a threat to the might of Mercatorius if it were really such a primitive place was a question no one seemed to consider. But here below her Verna saw paved streets, well-made houses and imposing public buildings all laid out in an orderly grid, their walls shimmering white in the daylight. Seemingly unassailable fortifications surrounded the whole city and the gilded roofs of a dozen palaces shone like little suns. She could see no part of the city that corresponded to the squalid Poor Quarter of Mercatorius.

'This is beautiful,' Verna murmured.

'Yes,' a man's voice said behind her. 'The most beautiful place in the world.'

Verna turned round so quickly she nearly fell. She clung to the balustrade for support and saw a man dressed in a crimson robe of silk, tied with a golden sash. The balcony ran the whole length of the building and he was sitting in an ornate chair outside one of the adjoining rooms. He stood quickly and held out a hand that was covered in jewelled rings.

'Gemmax?' she said.

Then, despite her wobbling legs, she hurried towards him and seized his hand in both of hers.

'I thought I was the only one,' she said. 'The only one who'd survived.'

'You were the last one out of the water,' he told her gently. 'After you, they gave up. Bodies from the Fulmina are still being washed up – but no one else has been found alive.'

'My sister!' Verna said. 'Is she alive? Where is she? Take me to her – I have to see her!'

But Gemmax loosed her hand and moved away. He turned to rest his back against the balustrade and looked thoughtfully at the elegant building which the balcony fronted.

'My home,' he said. 'Mercatorius may rule the seas, but Sordesian land routes bring enough trade to pay for a little beauty in our lives.'

'I'm not interested in all that,' Verna interrupted. 'I want my sister, I must see her!'

'You have nothing to fear in Sordes – you are my guest here,' Gemmax went on doggedly. 'I've had an audience with our Duke and explained how you rescued me, so he has allowed me to offer you hospitality... and the others of course—'

'I want Beata!' Verna insisted.

Gemmax seemed distracted and wouldn't meet her eyes.

'You're not strong enough yet,' he protested.

'Nonsense,' Verna declared. 'How long have I been in bed?'

'Five days,' Gemmax told her. 'You've had a fever. You're very weak.'

'Five days is long enough to get over a fever,' she announced. 'I must see my sister at once!'

Although her body was indeed still weak, Verna's will was strong as ever. She brushed aside all her host's protests and minutes later she left her bedroom leaning heavily on Gemmax's arm, with the rich silk robe of a Sordesian noblewoman wrapped around her. A broad, marble staircase with curving banisters swept down to the main reception hall and Verna paused at the top of it to look at the group that Gemmax had sent a servant to summon. Her eyes travelled urgently from face to face, then back again, searching. She saw the men she had gathered in the Poor Quarter to form her rescue party, four of them heavily bandaged; she saw Captain Ebrio; she saw Nefa and Fallax; but that was all.

'Where's Beata?' she asked desperately. 'Where's Uncle Crasto? Where's Amisso?'

No one dared answer her, and she suddenly noticed that every one of them was wearing black. Then a tall figure, dressed in court uniform, stepped out of one of the side rooms and came to the foot of the staircase.

'They're gone, my dear,' he said. 'All gone.'

It was Ambassador Capax, the Mercatorian envoy to Sordes. Verna gave a wailing cry, staggered down the stairs and fell sobbing into her father's arms.

17
Discoveries in Sordes

Verna felt dazed, as if she had had a blow to the head. Gently, her friends led her to a sitting room and lowered her onto a richly upholstered settee. They each told her the story of their individual rescue from the storm, at least the fragments they could remember, and how they had passed the last few days. But Verna found it hard to concentrate. The others had all had time to try and cope with the death of Beata, Amisso and Crasto, but for Verna, it was as if the three of them had been wrenched from her that very moment and their loss was all she could think of. She clung to her father's arm as if he too might be torn away as soon as he had been restored to her. She felt as if someone had clamped a giant shell to her ear so that all she could hear was the roaring of the sea.

After a while, Verna became aware that the others had stopped talking and her father was speaking to her now.

'I've been well treated, my dear,' he was telling her. 'They've kept me under guard, to be sure – there are soldiers outside Signor Gemmax's house now. They have to go with me everywhere, but I've been allowed to stay in my residence. These are civilised people, Verna. I doubt that their own ambassador has been treated as well in Mercatorius.'

Verna had a fleeting image of the Sordesian ambassador being paraded through the streets on a wagon and pelted with rotten fruit at the start of the war, and she remembered how anxious they had all been for her father Capax then, fearing that he would be murdered, tortured or at least starved and beaten in some foul prison cell. She forced herself to focus and looked at her father carefully. His handsome face was drawn and worried, but he seemed healthy and well cared for. His hair and beard were immaculately trimmed. His fine court clothes were clean, and his ambassador's chain and medallions shone.

A black diamond of silk had been neatly sewn onto the ambassador's sleeve to show that he was in mourning, and Verna ran her fingers gently over it.

'Is there no hope?' she said.

'No, my dear,' he told her. 'We must give them up for dead. With no bodies, we couldn't hold a funeral. But we've done our best to mark their passing. The Duke sent us musicians, and we held a small ceremony yesterday.'

'They let us use one of the battery towers at the harbour entrance,' Fallax explained. 'We threw flowers on the water.'

'All this lot from the Quarter spoke up for Mistress Beata,' Nefa said, indicating the men who'd crewed the Oryx during their escape.

'Your sister was a wonderful girl, Mistress,' one of them said, trying to make his deep sailor's voice as soft as he could. 'Everyone knew her in the Quarter. It can't have been easy – a girl from her sort of background, braving it among the likes of us to bring us the Almus.'

'And Captain Ebrio spoke for Master Amisso,' Nefa went on. 'How the young master gave him a drink when his brother was all for having him whipped.'

'And how we'd never have had Almus at all if Master Amisso hadn't gone on his adventure,' Ebrio reminded her. 'Maybe it was a stupid thing to go and do, but it took some guts for a boy like that.'

'And your father gave thanks for Senator Crasto's life,' Gemmax said.

'He was a man of passion, Verna,' the Ambassador said. 'Perhaps it's not what most people would remember about him, but it's what I remember. He loved his city, but he also loved his family: his wife and his boys. And he loved you too, Verna; he was overjoyed when we agreed that you would be his daughter-in-law—'

They were interrupted by a servant entering the room. The man spoke hurriedly to Gemmax and handed him a note, which the merchant passed over to Capax. The ambassador read it, then rose quickly from his daughter's side.

'I must go, my dear,' he said. 'For the first time in a long time I have a task to perform.'

'No, Father,' Verna cried, gripping his hand in both of hers.

'It's my duty,' he told her gently.

'Then let me come too,' she said.

'You're hardly strong enough to stand,' Capax reminded her, 'and this is not a social occasion. The Dux requires me to join him in negotiations with the Duke of Sordes.'

'The Dux?' said Verna in astonishment. 'Is he here?'

'Oh yes,' Capax told her. 'He was aboard the Fulmina with Senator Perdo. The pair of them were fished out of the water by the Sordesian navy and have been under lock and key ever since.'

'The war is lost, then,' his daughter said dully.

'We shall see,' Capax replied. He freed his hand from Verna's grip and bent to kiss her forehead. 'I'll be back,' he assured her. 'I promise.'

'Everything is lost,' Verna murmured as her father left the room.

The State Buildings of Sordes had much less gold and much more light in them than those of Mercatorius. The hall into which Capax was shown in the Duke's Palace was spacious and its high, vaulted roof was supported by two rows of snowy marble pillars. It was a room the ambassador knew well. Sunlight streamed in from the tall windows that made up most of its two long sides. The guards who had accompanied him stationed themselves at either side of the gilded door, and Capax walked slowly across the black and white chequered floor towards the dais at the far end of the hall. As he approached, the four figures seated there rose to greet him. They were the Duke, two senior ministers from his Court and the Commander of the Sordesian armed forces.

'Ambassador, we trust you are well,' said the Duke.

246

'As well as can be expected, your Highness,' Capax replied, bowing. 'I thank you for your concern.'

The Sordesians bowed in return and the Duke sat down again in his gilded seat. His three advisers did likewise and he waved towards three seats that had been arranged facing the dais.

'Please be seated, Ambassador,' the Duke invited. 'We were so pleased to hear that your elder daughter had been rescued. You must be delighted.'

'Indeed, your Highness,' Capax replied. 'She is weak and in some distress, having only just learned of her sister's death. But it is a great comfort that Verna has been spared.'

'And you will be in much need of comfort at this time,' the Duke continued softly. 'Please accept my deepest condolences and those of the whole Court for the loss of your younger girl. War or no war, we take no pleasure in your sadness.'

The Duke of Sordes was a vigorous man in his thirties, clean-shaven and with his dark hair cut short – as was the fashion in Sordes. He had brown, serious eyes and they were full of pity now as he looked into the Mercatorian ambassador's face.

'You are most kind, your Highness,' Capax replied. 'And I am thankful for your assistance with our memorial ceremony yesterday.'

'You are welcome, Ambassador,' said the Duke. 'I'm only sorry to have to call you to business in your time of mourning.'

'I'm here to do my duty,' Capax responded. 'The world continues, regardless.'

'The war continues, at any rate,' the Duke commented, 'and as you will know it has taken a very interesting turn in recent days. We have two unexpected guests in Sordes, whom you will be glad to see safe, but not necessarily in my custody.'

The Duke clapped his hands, and a soldier guarding one of the doors at the other end of the room stepped outside. He returned a moment later with Senator Perdo and the Dux of Mercatorius. These two advanced towards the dais. The Dux had his arm in a sling, but otherwise they looked unharmed and had been provided with clean clothes appropriate to their rank. The Dux walked with a firm tread, and head held high, but Perdo seemed to stumble forward and there was something slightly wild about his expression. When the Mercatorians reached the dais, the Duke and his advisers rose to greet them, as did Capax.

'Brothers, you are welcome,' the Duke said, bowing deeply. His advisers followed suit.

The Dux nodded his head slightly but Perdo suddenly threw himself on his knees before the Duke.

'Mercy, your Highness!' he cried.

'Peace, man,' the Dux said in astonishment. 'Get on your feet at once – no Mercatorian kneels in Sordes.'

'Nor is expected to,' the Duke added. 'Please be seated all of you.'

The others did as instructed but Perdo merely shuffled nearer to the Duke, still on his knees.

'Take no notice of him,' the senator said. 'Do what you like with him, but have mercy on me, your Highness. I am a true friend to Sordes.'

The Sordesian ministers exchanged puzzled looks.

'You have a strange way of showing friendship – bringing your most powerful warship into our waters,' the commander remarked.

'I was going to surrender it to you!' Perdo replied, glancing desperately from one Sordesian face to another.

'It rather looked to us as if you were chasing one of our leading merchants,' the Duke told him, a hint of contempt in his voice.

'Escorting him!' Perdo whined. 'I was escorting him.'

'Be silent, you scoundrel!' the Dux commanded. 'This is intolerable.'

'It was me who set your merchant free!' Perdo explained, ignoring the Dux. 'I arranged it with the sentries. I did it all. I got him out of the Palace.'

'You did what?' the Dux interrupted. 'Do you swear to this?'

'I swear it,' Perdo said. 'It was me – I let Signor Gemmax escape.'

Before any of the astonished spectators could move to stop him, the Dux leaped towards the grovelling senator and kicked him hard in the stomach. Perdo keeled over with a groan, and the Dux kicked him again. Capax was the first to act. He moved swiftly to the Dux and restrained him. For a moment it looked as if the Dux would try and fight with Capax despite his injured arm, but then he regained control of himself.

'Thank you, Ambassador,' he said, lowering himself slowly back into his seat.

The Dux took a moment to steady himself, then he drew a deep breath and levelled a searing look at the fallen senator.

'Everything you've said is a lie, except this last,' he said. 'And that's only half the truth. I can well believe that you let Gemmax escape – but for his money and not the love of his state! If only Crasto were here I'd grant him a free pardon on the spot. He shall have a posthumous one, at any rate.' The Dux turned to the Duke of Sordes. 'Do what you like with me, Duke,' he said, 'but if I am to be executed, grant me pen, paper and seals so that I can make out a pardon for Senator Crasto, the most faithful senator Mercatorius ever had. And promise me that you will have his pardon delivered to the Senate. As for this treasonous wretch... if you don't have him executed and we ever get back to Mercatorius, then I most certainly will.'

'There will be no executions here,' the Duke assured him. 'The two of you are worth far too much to me alive. What do you think the Senate would give for your safe return – a ceasefire? A treaty?'

'Nothing!' the Dux snapped back. 'They'll write me off as dead and elect another Dux.'

'You underestimate yourself, Dux,' the Duke said with a smile. 'Your people value you more highly than you think. Ambassador, would you care to give this to your Dux.' He took a folded letter bearing the seal of the Mercatorian Senate from the inside of his robe and handed it to Capax. 'Our envoy travelled night and day under flag of truce to bring the news of your capture to Mercatorius,' he explained. 'This is your Senate's reply.'

The Dux beckoned Capax to join him in reading the paper, while the Sordesians waited patiently.

'The fools,' the Dux declared at last, and he tore the paper up, throwing the pieces on the chequered marble of the floor.

'Perhaps, with your ambassador's help, you and Senator Perdo would like to negotiate some other terms for your release,' the Duke suggested.

'Capax and I will negotiate with you,' the Dux told him, 'but not that dog.' He pointed to the crouching figure of Perdo, who had got his wind back now and was trying to rise. 'Whatever you do with him, keep him away from me or you'll have to execute me for murder. Throw him in the dungeon and let's get down to business.'

The Dux was allowed the use of a small chamber to consult with his ambassador in private before entering into negotiations with the Duke and his advisers. Capax agreed with the Dux that the terms offered by the Senate had been unacceptable. They represented a surrender, giving up almost half of the trade routes belonging to Mercatorius.

'We must find a way to force them into a better deal,' Capax said.

'We must offer them no deal at all,' the Dux told him. 'They can keep me locked up till I die. I'd rather that than sell the city's trade routes to be free.'

'But it's not up to you, my Lord,' the Ambassador pointed out. 'The Senate wants you out of Sordes, whatever your views on the matter. You may have torn the paper up, but the Senate has made an offer for you and that offer will stand unless we can find a way to bargain the Sordesians down.'

Both men were silent for a long time – by turns sitting, standing, pacing or looking out of the small latticed window at the streets of Sordes – until at last a smile broke across the face of the Dux.

'What about this for an idea?' he said.

Half an hour later, the Duke of Sordes had deep furrows of worry between his dark brown eyes, and his advisers were shifting uncomfortably in their seats.

'But the whole system would collapse,' the Duke said. 'Trade would be finished. Sordes would be finished.'

'Exactly,' said the Dux. 'If we unleash Almus on Sordes, your city is doomed. It would only take one Mercatorian agent disguised as a beggar, a traveller, a trader from another land to wander through your streets, silently scattering seeds like a disease. And as soon as the plant spread your city would be brought to its knees. A trading city can't seal its gates – and who would want to trade with a city that searches every last bag and purse and pocket of every traveller who enters it?'

There was a shocked silence.

'So our terms are these, Duke,' the Dux continued, with a hint of a smile, 'in return for my freedom and safe passage back to Mercatorius, we will destroy the stockpiles of Almus seeds held in Mercatorius and remove this scourge from the world of commerce for ever. But most important of all, we will agree ceasefire terms with you that are fair to both our states and put an end to this foolish war.'

'But how can we be sure that you'll destroy the seeds?' one of the ministers asked.

'Send inspectors with us,' the Dux replied. 'They can go wherever they like and look wherever they like in our city.'

'A seed is an easy thing to hide, Dux,' the commander pointed out.

'Granted,' the Dux agreed. 'In the end, there must also be an element of trust, gentlemen. But one thing I would say: we in Mercatorius have as much reason to be fearful of this pernicious plant as you. We have no interest in preserving it; it is a danger on our own soil and we have only kept it for use in this war. With the war over we will no longer need to take the risk of storing the seeds. We will be as glad to see them destroyed as you will.'

The Duke had been silent for some time, and the ministers now looked to him for a decision. The young ruler smiled at the Dux. It was indeed a matter of trust, and the Duke was beginning to like the leader of their ancient enemy. He respected the way the Dux had rejected the cowardice of Perdo and been ready to face death rather than betray his city. But most of all, as the Dux had explained the horrors of Almus and the devastation it could cause in trading states such as their own, the Duke had realised how much Sordes and Mercatorius had in common.

'One thing must be discussed before I can agree,' the Duke said, 'and that is the peace conditions between our two states.'

Capax opened his mouth to speak, but the Duke held up a hand to silence him.

'Ambassador,' he said, 'bearing in mind that your Dux is a prisoner of war here, I think Mercatorius has done quite enough laying down of terms. Allow me to make some demands now, if you would.'

Capax looked to the Dux, and the Dux nodded assent.

'Very well,' the Duke continued. 'When Mercatorians write the history of this war they will no doubt claim that Sordes provoked it by its pirate raids against your shipping. However, when Sordesian historians write the story, they will say that Mercatorian bandits ambushing our overland caravans were the cause of all the trouble. Yet you and I, Dux, know the truth, which is that both our cities are to blame. My terms for peace are simply these: Mercatorius will agree not to interfere with our land trade and in return Sordes will cease to harass Mercatorian shipping. Your traders may pay to join our caravans and we will be allowed to pay for your protection at sea. Wealth is what we exist for. Trade builds wealth and war destroys trade, so in the interest of business we must end our fighting. Are we agreed?'

The Dux and the Duke looked into each other's eyes. They both knew that it was a moment of cool calculation – each had a clear estimate of how much money their cities had lost in the conflict so far, and how much more they stood to lose if the fighting continued.

'Agreed,' said the Dux, and much to the surprise of everyone else present, the two leaders sealed the bargain by shaking hands.

It took time. Envoys had to pass to and fro between the warring cities under white flags of truce to make arrangements. But eventually Ambassador Capax travelled back to Mercatorius to address the Senate and in due course returned with the Senate's agreement to the terms. He returned in the Mercatorian galleass which would take the Dux and the others home. The vessel was not the equal of the Fulmina – no ship afloat could match the lost Mercatorian flagship – but she was still a fine sight with sails billowing and gaudy flags flying from every masthead as she approached the entrance to the harbour of Sordes.

Verna watched the ship's arrival from the balcony of Gemmax's mansion and saw with relief that a huge blue, red and gold banner was streaming from the stern of the vessel. She turned to her host, who was standing a little behind her.

'Father's aboard,' she said, pointing to the Mercatorian warship. 'Look, she's flying the ambassador's colours.'

Gemmax took a step forward and stood beside Verna. He had been studying her as she watched the ship and thinking how noble she looked – she had the poise and elegance of a queen, and yet she'd had the courage to organise their escape and the strength to swim across a harbour. She might be an alien, a Mercatorian, but Gemmax had to admit she was an extraordinary young woman. He'd overseen her recovery, supervising her care, and it made him glad to see that now she was fit and well. She still grieved for her lost sister and friends, insisting that she would wear a black mourning robe for a year and a day, but her will was unbroken and her body had grown strong again. Her chin was high and her shoulders squared with determination.

'What will you do when you get home?' Gemmax asked her.

'Father told me he should be given some leave now the war's over,' she said, not taking her eyes off the galleass. 'I shall have to help him with Mother. I don't know what she'll be like, now that Beata's gone. I shall have to manage the estate – there'll be plenty to do.'

'I expect I'll be travelling to Mercatorius again on business, now that we're not fighting any more,' Gemmax said. He paused as if he expected some response, but Verna was busy watching the manoeuvres of the warship as it furled its sails and the steady strokes of its oars brought it past the gun batteries at the harbour entrance.

'Perhaps I could visit you,' Gemmax suggested.

An unusual intensity in his voice made Verna look at him. His eyes seemed very dark and serious.

'Would you like that?' he asked.

As far as she knew, a Sordesian had never crossed the threshold of her father's villa. It was a strange idea. And strange that a Sordesian should want to visit a Mercatorian home. Stranger still that any man should want to visit her. Despite the understanding that Bardo and she would marry, Amisso's brother had never actually shown any great interest in his promised bride. She suddenly thought of the daydream she had had on the day of her recovery – Beata and Amisso and Crasto, in her house at a musical evening. She had not seen Bardo in her vision, nor had she pictured him in the three weeks that had passed since then, although she had seen the faces of the others almost every time she had closed her eyes. Verna looked at the kind face of this Sordesian who had shared her adventure, who shared her grief for those they had lost and who had nursed her back to health, and she realised that it would be good to see him again.

'Yes,' she said. 'I'd like it if you visited. Thank you for looking after us.'

She held out her hand to shake his, but to her astonishment he took it to his lips and kissed it.

At the front of Gemmax's mansion was a terrace garden. Nefa, Fallax and Ebrio were sitting together there, in the shade of an orange tree, sipping lemonade. They had been told that they would be sent for within the hour since all was now ready for them and the Dux to begin their journey home. Such was the Dux's fury against Perdo, and his sense of frustration at being unable to make amends to Crasto, that he had extended a free pardon to all who had been accused along with the dead senator, although they were commanded not to repeat the allegation that the victims of Almus poisoning had really been Sordesians.

'We'll leave that to Gemmax,' Nefa said, as the three discussed their plans in low voices in the garden. 'The Dux can't command a Sordesian merchant. Gemmax can spread the word around the docks when he comes again. And in the meantime we'll have to organise getting supplies out of the prison. If the three of us keep on eating Almus and don't die, people will see it's not poisonous anyway. But we'll have to be careful this time. We'll have to be organised. If the Senate gets wind that Almus is alive they'll try and wipe it out like last time, and we mustn't let them catch us out again.'

'And if you can get seeds out of the prison, I'll take them abroad,' Ebrio said. 'After that sea chase, the Dux says he'll get me a navy job, escorting merchant convoys. I can take seeds with me and make sure they get ashore wherever we anchor.'

'What about you, Fallax?' Nefa asked. 'Are you still with us? Will you serve Almus?'

The taxman was silent. He had been quiet and withdrawn for days, and the news that they were going to be allowed to go home to Mercatorius hadn't seemed to move him at all.

'I'm not going back,' he said at last.

'Why not?' Captain Ebrio asked.

'There's nothing for me now in Mercatorius,' Fallax explained. 'I've no money – every last coin went down with the Oryx – and I don't want to go back to collecting taxes for a living. Not after everything that's happened.'

'But what about Almus?' Nefa asked. 'There's that to go back for – we have to work for Almus now. You don't need your gold when you've got Almus.'

'I know,' Fallax said. 'Perhaps I ought to come back and help, but I've got a feeling there's something different for me to do. It's been in my mind ever since we arrived here, and I haven't been able to get rid of it. I want to go to the mountains where the Almus came from in the first place. Amisso said there are people up there who live on nothing else. I want to find them if I can and stay with them if they'll have me.'

'But it could take years,' Nefa warned.

'A lifetime,' Ebrio added.

'There's no point arguing,' Fallax told them. 'It's what I have to do.'

The clank and scrape of iron was the only unpleasant noise as the Dux made his way to the cutter that would carry him to the waiting galleass. It was the sound of Perdo's chains dragging on the stone quayside as the disgraced senator was hustled along under guard at the back of the little procession of Mercatorians. A small band played, and the Sordesian Court had gathered to bid a fitting farewell to the leader of their rival state. The Dux and the Duke bowed to one another with great ceremony and exchanged gifts, and a guard of honour saw the Mercatorians safely into their boat.

'So our traders must pay to join the Sordesian caravans,' the Dux said to Ambassador Capax as the cutter made its way out into the harbour and the two stood in the stern, saluting the figures of the Duke and his Court on the quayside. 'Not a bad bargain, after all, since our merchants will be learning the secrets of their trade routes as well as paying for their protection. I think the time may come when we can turn that knowledge to our advantage – don't you agree, Ambassador?'

On the quayside, the Duke held his hand up in a solemn farewell gesture until the cutter had carried the Dux to his ship. As the boat carrying the Sordesian Almus inspectors pulled out towards the Mercatorian warship, the Duke turned to the commander of his forces and put a hand on his shoulder.

'I wonder how long it takes to build a galleass,' he said.

'It's not the length of time it takes, your Highness,' the commander replied, 'It's the know-how – the plans.'

'Which is exactly what we'll be able to get if we pay to sail with their convoys. If we put a shipwright on every merchant vessel of ours that sails with a Mercatorian convoy, they can make detailed drawings of their galleys and galleasses at close quarters. This time next year we might well have our own fleet of flying ships.'

The Sordesian band played joyful music as the Court processed to the Duke's palace for a sumptuous banquet in honour of the peace. Out at sea, they heard the galleass fire a salute with all its guns as the Mercatorians sailed for home. Gemmax wasn't with the Duke. He wasn't in the mood for celebration. For a long time he watched the departing warship from the balcony of his mansion before turning back to the empty bedroom that had been Verna's, and his rich but silent house.

In the foothills that rose to the mountains above Sordes, a traveller in simple clothes leaned for a moment on his staff. Fallax looked out beyond the harbour below him and watched the galleass, like a colourful toy, moving slowly across the silky, turquoise sheet of the sea.

18
A Place without a Name

To the bright yellow eye of the solitary seagull, the world below it was nothing but water – within the vast circle of its horizon there was only one tiny speck to be seen on the shiny, shifting surface of the ocean. The roving gull tipped its broad wings and slid down the air to investigate. It swooped low over a small rowing boat making its way steadily westward and gave a raucous cry of salute. The crew of three looked up, but the regular rising and falling of the oars didn't falter. The gull circled the boat several times, but seeing no offered scraps of food it finally skimmed off across the surface of the water and powered its way back up into a pale, wintry sky. Still rowing, Amisso looked over his shoulder and watched the seagull cruise towards the western horizon. He smiled to himself. That seagull was just what he'd needed to confirm his suspicions.

The gull knew for certain what was over the horizon, and now so did Amisso. A subtle change in the smell of the fresh sea air, floating weed and a shift in the currents, together with his own calculations, had led him to hope for the last couple of days that their long journey was nearing its end.

But still he said nothing to his father, resting in the stern of the little boat, nor to Beata, pulling firmly at the other oar beside him. From the beginning of their voyage it had been accepted that Amisso would set their course since he was the only one of them who had any knowledge of navigation. Crasto was a merchant not a sailor and so, despite Amisso's youth, the father had deferred to his son's judgement. But Amisso had insisted on keeping their destination a secret and now he intended to keep their arrival a surprise as well. Crasto had closed his eyes and Amisso looked at his father's face with pleasure. Two months at sea had tanned Crasto's skin to a rich, healthy brown and his flowing white hair and beard looked dazzling by contrast. Amisso glanced quickly at Beata. She too was bronzed by exposure to the elements, and her arms and shoulders had become powerful with the constant rowing. Crasto took equal turns with the oars, despite his age, and all three were as fit as they could be. The secret of their health and strength and their very survival stood proudly at the bow of their tiny vessel like a figurehead – a sturdy Almus bush, laden with its fragrant, golden fruit.

Almus had been their only source of food and its juice their only drink for the two months that had passed since the sinking of the Oryx. For Amisso and Beata, the experience of eating Almus had been nothing new; but for Crasto, who had finally been left with no alternative but to eat the fruit he had once scorned as too poor for his table, this had been his first taste of Almus and at last he had come to realise why it meant so much to those who ate it. He had set out to escape from Mercatorius filled with shame at his own failings and anger at the failings of the city. But now he found that he shared his son's sense that they were not running away, but running towards something, not filled with shame and anger, but with the hope of something better.

When Amisso had hauled Beata retching and groaning into the rowing boat, she had immediately searched for her Almus seeds. But she had searched in vain – they had been washed away during her time in the water. Nefa too was to find after her rescue that her precious seeds had been lost. But before the sea battle, Beata had given two seeds to Amisso and it was one of these that had rolled out of his pocket when he had heaved himself into the boat. Late on the day after the shipwreck, famished and parched, the three survivors had noticed to their amazement that a tiny Almus bush had begun to grow in the bows. The seed had lodged there and spread a net of fine tendrils across the wooden bottom of the bows. It appeared that Almus could turn even the bitter brine that soaked the planking into nourishment. If anything, the Almus grew more quickly on the salt water, as if the plant knew that its sustenance was urgently needed. The next morning, the bush was already 30 centimetres high and the first fruits had appeared to quench their raging thirst, give them strength and help them withstand the cold weather of the dying year. When he saw the fruit, Amisso remembered his master telling him that he would get a feeling for what was required in serving Almus, and straight away he had known why they had been given the boat and what they must do.

The boat had indeed seemed like a gift. It was the one in which their executioners had been supposed to row back to

Mercatorius after they had set off the bombs in the hold of the Oryx and left their prisoners on board to die. During the chase, it had remained on deck where Ebrio had ordered it to be secured. But when the Oryx had broken up in the storm, it had floated free among the wreckage and Amisso had struggled to the surface, after being pitched into the heaving waters, to find it bobbing by his side. As soon as he had dragged himself aboard, he had started to search for other survivors, but he had only managed to pull his father and Beata from the water before a huge wave had thrown the little craft clear of the shipwreck and powerful winds had driven it on until it was far away from the scene of the disaster.

By the time the storm had abated and the skies cleared, the coast of Sordes was no longer in sight and it seemed pointless to go back. Beata pleaded for them to return to look for Verna and their friends, but Crasto eventually made her see sense.

'Think how far away we are now,' he'd said. 'Think how long it would take us to row back. If they survived the storm and the wreck, they'll already have been picked up and be in the hands of our enemies. If we go back, Beata, we'll only meet the same fate. We must come to terms with it, my dear – there's nothing we can do for them now.'

Crasto had already had to deal with the loss of a wife and a son, and all that he held dear in his city, but Beata had neither his age nor his experience to help her cope with what had happened. Even the appearance of the Almus didn't comfort her at first, but it gave Amisso a sense of hope for their friends as well as for the future.

'They'll be safe,' he'd assured Beata.

She'd scowled at him, almost angrily, and demanded to know how he could be so confident.

'Almus will be protecting them,' he'd told her. 'Look at all we've been through – and how we've survived. We've escaped from prison. We've survived a shipwreck. A boat's been provided to take us away from danger, and Almus is still here to feed us. It's as if Almus is protecting its slaves. I'm not the only slave now: everyone who's helped Almus on its journey has become one as well. Almus will look after them all; I'm sure of it. And Almus wants us to take it onwards to the place I'm aiming for; I'm sure of that too. That's what this boat's for. I know it's hard, but we have to look forward, not back. That's our job... for Almus.'

Now, two months later, they had crossed an ocean and the wooden store-chest that had once carried bombs was now filled with the seeds of all the Almus they'd eaten, just waiting for a new land to grow in.

~

Amisso and Beata rowed on in silence after the seagull had disappeared over the horizon. They felt easy in the steady rhythm of their labour and the peaceful quiet of the ocean, broken only by the gentle slap of water against wood. Time, talking, work and Almus had helped Beata through her grieving, and now she felt able, like Amisso, to trust in Almus for the safety of Verna and the others. Her sense of loss was still with her – even if her sister and their friends were safe, it might be that they would never meet again – but she found she was able to look forward now, forward to the next adventure that serving Almus would bring. Crasto, too, old though he was, had discovered an appetite for the future. He had lost so much but, in these weeks at sea with his remaining son, he felt as if he had gained something new and unexpected – something to live and work for again.

Crasto was still resting in the stern as the youngsters rowed. He had had his eyes closed, but now he opened them and what he saw made him start. He took a moment to focus but then he leaned forward, peering intently between Amisso and Beata at something in the distance. Suddenly he was on his feet.

'Look!' he shouted, pointing.

The two teenagers swivelled on their bench and saw at once what had caught Crasto's attention. A low, dark shape had appeared on the horizon. It wasn't very big – a hand could blot it out – but it was definitely not a cloud or a trick of the light.

'It's land!' Crasto cried.

'It's so small. Is it an island?' Beata asked.

'Keep rowing and we'll find out,' Amisso told her.

He struck up a sea shanty that he used to hear the sailors sing down at the harbour in Mercatorius. It was a song about the dangers of a long journey and the expectation of homecoming with all its celebrations. During their time at sea, Amisso had taught his father and Beata all the songs he'd learned from the seamen, and they joined in with him now. Amisso and Beata bent to their task with new strength and every so often they looked over their shoulders to see the shape lengthening ahead of their boat.

After an hour, the silhouette stretched across the whole of the horizon and the rise and fall of hills and valleys could be seen.

'That's no island,' Crasto declared. 'That's real land. But I don't know what land it is.' He threw his head back and laughed. 'I've sent ships all over the world,' he went on, 'but I've no idea where we are now.'

Amisso realised that he hadn't seen his father laugh like that since he and Bardo were children and their mother,

Summata, was still alive. He had a vivid picture of his father, with jet black hair and a face unmarked by the worries of age, holding Bardo high up in the air, then putting him down and stretching out two huge, loving hands – one to his mother and the other to Amisso himself.

'Tell us where we are, Amisso,' Beata said. 'You've been deciding our course all this time, you must know.'

Amisso smiled and explained how he'd been using the stars and the sun, keeping track of the days and estimating their speed.

'I could draw every one of the charts in your map room from memory, Father,' he said. 'I've got them all in here,' and he tapped his forehead. 'I can close my eyes and it's as if I'm standing in that long room right now. I can see the chart of the western ocean in my mind and I've been drawing a red line on it day by day to show where we've got to.'

'But where is it?' Crasto asked. 'You still haven't told us.'

'A place without a name,' Amisso replied, 'without ports and trading stations and markets. It's just a vague outline on the edge of the map. Somewhere that's only known from half-remembered tales of long ago. A place that might even have been a myth, except that we've found it. Somewhere the empires of Mercatorius and Sordes have never touched!'

Both Amisso and Beata had stopped rowing now and all three travellers gazed for a while at the ever-growing outline of the coast.

'Move over, Beata,' Crasto said at last, 'it's my turn.'

Carefully, they changed places and Crasto settled himself shoulder to shoulder with Amisso. The two met each other's eyes for a moment, then Crasto spat on his hands and took up his oar.

'Come on, son,' he said, 'let's pull for shore.'

Notes from the Author

I feel as if I've heard stories from the Bible all my life. Certainly, I would have been told them regularly from starting school and they've been with me ever since – a part of my picture of the world. My understanding of the Bible has changed and developed over the years though. Just as life stays fascinating and exciting, thanks to all the new things we find out about it, so the Bible is as alive for me now as it was when I was a child, thanks to the new things I continually find in it, about it and through it.

Christianity is a forward-looking faith. We're on a journey and we have our eyes turned towards a brilliant destination. I'm always developing; the world is continually moving on – that's the way God made things. And Bible study is a journey to new insights and understandings. As I change, and the world changes, and my understanding of the Bible changes, so the Bible stays fresh for me, just as a relationship with a childhood friend can stay fresh if you journey together through all the twists and turns of life. Friendship goes stale if all you ever do is reminisce about the past. It stays alive if you're always looking forward to the next adventure you can share. That's the kind of companionship I try to have with the Bible – always wondering where we're going next together.

One of the great things about the Bible is that there are so many different ways to look at it and relate to it. And one of those ways is to do what I've done in The Slaves of Almus – that is, write stories about it. If you've just finished reading The Slaves of Almus you might be surprised to hear that it's a story *about* the Bible. 'Which bit of the Bible is it about?' you might ask. Well, that question's easy to answer: it's specifically about the writings of Luke – mainly his Gospel but also the Acts of the Apostles. But how *The Slaves of Almus* is 'about' Luke's writing is perhaps a little harder to explain. It certainly doesn't retell his stories, or try to explore in detail, bit by bit, what's special about each part of what he wrote. It doesn't investigate how Luke's Gospel and Acts might have come to be composed and for what purposes, or any of the other things we can do in writing about the Bible. Instead, I like to think of *The Slaves of Almus* as a personal 'response' to Luke's writing – a response of the imagination.

It's very easy to underestimate the importance of the imagination in life – particularly in a life of faith. There is a tendency to link imagination with 'made up', 'fairy tale', 'make believe' – in other words, with things that are not true. But that is to have a very narrow view of 'truth'. The story and characters in *The Slaves of Almus* are obviously made up, but have you ever met anyone who acts like Verna or Crasto? Do people with power ever behave in the way that Perdo does in the story? Do people ever resist things – even good things – that threaten their way of life, as the Mercatorian Senate does? If your answer is 'yes' to any of these questions, then you are saying that although *The Slaves of Almus* is not a 'true story' the story is true to experience.

Our imaginations are part of the experimental equipment that God has given us; they let us try out all kinds of 'what if?' questions that might be too difficult or dangerous or simply impossible to experiment with in real life. And if we are honest in the use of our imaginations rather than steering them to get the kind of results we want, then they can lead us towards truth, rather than away from it.

Apparently, Einstein reached some of his scientific conclusions after imagining what it would be like to ride on a beam of light; so even the great scientists can find a value in letting the imagination loose on life. We can also look for spiritual truth through an honest, Spirit-guided use of the imagination. In Bernard Shaw's play *St Joan* a character suggests to Joan that her 'voices from God' are actually from her imagination. Instead of being upset by this, Joan replies, 'Of course. That is how the messages of God come to us.' Imagination is at the heart of creativity and creativity is at the heart of God, so it shouldn't be surprising if our imaginations turn out to be a channel of communication between us and our Maker.

So what, exactly, was I letting my imagination explore when I set to work on Luke's writing? To understand the answer to that, it's important to grasp that the four Gospels have different characteristics. These differences show how, even in the early years of Christian writing and thinking, people's way of looking at things changed with changes in circumstances. The four Gospels were written at different times and locations for different purposes, and this has had an effect on the way they portray the life of Jesus. Sometimes this means that different material has been included; sometimes it means that things are expressed in different ways: and this means that each Gospel has a different 'feel' about it and highlights different themes.

The Gospel of Mark could be said to give the basic story of Jesus, and I used that storyline for the structure behind my first set of imaginative responses to the Gospels: the *Rumours of the King* trilogy (also published by Scripture Union). But in writing *The Slaves of Almus* I haven't used the storyline of Luke's writing. Instead I responded imaginatively to what are generally regarded as the special themes of his Gospel, such as the spreading of the good news in the world and the importance of outcasts and marginalised members of society to God and his work. I also wove into my plot the storylines of some important parables that only Luke records. The Acts of the Apostles deals with the experiences of the early Christians, and hints of some of these experiences found their way into the plot of *The Slaves of Almus*.

But perhaps you're still wondering why I should have written stories about the Bible that aren't set in the Bible lands and are about characters whose names are not in the Bible. Couldn't I have written some imaginative stories about Jesus and his friends? Yes, I could, and some writers have done this very well. However, for me, setting my stories in different times and places and with different characters was a way for me to explore how Jesus' life and teaching can apply anywhere, anytime and to anyone. Most of all, though, I wrote *The Slaves of Almus* to be an exciting adventure – a reminder that to try and live out the good news means living adventurously. This won't necessarily take us through an outward story like that of Amisso and his friends, but it will take us on exciting inward journeys to new understandings that may often involve conflicts, false starts, risks and rebellions inside ourselves and it will certainly have some outward effects in the fruit of our lives.

Reading groups are a popular new development: groups of people who agree to read a particular book then meet up to discuss their ideas about it. In a way, all of us who read the Bible, reflect on it and share what we come up with are part of a massive reading group that stretches all round the world.

Perhaps you and your friends might like to get together after reading *The Slaves of Almus* and talk about it. If you do, remember that it's important to ask each other 'open questions' – questions which don't stop at a simple yes/no response or have a single 'right' answer, but which open up places for your imaginations to explore in the light of the Spirit.

Here are some suggestions:

- Amisso starts the story with a dream, which changes as the adventure develops. What are your dreams, and how have they changed?
- Almus changes lives. What kind of things have changed your life, and how? Would you like your life to change in any way? If so, how and why?
- Different characters respond differently to Almus in the story. Talk about some of these differences.
- Almus brings together some unlikely allies to defend it and to oppose it. Why might that be?
- Do you know any places like Mercatorius?
- Amisso said, 'I'm useless', but he managed to carry out a difficult task. What advice would you give a friend who feels that he/she is not valued by anyone?
- 'You will get a feeling,' said Amisso's master. Have you been aware of times in your life when you have felt it was right to do something that others may have found strange or unexpected?
- What do you think might happen next in the 'new land' that Amisso has found, and in Mercatorius? What might have happened in both places in a hundred years' time?
- Where do you think the 'new land' could be?

Steve Dixon

Steve Dixon

has written the Rumours of the King trilogy.

Out of the Shadows

is the first of the three books.
It was short-listed for the 2004 Christian Book Awards.

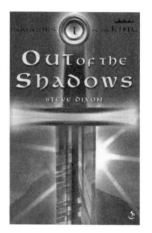

'A horrible feeling, like something squashing his heart, sent Ruel racing from the forest. He arrived just in time to see two men leading the latest sacrifice up towards the trees. The victim was Safir.'

The village of Hazar has lived under the shadow of The Reaper for a long time. People are taken and never seen again. But when Ruel's sister is chosen he decides to find out what happens to the sacrifices; he decides to fight back.

ISBN 1 85999 671 X

Also in the same series:
What the Sword Said ISBN 1 85999 672 8
The Empty Dragon ISBN 1 85999 746 5

You can buy these books at your local Christian bookshop or online at www.scriptureunion.org.uk/publishing or call Mail Order direct: 08450 70 60 06.